# UP
# FISH CREEK
# ROAD

## and Other Stories

David Matlin

SPUYTEN DUYVIL

New York City

Grateful acknowledgement is made to the following magazines for publishing excerpts from this collection: *Golden Handcuffs Review* and *Green Integer Review*. And my special gratitude to the family of Charles Ireland, a Truth Teller who stood and faced the ruins personally.

Library of Congress Cataloging-in-Publication Data

Matlin, David.
Up Fish Creek Road and other stories / David Matlin.
p. cm.
ISBN 978-1-881471-60-8
I. Title.
PS3563.A8367U6 2013
813'.54--dc23

2012025955

*Just for Gail*

# Contents

# A
# Mud
# Loosened
# Tree

"W hen wood's thickness won't do."

Dr. Blanchard wondered how that phrase from his mother's spring observations mixed with the scents of raw garlic washing over this corner of land he'd been assigned to as a Conscientious Objector; Sanger, California, the small town lying in its bed of 1942 mid-summer heat. The news of the War, in both the Pacific and Europe, came in savage dribblings and no one in those months after his arrival was sure, either of him or of a "victory" which seemed as remote as the Sequoian Giants hovering in the Sierras where he went sometimes to draw and write and organize his medical notes on patients. The people he treated, though they needed medical care, were suspicious and often, overtly distant. One result was the grinding isolation of his young daughter and son; the other: his wife who had become increasingly moody. His alternative service was based on his Quaker beliefs not just in non-violence, but the adorable mercy of peace and its defiance of the sword as a Truth still in search of completion.

He did not think his devotions were mystical and would have scorned such notions as deep and useless pretension that had nothing to do with his practice of medicine among the people he gently treated and respected who thought he was either an odd foreign agent or a Temptation whose kindnesses were to be used and then discarded.

Joe Blanchard was up most mornings by 4:00am tending to births, fevers, infections, sunstroke, discoveries of cancer, and farm injuries which included lost fingers, lost arms, lacerations, and sometimes just drunken angers over work, gone to dead marriages, the moveless, looming High Sierras that seemed to scavenge men's dreams, broke them and prompted them toward carelessness and its translations into women and men and children with cut lips and bruises. Dr. Blanchard also knew the constant weighing of absent sons and occasional daughters on faraway islands or continents killing and dying, nursing and being killed; everyone, home and homesick, scared and trying not to be scared, but being cinched tighter and tighter as to a sneaking sort of drought and its rainlessness, its swirls in a kind of helpless barrenness over the terrible war so distant and so horribly near.

House calls. Mothers and kids. The young fathers gone to proverbs that evaporate the living. "Add to this recipe," he noted one morning, "My own intrusions."

The absence of young men gone off to war inclined those who were left to feel like "leftovers" as a workable, partially maimed condition of their lives. The young, not of war-age boys, girls, women, and older men, had to somehow fill the space of desertions no one at that point knew the end of. Dr. Blanchard's arrival, a healthy war-age man and medical doctor, escorted by wife and children caused many who saw or heard of him to sulk, as one might, in the beginning, over a leaf-eating caterpillar or two, observed while watering and seeing to a peach or plum grove; not a threat, but a small disorder that would allow no further gathering.

"A Doctor's skills? Sure we need'em. But our boys need'em more. And what the hell kind of Doctor is this anyways who'd let 'imself ride it out with wife'n'kids while a million others bleed alone?"

No one really wanted questions like this to take root because of Dr. Blanchard's fine care and gentle way.

"A Doctor's Doctor. Rare enough. And don't make you feel like a dog neither," one of the isolate, first settlement ranchers was heard to say while getting once-a-month supplies in town as if that pound of saying might dispel what sometimes grows best in any seasons of rainlessness; "seeds of gossip" which the rancher pointed out "cin sprout inna drop'a piss or pinch'a fire" by way of a reminder that though the war ran deep, it hadn't yet conspired to make a total waste of their world, that they could still see it and live it everyday and "trust could start with one man going to another for simple help."

"Theo" was the rancher's name. His father, a Civil War veteran, had come into the Sierra foothills in 1870 or so, when the San Joaquin still had grizzlies and tule elk herds and sky blackening migratory bird flocks that took as much decided concentration to kill off as Indians.

"No formal count. But it was by the millions. And

my dad arrived in the last stages of the slaughter. An amputee whose one arm and hand," Joe Blanchard heard from the fifty and more year-old son and other older patients, had more than enough strength, the understatement holding to itself even after seven decades, a respectful austerity having to do not only with physical strength, but the fact that he sheltered the occasional desperate Indians who came his way, would not allow any murderings, and was said to have broken the backs of two or three Indian Shooters who couldn't seem to let go of earlier habits along with an expected bounty and received, with equally applied understatement, "some payment for their trouble." Theo's father stayed his remaining life among these people, in that way, a kind of precisely defined but not distressful embarrassment, reminding those who had gotten, in those murderous years, to place in the whispered local terms, "How the gottings took place."

And the town wasn't always glad about Theo. Thought what had landed under the tree had a full complement of body parts. Otherwise that was probably the only difference.

Dr. Blanchard had treated Theo.

"Gone partially talkless, Doc. About to turn into a bad neighbor," as the physician held the older man's arthritic hands, touched them at their various swollen points, asked that fingers be flexed and unflexed, and then said little could be done; a good soaking in hot water once or twice a day with a shot of a man's favorite whiskey would ease things up a notch or two, hold back at least some of the pain.

The hard rancher noted how the physician had conducted the "house call"; rode the nearly trackless fifteen miles, took notes, asked questions, keeping in mind he was a stranger asking these questions that needed some precision so as not to pull up the wrong weeds about who died, who'd got sick and who didn't and from what and knew enough about horses, cattle, the smell of fall in the air and color of midday sun to attract his four half-wild dogs.

And the "minor" earthquake that took place while the "general practitioner" held the older man's hands; the walls of the house swaying, chairs seeming to float a yard one way, then back approximately to their original position. And outside, the windmill creaking, the live oaks in their livid twisted rupture hovering over a creek dropping some of their limbs, a crack appearing in one of the oldest trunks (that would surely kill the tree in the last five of its five-hundred year life), the hills lifting up mists of displaced dust; the Doctor placing his glasses properly again on the bridge of his nose when the swaying stopped as if this were also a part of his vocation, not exactly companionable, but supposable as the rattlesnake bites he also sometimes treated if he could get to the victim or the victim to him in time.

Theo did not ask though, "What is a Doctor doing here?" He could readily see for himself what was being done to the best of one man's abilities, pouring an intelligence into the daily needs of a practice, keeping the hours exact and spare so as to get to know patients and their ways. He left "The Question" up to his neighbors and fellow townsmen. It was to Theo a "Democracy" and young men and women were dying for the price of such painful inquiries as the one beginning to emerge in the Valley that shifted and trembled below him. More than that and old Theo saddled up a horse to ride fences or shoot a hawk taken up a habit of raiding his chickens. It wasn't that thought was certain, but that there were certainties and the immediate business was to know how far they'd come and go otherwise the exposed fronts caused a man to slow down some and sharpen his knife.

The rancher had also fought in World War I, and the Doctor, as he examined the increasingly arthritic hands, noticed the burns on wrists and forearms.

"Mustard Gas?" Joe Blanchard looked up into Theo's eyes.

"Can still see the fog making its mess, Doc. Part of my lungs too. Not enough yet to stop breathin' though."

"Haven't seen such burns very often, Theo," as the younger man touched the still traumatized skin, applied stethoscope to chest, listened, took a salve from his bag, left it on the kitchen table and said, "When you run out, I'll get more."

Theo remembered, equally, the young Doctor's

hands. His finger's were short, the flesh thick and seemed unrelated to the physician's tall, thin body until he touched a patient's veins or joints, or felt an arm pit.

It was hot that day. A 110 degrees and more and the younger man was grateful for the lunch of cool well water, hard boiled eggs, and smoked venison, along with some pick-me-up slices of lemon, peaches, and a pot of fresh honey.

"Never had a better lunch, Theo. And never expected fruit or water this good".

"Father hauled the first trees on a pack horse. Made sure they wouldn't get too rain resistant and break someone's teeth. Got a small orchard now and some hives".

"Any more rain than the Valley?"

"Can't say much more. But the snow piles up pretty good. Poor man's fertilizer won't git anyone rich up here but down there it attracts the funniest gamblers ready for their hand of poker with the Creation. No other way I know to think about farming or ranching. Beautiful a devil as ever boiled up in a man's mess'a dreamings depending on your brand. If you're ever ready to try it Doc, lemme know."

"Think I'll let that epidemic pass me by for now."

Theo liked the younger man's refusal. Its lightness gathered, but not too hard, and it was, with a little rummaging, given to the form of leisurely ambiguities that caught Theo's respect for men who might find a way to belong anywhere in any world without having to scheme.

"Yep. Don't come lookin' fer no company up'cher," Theo added with a touch of the "listener" grown shrewd before the slippage of his own words.

"Cattle running OK?

"Help's away fighting the war. But the sons help out when they can."

Dr. Blanchard knew Theo had sent at least four of the sons and daughters of his hired workers to college. And that the town whispered about this; the gossip reaching to Fresno and beyond; the too easy whispering about wasting money on Mexicans, Indians, Okies. The local and not so local people sneering over the thought, the intolerable proclamation of it. The other, perhaps more fearful whispers, had to do with Theo's boyhood, specifically his earliest fascinations with geology and the rock boiled world that thrust itself up nearly three miles and held only the most fleeting possibilities for both the prosperous and the damned who might inject themselves with its invitations.

"As a child he was a rock-hound. Didn't you know?" As if that would explain a certain kind of helpless error akin to retardation, or, worse, a calling of the "Spirit" lying outside of the local Christian appetites for the "Rapture" and any messages to be sent to the sinful inhabitants of the Fallen World. The boy's wanderings in places like King's Canyon posed for the most faithful and devoted an insidious mischief. And a "committee" was gotten together once, before the turn of the century, for a "Visit."

Those visitors one Monday after the Sabbath saddled up some horses and for insurance took wives with baskets of food "in case of some sort of trouble," said a local pastor.

"Fear'a God must'a made'em unafraid to hide behind a woman's skirts," was the comment Theo's father was said to have whispered through his gritted teeth after the "incident."

The party of five rode up into the foothills, their horses and a mule to carry water and even a passenger if the footing became too loose or hazardous. The journey was said to take then five hours; late spring in that third year after Theo's mother's death. Sun was full out, so too the rattlesnakes and scorpions. And there were still scattered grizzlies in those decades as well as Yokut and Miwok burials with fine baskets the "ladies" used to decorate their parlors. The mother died a year after the son's birth. "Valley fever" it was said; the mysterious infection named after the San Joaquin itself but also called "desert rheumatism" may be because no one knew what the hell else to say about such kinds of dyings. Theo told Dr. Blanchard as he took his notes, "Son-of-a-bitch wind, my father was heard to mumble when he'd gone a shot too far into whiskey after his visits to her grave. No one knowing in those decades what it was. Middle finger was where hers began. A small abscess along with the flu and

11

some pain in the right side. Not a thought more than that as it was told to me other than rest in bed for a day, two at the most. Skin boils came. The other; crushing headache, hallucinations. Whole thing carried her off like the petal of a poppy without touching me or my dad."

Dr. Blanchard listened carefully. He'd seen other less dangerous symptoms, but ones that were persistent in their deliberations; fatigue lasting for years, a month only without explanation. No one knew exactly how it might turn out once the infection came. Dr. Blanchard knew its name: "Coccidioides", a fungus hibernating in the dry alkaline soils, stirred by wind, or hoe, tractor blade, a simple footstep and flying like some misaligned pollen from an earlier geologic age to the lungs of more recent species, human and non-human. The physician knowing the name, knew too that wasn't quite enough. The disease was often difficult, chronic. So he noted Theo's story having already attempted to treat others.

The husband with his war ravaged body later thought when grief had subsided and he carried his longings after that, for "the Boy," about not wanting any further wonder as to which or what women found dismembered men attractive. So he watched the small procession climbing toward the plateau; the "retreat" he constructed before his wife's death to escape the stifling summer heat of the Valley. The women with long dresses and hats and scarves to ward off sun and wind, the men stiffly suited riding their horses badly. He had a world to water, a cow ready to drop a calf so as to show his son birth. He looked at the surrounding granite spires looming over his one thousand acre plateau with its arroyos and year-round streams, stands of oak and sycamore and cottonwood and wild flowered shadows, knew it would all still be around when the uninvited arrived.

Amputation at the shoulder of his left arm; a sniper at Chickamauga, the inflammation of the Cherokee name, "River of Death," rising up, perhaps as terrible as the original bullet itself to send those parts of his body into hungers more rapacious in their invisibilities than the visible at the farthest boundaries its senescence could bear or comprehend. Such personal speculation had risen up out of the "absence" as Theo's father referred to it, "the ocean where the soul might swim having its shores reduced." So he walked two thousand miles learning in that after-war immensity to re-direct the balance of his body and it appeared to those who reluctantly marveled over it that he had far more arms than the countable comprehendable one with a hand that could lift a common man up to dangle in the air, which he'd done when necessary, "To prove that the end of the day will surely come," and to further surprise the unsuspecting with the hid mysteries of the landscape.

"Born on Long Island. Father's people fishermen. Mother's people farmers. 1839. Far from the clank of crowds," he was heard to say, adding "I too started from Paumanok" and recited Whitman's poem to his son as they shod and checked horses' teeth, chopped wood and built a local fortune from land purchases and when the Southern Pacific came, that too, sending crops of fruit around the world. Sagaponack, the exact place of birth and a boyhood spent exploring the local bays with their old defiantly firm names, the depths of their insinuations not yet broken at that point when he canoed as a fifteen year old, the watery swells of the Shinnecock, the Peconic, the Mapeague Bays. He liked both fishing and farming but the storms and tides of the sea drew him more against his uncle's fate (his mother's beloved brother following a plow horse turned up a nest of ground hornets and was stung to death). And he the nephew could smell the currents, had an eye for sea distances, lay for sea colors, bones for weather. There was no decision really, no dilation of the will along with the memory of his uncle, bloated in his suffocation from at least two hundred stings; the plow-horse found nearly a mile away pulling at tufts of sea-grass on a dune overlooking the Atlantic with twenty or thirty dead hornets woven into the mangy disarray of its tail. What his pre-Civil War memories allowed him against the mountainous creature horrors which wanted him, wanted to immerse him, he knew, as another ocean memory could barely resist. The waters of Long Island Sound cutting his arms and shoulders from the thinning ice of early spring to the thickening ices of early winter, the haul of fish and nets (his and other waterlogged faces), fish and net weight cutting at his endurance, the smell and glistened bodies of sea lions waiting for their thefts, ocean spray burning his ears and eye lids, heaving sea and horizon close to the nose, porpoise timing their watchful passages into the air with the heavy or light undulance of sea swell: "Keep an extra eye for sharks, and if you got one, an extra hand," the elder fishermen joked, their own nostrils wet with sea washed fish oil, fish blood; hair and ears under that sun glinted with scales of freshly clubbed sea creatures, the piles of flesh fishripe and slippery and one needed to watch for the clandestine gaff prong which could butcher either men or that unlucky sea serpent come for its lone mistake.

One mid-day meal, along with a bowl of steaming cohogs, his mother set beside his feast for her son the collection of Walt Whitman's poems "Leaves of Grass" which he memorized and recited to himself as he either re-strung or set nets, the labors and the poet's phrasings setting a pace that brought him into and through the days "without feeling like a heaped up shade." The book of poems appeared in his sixteenth year, 1855. When he later asked his mother about the gift, her explanation was "A fellow Long Islander had written them," as if that response might admit light into shadow escorted by the calming practicalities of household chores as relief from the glancing darknesses which had stolen the life of her brother.

On that basis the family subscribed to the "Freeman," Whitman's newspaper in Brooklyn, and though it more often came late or not at all, Theo's grandfather read the news, avidly looked for the poet's journalism and recited it to Theo's grandmother as she prepared Sunday chowder, baked bread, planned her garden for the summer. The maternal great grandmother; her name was Ora as if the tones of the central consonant encircled by the orbiting vowels were a well-footed not at all unpleasant solar system which in its gatherings also included her habit of befriending a new female goose of each generation who cried whenever she the mistress of the farm was seen to leave by those other feathered mistresses and protectors of the barnyard. She preferred not to be aligned, however, with any members of the family of orators no matter how persuasive except the one who struck the deepest chords of her admirations: Elias Hicks. Both her own and the Whitman family had gone to hear the great and compelling Quaker theologian whom the poet, in 1888, recalled in a scrupulous, intimate prose, the recollection tender and close, Whitman remembering himself as a boy of nine, no more than ten, and his father's voice calling "Come, Mother, Elias preaches tonight," and the young Walt allowed to go. Four years before his death, the old, partially paralysed poet wrote of the Quaker Speaker's "agonizing conviction and magnetic stream of natural eloquence ... (different as the fresh air of a May morning or sea-shore breeze from the atmosphere of a perfumer's shop)." In trying to define and hold (after sixty years) the presence of Elias Hicks, a fellow Long Islander "from Hemstead Township" Whitman said in his essay "There is a sort of nature of persons I have compared to little rills of water, fresh, from perennial springs—(and the comparison is indeed an appropriate one)—persons not so very plenty, yet some few certainly of them running over the surface and area of humanity, all times, all lands ... sparse, not numerous, yet enough to irrigate the soil ..." Theo in his boyhood, wanting to have a more definite sense of his father's origins and what "look" the faraway Paumonok had was shown another paragraph from this essay his father thought contained some of the expression he would only stumble before, though he had been sharpened and fashioned by his apprenticeship of walking and discovering such sea and landscapes: "How well I remember the region-the flat plains of the middle of Long Island, as then, with their prairie-like vistas and grassy patches in every direction, and the 'kill-calf' and herds of cattle and sheep. Then the South Bay and shores and the salt meadows, and the sedgy smell, and numberless little bayous and hummock-islands in the waters, the habit of every sort of fish and aquatic fowl of North America. And the bay men-a strong, wild, peculiar race-now extinct, or rather entirely changed. And the beach outside the sandy bars, sometimes many miles at a stretch, with their old history of wrecks and storms-the weird, white-gray beach-not without it tales of pathos-tales too, of grandest heroes and heroisms ..."(the fragment from Whitman also calling for and giving courage-something about "hands tight to the throats of kings ...").

Theo memorized the passage and asked about its details as he examined the geological wonders surging thousands of feet into the skies of his own homeground. The father, at that point in his son's obvious growing hungers for knowledge and curiosity, committed himself to the writing of "a kind of stack of memories, each of them to be thought of as a bail of hay personally harvested, bound, and stored up as a pile" along with Whitman's "Leaves of Grass" and John Muir's "The Mountains of California" with its descriptions of "The Bee Pastures"; plains of wild flowers creating various auras of light as far as the eye could trace the luxuriant sheets of wild colors vanishing into the distant hazes interspersed by groves of ancient oak casting their interlacing shadows and producing a sense in the walker of "wading in liquid gold" full of bird song and waves of fragrance. How would one in a time even of Theo's emerging adulthood, just mere decades from these witnesses, consider their truths before the carnage-like transformations of those spaces -"the ambush'd womb of shadows" Theo's father quoted Whitman trying to release both himself and his son from the bitterness of those negations and their powers.

Maidu, Wintun, Yokut, Miwok. Theo liked to wrap these syllables into his explorations of the high meadows and granitic fastnesses which surrounded his boyhood world looking for big-horn, the remnant herds at his end of the Sequoia country not yet destroyed by the "hoofed locusts" as Muir called the domestic sheep introduced directly after the Gold Rush, denuding ancient forage and meadow, spreading disease for which the wild ungulates had no immunities. The sound of the rut, the bloodshot smaller thunder of the male bighorn collisions echoing off ice-grooved cliff faces was one of his favorite observances and studies, though it too, strong as it appeared to be in its immense sensualities and desperations, was "tentative"—that word striking the ancient syllables of Indian nouns he pronounced below the warping granite spires with everything of a language clipped off but a core of leftover, hanging sorrows.

The older mustard gas scarred rancher told the Quaker Doctor that as a boy he still saw many of the western hills covered with the original grey-green and green grasses rather than the brown and golden forms that strike the mind in a sweep of sun-creased, grudging distances. "Wouldn't believe it, Doc, but those old colors offered a gentleness to these spaces" as the Quaker watched the rancher almost sight the trail of his words moving toward the stories where no famine marked the earlier dwellers in a region rich in rivers, marshes, swamps fed by the unimaginably huge yearly snowpack melt of the Sierra Nevada and pelagic plains where tule elk, deer, pronghorn antelope and grizzly bear grazed lakes and riverine mazes provided nutrient plants, trout, salmon, and migratory birds. "Foundation for thousands of years, Doc, where the great Valley Oaks and their acorns cleared enough room for thirty human languages." Come up here at night and you can see the lights of small towns named "Tuolumne" "Mokelumne" "Chowchilla" "Kaweah" and in invoking the extinct vocabulary and its strangeness, Dr. Blanchard thought at that moment the thick finalities (as if they too were geologic forces) might shrink back with the pronunciations of these isolate but still breathed relicts.

"Some say those speakers didn't have a word for war or peace," and as Theo let the speculation settle on the paradox of that double absence Dr. Blanchard, the "modern" Quaker in the shadow of a second twentieth century "World War" thought of William Penn's "Holy Experiment" and how the "Founder" of that province had been generous and scrupulously fair with the Indians believing each of their ideals regarding Justice "were much the same" and that both peoples could live "side-by-side in peace." It took only a hundred years, the younger man remembered, from those living moments when the "Founder" was most creative in "Kindness" and what he, the young physician thought was the recognition of the Carnal Presence of the

Cross to remind women and men of the holiness of their dying and having lived, to the deadened seconds when the grandson, John Penn, in 1763, proclaimed a bounty for all Indian scalps sending the grandfather's "Holy Experiment" into hollowing ruin.

Theo's father knew the small contingent of townspeople held "the Boy's" studies and wanderings in the same suspicions as the fossil skulls of sea lions and whale vertebrae uncovered by the spring floods of Valley rivers or by the simplest act of applying hoe to soil in an "innocent" garden where the upheavals of the "Fallen World" could challenge the purest forbearances of the devout, upturning Satan's Vulgarities posed as the cleverest lie before the real age of the Creation. And "the Boy" after being allowed to read the works of von Humboldt, Lyell, von Beyrick, and the Lord's acutest enemy, Charles Darwin, would explain to other children the "Miocene" or "Pliocene" fossil leaf impressions in rock or animal skull fragments and huge sharks' teeth aswim in the roots of peach trees (a backyard patch of a good Believer's simple strawberries) he carried in his pockets weren't three or four thousand years old but thirty and fifty million; an exaltation of the Abyss. One prominent minister's wife hearing of Theo's "facts" actually broke one of her molars over the thought of her children receiving "such terrible sorts of vice" and so swept up her skirts along with the others for this "visit."

The Civil War veteran understood the party had a

kind of natural force to its determinations and thought for a moment some well-placed this side-of-fatal bullets would be a welcome rain but one, no matter the intent, that'd land all over Theo. For himself harm had little mystery to it, arriving as it could or must dry or moist. The two extremities a sort of cluster reminding him of the "where" he had come from and his arrival in this Valley which seemed to attract in its seasons mist and rain wind and lightening, dust-storms and a summer heat to turn the nerves into a vocation of threat; one to upturn trees or snap off a roof like it was a piece of brittle finger-nail; the other to char a horse from mane to hoof, kill anything trapped in a too open space, the mind searing snap of thunder equal to the dispossessing, explosive tremors which unfoot beast or person, ship-sized boulders from a one hundred thousand year perch. He and Theo watching the huge cliffs for those seconds tremble as parts of what had been four or five thousand foot faces of sheer granite walls turned to a peculiar dust at those moments. The "solidity" of any present world as he thought then, to be drifting and splitting as these five people were drifting, toward him. The lead woman's husband had helped to bring in the railroad (Leland Stanford's personal letter guaranteeing lasting prosperity was displayed in in-framed glass hanging prominently in the man's study) and with it the exportation of every crop a farmer's imagination could force upon any soil and begin from there a transformation into salt. He was a childhood acquaintance of Theo's mother and had been in the process of courting when the Civil War veteran arrived "afoot in a dangerous country" as the locals still had it and reported it.

# II

He had in those years been mostly "afoot" from Sagaponack. Came home from 1865 to late 1867 to recuperate; help and be helped by his family and to begin reading again, his beloved Whitman and the image, for him, of Benjamin Franklin in last days praying "that God grant us that not only love of liberty but a thorough knowledge of the rights of man may pervade all the nations of the earth"; that the whole world be "Home" for everyone. But he didn't any longer quite know what "Home" was. And in thinking about both the "Printer", and the Poet from Long Island—his works of seeing and hearing were a discord the newly one-armed man felt was irresistible, felt that if he didn't walk he would rot. It was in the beginning "for balance"—he didn't know anymore how to literally hold himself—the sensations of falling over on one side, feeling undermined, betrayed in the visible, this other portion residing in death, pulling at him (his family also unable to bear his anguish). So he set out one morning in 1867 to try to regain what poise there was left for him. What would "nature without check with original energy" be, every hazard of it permitted to speak as if that possible freest speech could quell the stale residual war sensations that aroused a craving in himself for something just this side of disintegration, to bluff his grief, his unworthiness before the deadnesses he'd personally conjured and could not subdue, walking as his mother said one night through her tears as if he were "a mud-loosened tree about to fall on everyone." He took new courage from where, anywhere, he could find it and distinctly from the lines of "Song of Myself":

"Undrape! You are not guilty to me, nor stale nor discarded ..."

He went out and netted fish with his father for that last month; fish and boat and sea-weight making his hand and wrist throb and burn, the wave lurch, the bunching slanting heave pressing at him and the stump of his shoulder. He desired to meet the Poet but he was gun-shy; the weight of a rifle, the small mounds of blood-stained bullets, unhinged teeth next to a man's body, the moments when hate had taken him in hand-to-hand combat frenzy. He had killed with the bayonet and that made him shy as he remembered equally stray fragments and phrases from "Song of the Open Road":

"None may come the trial, till he or she bring
        courage and health" or

"These are the days that must happen to you..."

Their insinuation made him withdraw further and there seemed less and less any safe distance to withdraw to. The fish which he hauled in, learning the world of one-handedness and its smallest rituals from grooming to dressing, staring even at the disfigure; wondering at his sleeper's weight and where it would land him, sorting through that unreality—the privacy of himself corpse-like, dazed with the busy peculiarities of it. His mother smoked fish, dried apples, prepared for, at the most as she knew it had to be, two weeks of his journey wanting her war-broken son not to die, and no longer knowing what his life was nor how to keep him alive.

That morning in late spring of 1867; it was before sunrise and his mother cooked his favorite breakfast of pancakes with fresh churned butter, maple syrup, blueberry jam, thick slices of bacon, milk directly from the udder rich and warm and creamy, his pack with a copy of the Poet's book and it additions to 1867, fresh cobbled boots, fresh clothes, a walking stick his father carved from black walnut and whale-bone. The leave-taking was quiet. He remembered his mother kept her hands under her apron, his father ready for his own day fixing nets and boats for an new fishing season at sea, those hands forever swollen, more callous than skin. Every finger broken at least once. These images almost more than his parents faces a parasitic anguish at the beginning of his journey fixed to the smells of kitchen and heavy thaw breezes that seemed to stick under the lids of his eyes. He could barely swallow his mother's lovingly prepared food.

The dawn filled with robins hopping, the deliberate, careful stuttering motions of their listenings helped to rouse him as did the returning Canadian geese (the fierce, watchful ganders that awed him as a boy and man with their deliberate courage whenever the hint of threat appeared to the resting, ground-borne flock), the taste of pancake and kelp-tinged wind on his lips.

The journey took three years. In the winter he stopped and offered himself as a laborer for farming families in Ohio. At first the suppositions were a torture and threat of starvation. A Civil War veteran was fine, but a one-armed man and Yankee, what could he do that wouldn't embarrass their charity? Such creatures came back to their home country-sides, many to give up, become drunks either of various violences or passivities; become a shambles gathered at the corners of everyone's eye, the mutilations pure and simple in that way filling the villages and towns with a watchful futility. And here was yet another drifting through under what terms of vagrancy?

Without work, work for food, no food. The simple mathematical reduction harbored no lies. He had to think of equally simple questions. The simple granite-like merciless bunching against him demanded it. The visible cliffs of Kings Canyon which surrounded him, he later thought, wonderful as they were, were the awkward twins to the more invisible geology he earlier experienced on the shores of the Ohio River as it plunged toward the Mississippi and the edges of the

Confederacy. Was he the "erysipelite" of Whitman's "Sleepers", the "Idiot" or one of the "transient" meteors disappearing from the poet's "year of forebodings" at the precipices of the Civil War?

"A day? Let me show you what I can do in a day," he offered without beggary, wondering at that point what kind of slow ruin a three thousand mile walk can visit on a man, one like himself hauling death, not by name, but by the breathless residues come to drink at the springs of hostility he could not discard. And he saw himself asking this question as if he were the single actor in a traveling carnival offering carefully chosen temptation. He was as surprised by these words as the farmer who with thinning hesitation allowed him exactly that:

"A Day."

To do what?

Stack and fork hay.

"Enough for a man with five arms. Didn't use them words with the wife, though. She's scared of strangers. Scared of the violent men who come home after the war as if they'd ate the Face of Doom, the meat sweeter than anything they'd ever had or got again. But yer hired. You'll sleep and eat in the barn. A plate'a food'll be waiting at sunset."

With that Theo's father was left alone and astounded by his capacities. The fish and sea weight carrying over into the central continent as he reckoned it, those waves of Sagaponack undermining the relic sensations of his previous body; the oddity of the mutilation a too arousing curiosity at his edges, and thereby even more suspect; a war-wraith.

His hand was swollen, blistered, and when he woke from an exhausted doze there was a plate filled with gone cold pork, a pitcher of water, a metal cup, two dried peaches he ate hesitantly having been already at the fearful borders of this life and breathing from his own partially entered bodilessness helped him to drift into sleep.

The land-bound winter came in a different fury from the one he knew. The Bays so direct then to his recollections might freeze over but the sea swelled and rolled, ate the land-ward edged ice with tide and spray, rotting sea-kelp. Here wood needed chopping, trees downing, horses fed, groomed, tools oiled, harnesses and other leather mended and tended, machinery and buildings repaired even as blizzards came, subsided into searingly light cracked days, the sun unable to break even the smallest eye-blink of the cold as he chopped oak for its density and prolonged fire heat, wood chips from his axe acrid, spilled fresh from blade as they piled at the foot of an about-to-be severed trunk. He learned the arts of sharpening; wood-saws, axes, knives, scythes, harrows, thresher blades. Spent hours under a whale-oil lamp smelling this sea remnant and applying file to steel, learning the new forms of coordination, body and tool, mastering leverages, what could be held and could not as he experimented and recalled the initial frustrations and despairs over lacing and tying his boots, simple dressing, tucking in shirts, synching belt after his return to Sagaponack, each small cluster of the new orientations gathering (always to him) in their slow arrangements as he thought in that winter of Whitman's "erysipelite" and whether this was the poet's secret image of sorrows for a Democracy, not their immediate fatalities, but the generating disfigurement, once able to stake its claim, its full powers of inborn reduction and subtlest enfeeblements?

When Theo's father had a chance, he walked the countryside of the Lower Scioto River Valley. It was late February as he and Asa Kendrick wandered over river bottoms which then still contained wild rye, white clover, and blue-grass meadows once grazed, the Long Islander heard from his hosts, by elk and bison.

"Stay until early summer," Mr. Kendrick said "and you'll see enough mallards to suckle at least two new armies risen from their graves," adding "when my great-grandfather came into this country most of it was forests of white and red oak; most trees at least six foot in diameter, and scary enough like those settlers said 'ta' fil'yer boots with the wrong color piss.' Place still got streams run like buttered blood, so slow the catfish and sturgeon bin known to eat one or two stupid horses come for a too easy drink, and at least three smart politicians." This said with a tone so flat you could practically ice-skate the syllables.

Theo's father liked Mr. Kendrick and his wife. At night, when his missing part ached, he thought of staying longer than he'd planned with the childless couple who were both half-Shawnee, who he learned, lost two daughters, one to measles, the other crushed under a suddenly fallen tree; "The Hazard of the Woods" not to be bribed by either devotions to sin or devotions to prayerful devotion put upon the deepest inquiries as to God's mysterious frownings.

"No warnin. Thing fell with hardly a sound, so rotted breath of a woodpecker could'a started the lean."

Asa Kendrick didn't want to say more at that point and Theo's father recalling his mother's words about himself, "A mud-loosened tree"; the name gathered and swelled with a now even more forlorn oddity that made him cringe with luckless drift and its warnings about artillery explosions, bayonet charges come to claw the valleys of this or other planets as he foraged for air and found so little. The "Democracy" to his after mind, when he walked the spectral edges of the Ohio at night, was the eyeless extremity he and hundreds of thousands of others had lost themselves to, himself among the uncountable "furthers" rising as airless, earth-held ruins.

The Long Islander, watching the delegation climb toward his plateau, remembered asking Asa Kendrick, "Wind ever die down?" further recalling his own childhood study of the ocean and shore; the glass-smooth surface of a bay where he knew the only breeze in all that space was his own breath, not even a grass-tip swaying in the stillness as seagulls watched and smelled and kept their distances. He still felt to his shock, the sudden hard gust which had scoured himself and his host, sprang and jerked as some broken possum tail to cut their faces. There was no thought of spite, he knew, in either himself or the older man. They had lived through winters more profound. "To what," he asked himself, as he heard his son, Theo, working his horses, "would we belong to if not this too without comment or wasted fuss?"

The Civil War veteran hearing Theo's horse work thought of his then young son, still at that point, without his knowing, was saving his father from starvation and suicide after the ravages of Chicamagua, and both were floating toward war soils that would set them to the dead and the lived having gone through with what they might or couldn't.

"Luck, whatever you are, you must be something like the nearest bowl of shit," Theo's father said to himself watching the townsfolk rise toward their inevitable visit, letting the sad humor uncurl and flutter to heal his numbness for that moment, luck's immensities as he knew it, coming with the earliest, barely discernable hints of any spring thaws and the no longer humiliating struggle of tying laces, buttoning pants or shirts, washing himself with the remaining hand as if that appendage and its fingers were spreading a chill over his human meat. The unrelieved touch of finger-tips which had been to him a kind of sickening left-over bulk, a cause of panic crushing him in vague inflammation; more ignoble, lurching disgrace. But the sharpening of tools, accumulation of small seemingly indifferent skills; the previously felt lameness and disfigurement did become unpronounced; the labors had turned him away from his weariness and its corrosions. "I did decide to stay an extra season" the whisper emerging nearly as a question under the Sierra monoliths. In that year he devoted himself to carpentry (setting nail to hammer at first without injury), planting and harvest, horsemanship, constructing a beautiful chair for Mr. and Mrs. Kendrick.

There was too his devotion to Whitman and to learning more about Tecumseh and the relationship of the Quakers to the Shawnee, the "Sa Wanna" as they were known to themselves, "People of the South."

Mr. and Mrs. Kendrick had old baskets, pottery, jewelry, turbans, a quiver filled with skillfully shafted poisoned arrows. "In case diplomacy failed," Mrs. Kendrick let it be whispered.

Theo's father was struck by the brave reserve of his hosts. They drew so little attention to the depths they belonged to. He asked himself if this was what Penn witnessed; the persons born of the malevolent, Godless wilderness who were diplomatic, reserved, knew the world "as home for everyone" as they well may have taught Franklin and what did these two remnants though of mixed race actually represent in the face of the earlier Quaker approach to their Shawnee neighbors as equals? On the basis of such experiments of conscience could the Civil War have been avoided, the earlier transgression of peace arising in the simplicity of a woman and man's heart and nowhere else?

The unexpected vicissitudes of the question nearly froze him. He remembered Elias Hicks, his mother's story of the Whitmans, and began to ask about violence, whether it is an obedience to evil even in the most favored circumstances and Hicks' statement as it was reported to him about the blood of Christ: "the blood of Christ-the blood of Christ-why, my friends, the actual blood of Christ in itself was no more effective than the blood of bulls and goats-not a bit more-not a bit." The humane challenge of Hicks' statement, its sweeping away of eighteen hundred and sixty-eight years of deception and heartlessness caused the Civil War veteran to look more closely at Penn's strict justice in land dealings with the Indians. Was this too a part of the Principle of Divine Light which initiated Penn's examination of Justice and "personal safety" and what "Union" could he belong to after committing his violences in what he had assumed was the name of "Union" and "Abolition." He concluded that body of thought may have held more injury than the body of injury he could never escape.

In the spring of 1869 he prepared to leave.

There was little ceremony because he could think of no proper way to tell these hosts how exactly they had helped him to want to be alive again.

Snow was rotting. Land bogging up finally after a brutal freeze.

"You've survived a second winter. Grandmothers told us the second winter after a war is toughest," Mrs. Kendrick responded and touched the Long Islander's hand as her eyes swelled with tears.

He had not expected Mrs. Kendrick's gesture.

The older couple smoked and dried venison for him, picked herbs, dried apples and peaches without his knowing.

"Sure you still want to walk to California? Mr. Kendrick asked and followed immediately with, "There is the Ohio. You can float down it. Mississippi's there too."

That said he handed the younger man a hundred dollars not wanting to impose any further intrusions.

"Can't take your money."

"Oh! We think you can. And you should," Mrs. Kendrick looked at her guest. "No trouble over it. I've got some eagle feathers for you too. They'll help when the dreamings come."

He didn't know how she knew about his dreams. Mrs. Kendrick kept to her guarded rhythms without display. The gesture was so peculiarly distant and kind he felt muffled, as if this elder had "supposed" him and would continue to.

"What do I do with eagle feathers?"

"Keep them near," she said, adding nothing else.

And so he set out on a flat boat late April, 1869

When he passed through the "Golden Gate" and landed in San Francisco he walked once more, this time in to the San Joachin, whose mapped outline looked to him, a Long Islander, as ancient a fish as "Fish-shaped Paumaunok."

# III

As the Civil veteran looked down from his plateau he saw the "visitors" still stumbling in what was for them risky mid-day heat. When they came over the first bluff he already had set out fresh well-cooled water for them, cut peaches and lemons along with smoked venison and brook trout. Their horses were lathered and rather than be angered over it he had Theo and his younger Miwok friend "Stephen" take the animals, to brush and water them slowly back to life again. About whether he could do this for their owners he didn't know, didn't care much, but they were here, not invited, and even so, he would honor their minor hardship getting to his second home. The hundred dollars the Kendricks gave him he transformed into, if not a huge fortune, then one based on shrewd land and water investments the "town fathers" could not touch since he owned what they most coveted. What they could touch was his son, give a useless misery to his young life that he would try to avoid. But there was a limit and beyond it he would pass their misery back to them. They knew too there were other banks, other investments which could "set back" their small town designs. They also knew he would try not to send Theo away to an Eastern school.

"Mornin' Reverend Petersen, Missus Petersen."

He also looked over Paul and Sally Eaton, the local banker and his wife who collected "Indian things." The minister's thin closely shaven face was reddened from the heat. His eyes partially glazed from the exposure. The dark suit he wore served only to procure him a more ample radiation. His wife; she wore a light grey linen dress, a substantial sun bonnet, red linen gloves to protect her hands and fared better under the on-set of heat and smell of draught-parched sage. Sally Eaton was a pre-49er "gringo" rancher's daughter. Her father was said to have led certain "Indian shoots" and house burnings of the earlier Spanish/Mexican settlers whose lands were ripe. She was short, hazel eyed, intelligent, cunning, used her religion and ambitions fanatically. Theo's father knew the surface of good manners, handsome cheek bones and complexion which accompanied her equally and memorably delicate facial bones and almost raven-black hair could be used as a "corner" the un-weary might wander into. Her husband was irritable, disciplined in his greed, the outward congenialities and public spontaneity of the would-be politician a drapery and token for the colder rigidities of their shared alliance.

"Sally. Paul. Looks like you could use some water."

They noticed his tone was friendly as they drank what was set for them in the crystal glasses he bought for his late wife on a trip to San Francisco. The air was still and hot as they ate the fruit, sampled honey, squeezed lemon over the smoked deer and fish.

"Wish sometimes you hadn't left the house after Julia's death," Reverend Petersen began.

Theo's father pulled trout off some rib, sipped the liquid, sampled a peach.

"Part of the town seems so empty. I especially loved her flower beds," Sally Eaton added, not wanting to wade much past her toes.

The host looked down at his one scarred and wind swept hand and thought, as he listened to this chatter, "Enough yet like a good shovel. Thirty sharpenings with luck. But not much goddamned more."

A third guest tried. Mrs. Petersen this time. "There are many mornings when we think of your Julia."

"Is that why you've come. To discuss Julia?"

They each looked startled knowing he had pruned their small talk, and set them prematurely adrift.

"Why, not Julia at all!" The banker was careful, not wanting to be too eager as his wife noticed the bent, sun-scathed fingers of this man who made her husband feel powerless, checked in his hungers for the lands of small farmers in their section of the Valley and herself less "prominent", uneasy in her assumptions of triumph with each mortgage foreclosure, each "artifact" accumulated for display in her home then "given" to universities or museums in her name while despising the fact of her "host" financing the educations of Indians or Mexicans.

"No. Julia, rest her soul, was our inspiration," Sally Eaton finished her husband's too hesitant declaration.

Their host took another sip of water from the crystal he held, looked at each guest, then asked, "What inspiration is that? I doubt if she inspired your foreclosures, Paul. But you never know about the mysteries of inspiration."

"Julia was a fine mother," Reverend Petersen said, wanting to tamp what he hoped was the so far minor bleeding of the conversation.

"Didn't have much chance, it seems to me. If she had lived, I'd have hoped to be the one to witness those virtues. If you'll excuse me for a moment, I'll go and see about your horses."

They knew they'd not be invited past mid-afternoon and while Theo's father was gone they rallied a bit from the initial stumble of their words and gestures. The women straightened themselves, the men drank too much water and fidgeted as they looked out at the huge cliff country surrounding this parcel of land, one of the puzzles Theo's father purchased and which allowed him further water rights. The banker understood a little more clearly from this vantage how the Civil War veteran had anticipated the need for vast amounts of water and irrigation and his fortune with or without the bank would shape the future of their town and Valley.

"Horses are getting better," Theo's father announced, his tone holding no reference to the way the animals were used. " 'Bout an hour and they'll be ready. Enough safe light for your return." His mood was polite and formal. "You can please yourselves with sitting on the porch. I'll have Stephen and Theo get comfortable chairs while you wait for the animals."

Sally Eaton asked then, "Don't you think Theo might be happier in town?"

"Is that what you've come for. Theo's happiness in his mother's name?"

"Well, since Julia's gone you've taken him so far from the home you made," Reverend Petersen's wife observed, regarding her words as a diplomatic triumph and containing the further unstated implication that to deny this would be to deny his wife and the welfare of his son.

"Who among all you wives will volunteer to be his mother?"

The challenge was obvious and cold and when Reverend Petersen started to say the first syllable of the dead woman's name once more the host stopped him.

"Please don't. I know her name. I'll be polite for the sake of that name. But don't say it aloud one more time. And I'll say this once. No discussion after that. Any more "visits" and I'll find another bank. Any more foreclosures, any more grave-robbing, I'll find another goddamned banker."

The "incident", though it didn't result in death or torn bodies, did become the foundation of the many family farms in their town, the "Backbone" the Civil War veteran thought, remembering the Kendricks and the world they held in their hands.

# IV

Dr. Blanchard gradually picked up the bits of story about Theo and his father. The linkage with the Quakers offered the young doctor a small forbearance and insulation, enough he thought to help his wife and children; the one wilting from loneliness and an increasing fear she felt dangling over them, with each hour more tense and less remote. The two children, a boy and girl friendless after a year, though their father gave medical care and expertise the local residents had never seen, letting payment come not always in money but vegetables, fruit, a tuned car for his house calls, baked breads, an oiled refurbished tool and when nothing could be afforded the best care he could offer without question. Still, his children heard whispers at school about their "coward" father, his strange non-violent ways; the son challenged once by three boys and beaten. He did not raise his fists, and that night humiliated with a black and blue face, their father attending to the son's bruises and the shocked helplessness of the daughter told them the story about the Irish Quakers in the uprising of 1797: "They were advised by their elders and leaders, as they considered the violences that would surely come for each of their families, to destroy their arms. The loss of the temptation to save themselves by force, increased their faith and their assurance in their teaching of non-violence. But each Quaker family, I suppose like ours too, had to decide and what they did was open their homes to the sick, the injured, and all those who had been made homeless whether English or Irish. The smallest acts of mercy could have resulted in their deaths. They knew it. For your injuries and your tears I only have my Doctor's hands and I'm not always sure if that will ever be enough. I don't think we're very much different from those earliest Quakers."

"I'm not strong enough, Dad," his younger son said in response to these references and as the father applied a cold compress to the boy's swollen eyes and lips, he answered gently thinking of one of his heroes, Thomas Hancock, a highly trained physician of the eighteenth and nineteenth centuries deeply committed to the rejection of war, the use of force, and inspired the twentieth century doctor's own pacifisms, "... and there is not, on the contrary, any one more truly bold who goes forth unarmed ... against the weapons of the cruel ..."

The older daughter, though she was muted and withdrawn by the ugliness of the school-yard incident, the teachers who stood by and let the brutality find its own end, wrapped ice in a compress of her own folding and held it to a mean rib-bruise, a kick she knew came from a more exaggerated anger over her brother's refusal to protect himself with his own violence as she pleaded for them to stop, that her family had done nothing to deserve this shocking hatred.

The father watching the daughter's gestures whispered to them both, "Violence does not stop and become peace, but leaves behind only loss and hatred and fury. My own father told me these exact words when I was also beaten as a boy and wondered too if the "Divine Light" and Liberty of Conscience were the beautiful words of fools and liars."

The acknowledgement of the bravery of his children was partially shattered as all three heard the mother's hollow sobbing behind a closed bedroom door.

Theo hearing of the school-yard beating decided to stay "in town" and came to Dr. Blanchard's office on the pretext of "runnin through that stuff you gave me for muh old sores."

"Let me look for more, Theo," the physician answered and unlocked a medicine cabinet.

"Heard about your son, Doc. Anything I can do?"

Dr. Blanchard weighed the two edges of the

question: the sincere inquiry about the damage to his children and family; the threat the rancher was capable of imposing causing more resentment.

"Thanks, Theo. Boy's better today. But can't say it wasn't a scare. Keep the kids home till the end of the week. It'll give their mother some reassurance and less worry."

Dr. Blanchard knew the words didn't hide much but that Theo would respect their sense of restraint and privacy.

As the doctor handed his patient the medicine, re-explained its application, and looked over the World War I mustard gas scars, the phone rang.

"An emergency. Farmer's son took a slice from his foot chopping wood. Better for me to go out than have them come here."

"So long, Doc. I'll be by next week with a box of figs."

"Appreciate it, Theo. And be sure to keep those scars from too much sun."

Theo watched the "Visitor" drive south. Figured he was headed to Dinuba, even Yettem. Anything further and you'd need a better car or phone wires. "And what the hell was a goddamned kid doin with his toes under an ax any way fer shit sakes. Little fart must be smart as a box'a goddamned stones." The rancher thought over that as he went about his errands and business over the next couple of hours. Went through his own mental list of local and near-local boys and none of the ones who came to mind were that stupid. He did remember one who picked up a rattler showing off for some girls, got a full bite on his forearm and nearly died from gangrene. "Father a dumb bastard too," he grunted under his breath. "The mother. Why, by God she'd only let herself be fucked in a pond so cool didn't know ever if you wuz the hungry boy which'd come first; yer withered balls or froze to a sawhorse dick while she laughed herself raw from that deep-freeze'a hers."

But he didn't appreciate the suspicions which did take shape and became more refined as he banked, discussed crop profits with the manager, forecasts for field hands and railroad space, food output for war, what families needed money to get through until husbands, sons, daughters came home. Or.

It was about 4pm when he stopped filtering the doubts. Wind had picked up and carried the smell of ripening orange blossoms, the coaxing sensuous perfume and white petals creased his face and arms and dropped swirling at his feet. He walked to a large in-town garage where he kept tools, irrigation supplies, tractors, parts, water and food in case of a really bad earthquake, and an extra pick-up for what work might be necessary.

All he cared about was that the piece of steel started up.

Theo drove first to Dr. Blanchard's home, hoping to see the Quaker's car in the front yard, the good Doctor back for a mid-day lunch, not having yet started his early evening rounds and home visits. He stopped, walked to the door, knocked. There was nothing. Neither wife nor kids. That told him more.

He got back in his truck, checked the gas gauge, heard noise of crickets and the calls of red-wing black birds, pairs still feeding late nestlings, off in a near meadow. The foothills below the great Sequoias were beginning to glow with a sun-down haze of magnifying gold so achingly resplendent in this region of dwarfing huge-ness as he began driving south through the fields and orchards whose labyrinths he knew. Fruit pickers were still stripping some trees, field hands hoeing weeds, bent over their hoe handles; men, women, and children harnessed to the bloodshot labors. He recalled the newly arrived Dr. Blanchard trying to treat a field-hand in his early thirties, poisoned by a constant exposure to insecticide; cancerous lumps all over his body and the Doctor going straight to the presiding rancher to see if that particular someone would help with hospital bills, a sure to be widow and kids who'd probably come down with the same ravages one day after years of drinking the contaminated irrigation waters meandering through the furrows as everyone else who sank into that other "Gold Rush" bigger than anything Sutter or Jedediah Smith with his fur hungers ever dreamed. Theo didn't completely know what to look for as he drove by drooping Valley oaks and sycamores getting through the rainlessness of summer as they'd done, each of them, for centuries. It was getting toward early evening and he could see workers stacking heavy ladders on trailers, women sharpening hoes and shearing knives, straightening bent backs, cramped legs and shoulders, tractors and their drivers covered with dust, a welt or two from an unseen branch across forehead, cut ear, a few wasps drawn to the blood and a few "growers" talking and smoking with their foremen about the closing day and where to begin the next tomorrow as harvest time was on the near and not far approach. But he noticed the number of "growers" and farm owners seemed damned small for the end of such days as they recognized his pick-up and waved. He reached over, opened the glove compartment, pulled out his father's old Colt .44 pistol, spun the cylinder to hear that little orbiter sing a tune, squeezed some of that salve the Quaker recently gave him, rubbed it on the old World War I burns to remind himself why he was traversing this maze. Thought of his father's single hand at the end, sun and wind whipped, hammer smashed, a gouge taken here and there, thumb nail that looked like the tongue of gila monster. Whole piece of flesh nearly used up. And how its touch in that final form could still calm a horse gone to fury; hold his collections of Whitman and other books, maps, and the things his mother sent from Long Island-China, linens, personally knitted sweaters, an eighteenth century silver tea-pot crafted in Boston as well as Theo's mother's beautiful gardens kept and manicured after she died.

Dr. Blanchard's wife had loaded their children in to a neighbor's borrowed car when he hadn't come home. Just gave into the general fears and started through the countryside having no idea about the labyrinths of fields, orchards, irrigation ditches, canals, dirt "roads" that ended with grower homes and often vicious dogs, suspicious wives and children unafraid to deal with strangers, shotguns and 30/30s nestled in an entrance door crook, trigger finger ready like some not yet classified chrysalis.

It wouldn't do to say she was frantic. The tone of disorder and loss lying at the confluences of the word's pronunciation had not yet caught up to her cold anger nor to her children who were looking out their back windows desperate to assist their mother who had advised them to "please notice" their father's car, a faded green 39 Chevrolet coupe, not very "respectable" but reliable even though it had, more often than not, bird splatter blotching it which went ignored sometimes for days as the "Visitor" did his rounds with the quiet, studied, calm formality which identified his view of the "profession" and its necessary demeanor in the face of human suffering (and occasionally, cure); hers now risen in the principle of a burning meteor, the stoic finalities of her personal Quaker guidances having crumbled into a fascination with the occult; vigorous, alert, suitable for the stark emptiness of the American West which her husband had not mistaken and in his distrust of her practices, formed a withdrawal which persecuted them both. She looking toward Atlantis, the spiritualism of the Secrets of Nature about to be in their unfurlings, but not yet unlocked and the intoxications that would become the Afterward advancing with the "End of Time": the secret details appearing only with one's initiation into these mysteries. He in their deepest reservations thinking them both somehow debauched by the abyss risen between them called upon the pronouns of their revealed non-conformity thus addressing his wife not by her name but in the Third Person; "Thou" or "Thee", depending. Adam and Eve once more as she saw their sadly emerging and inescapable repetition. How would they both abide for the sake of themselves and their beautiful children (even their, she still intermittently felt, beautiful religion) as she thought of her reading of William Blake's difficult prophecy "The Four Zoas" and who become in this world "Natives of the Grave" as they, four as "family" walked this strange earth and the even stranger "Valley" of her husband's assigned service in the veils of Conscientious Objection? She often thought of Hannah Whitall Smith whose honesty and ethics as a woman, whose comments upon the "loneliness of this world life" did not hedge in its forthright clarity either about "God" or a woman's experience:

"Thy loneliness is only different in kind but

not in fact from the loneliness of every human heart apart from God. Thy circumstances are lonely, but thy loneliness of spirit does not come from these, it is the loneliness of humanity ...."

Her own mother told her of, just after her birth in 1910, Hannah Whitall Smith's visit to their household where, in her infancy, she was held and rocked by the great woman who then, seventy-eight years old, and though wounded by the deaths of her children, remained "undulled." She the wife of the Doctor wondered still how her loneliness might call to her, take her as she searched for her husband's car, trying to shield herself from the images of his being mutilated; shot, pitch-forked, his gifted Doctor's hands cut off by some wrathfully crude farm implement and her husband allowed to bleed to death; the eruption of anguish over his imagined suffering causing an unbearable nausea and sense of being smothered as she reminded herself of her children alive and frightened in the back seat and endangered by her driving.

# V

It was nearly 6:00pm, the afternoon winds mixing with mirages and heat wave over fields of ripening tomatoes and lettuce, workers at break drinking insecticide-laced water, eating tortillas, jalapenos for enough energy till sunset and the end of a sixteen to eighteen hour day. There was a grower walking his potato field carrying a shovel, checking a stand-pipe, his gait a registration, Theo knew, of the burden of worries over what can and will go wrong.

One grower, Theo noticed. And the others in this busy time. Where the goddamned hell were they? A swarm of bees was gathering at the end of a grove tractor road Theo was driving. He stopped, closed his windows, then continued slowly through the boiling mass of insects slamming against the steel and glass of his machine. It was one of the largest swarms he'd ever seen, tens of thousands of bees in their frenzy of whirled almost vindictive, crackling flight. Theo stopped again, for another moment letting himself become immersed, to hear the sound of the bee mass, and to wonder over the spectacle.

He drove another two hundred yards thinking there was yet more dead end, the worry he felt suddenly arching and growing hot. But as he got closer he saw a bend. He came to its edge, stopped, rolled down his window and heard the combined buzzing of the swarm still vividly from this distance. He let the engine idle for that second, then shifted into first gear. The bend straightened out into a meadow full of draught resistant sun-withered weeds. A worn tractor path cut straight through the middle of the meadow and ended in front of a large barn bordered by lemon trees. There were also numerous cars and trucks parked around it.

Theo stopped. Cut his engine. Reached for the .44; instinctively checked the cylinder, inspected the barrel, pulled and re-set the hammer. He got out, shut the door soundlessly, whispered his father's name into the general emptiness and began walking toward the barn. Populations of the twilight had appeared; moths and butterflies, jackrabbits hurriedly nibbling tough weeds, ears nervously twitching, lizards open-mouthed, bodies flexing up and down, a startled covey of quail skittering for closest shadows, their fierce, shrewd defensive flight intensifying both the caution and hatred Theo felt.

Ten yards from an open side door he heard voices and was surprised no one had taken caution to stand guard or sentry. He thought too was this the day his life and had come to and if it couldn't be avoided, the shells in the cylinder of his Daddy's .44 would insure some company.

"Kill'im now. Don't deserve last words like other men," he heard a voice yelling in rage inside the barn.

"No! Give'im the chance to be heard first. Don't matter anyway," another reprimanding voice countered.

"Son-of-a-bitch worse than a nigger. Hung them in Indiana. Send this little bastard to hell with the rest of'em."

Theo appraised the parked cars and pick-ups. Estimated at least a hundred people; maybe more thinking this was a kind of swarm too made of a kind of spit nobody ever took the time to taste. But he would. Save everyone else the trouble so it wouldn't grow into some sort'a sneaking ocean as things tended to do.

"Cain't wait to see'im deyad."

Theo recognized the voice of a rancher's wife. A family he authorized a loan for just after the husband got shipped overseas to fight the Germans. "Both the women and men," he thought as he walked into the shadows broken by the rays of late-day sunlight cutting through the shrunk siding.

"Feels like a shit-sprung town or two," Theo squeezed up a throttled mumble as he looked up at the thick ax-cut rafters. There was a rope slung over one. Theo let his eyes spill downward to where the rope's noose joined Dr. Blanchard's neck.

The tight, sweat-drenched, curling viciousness of the spectacle nearly made the World War I veteran want to vomit. He looked around for a possible "leader". Figured a messy shot through an ear would give the citizenry a minor set-back; get their attention. And if he had to he'd kill one of the women in the crowd to let every person there know nothin was gonna be free at the end of this goddamned day.

Then he heard the Doctor's voice.

He was surprised by its fullness as well as his own sudden impression that he wouldn't be able to save the younger man's life even with the .44 ready to fire.

"What is the work of Death?"

Theo barely heard these initial utterances through the various angered breathings and resolved whispers of the lynch mob. Dr. Blanchard asked the question a second time and Theo wondered how he was able to gather a mysteriously stronger voice with a rope around his neck.

The crowd began to quiet in a kind of shock over the singularly risen words those participants had assumed would remain muted, or, Theo thought as he watched, a thing risen from the Shores of Death to startle the rage and murder about to crumble this barn. Theo wished at that moment he'd had a mind to empty a few cans of gas around the building, murder every murderer there, and shoot the ones able to get out the door but Dr. Blanchard's sudden vocabulary quieted Theo's about-to-soar deadliness.

"What is the work of Death," the young physician continued once more adding, "that you and I will go forward into. And what you kill with this rope tonight. And who will be deformed? The questions fell thickly on these people who had let the Quaker Doctor treat them and their neighbors and their children.

Theo looked at the crowd which had stopped milling and fidgeting with its secret business. He turned toward the waning light of the still open door and saw the Doctor's wife and children standing, the horror on their three faces caught him throat deep in an undecipherable shock he had not felt since watching clouds of mustard gas float over armies, hearing other soldiers across the lines and trenches retching up their lungs in last hell sounds that still woke him in malevolent night helplessness.

The wife and children saw the slung rope and covered their mouths. When they noticed the victim with a noose cinched around his neck the three moved forward toward him as the lynch mob, person by person, moved apart for them to pass, not knowing what to do either with the questions or these additional "Friends" who had come in "Kindness" and whose "Kindness" aroused this kind of fury and intent. The victim's lack of resistance and now these three others seemed to unnerve those who let them pass.

As the three went slowly forward they heard Dr. Blanchard continue:

> I announce natural persons to arise;
> I announce justice triumphant;
> I announce uncompromising liberty and equality;
>
> .
>
> .
>
> .
>
> I say you shall yet find the friend you were looking
> for
>
> .
>
> .
>
> .
>
> I announce a life that shall be copious, vehement,

> spiritual,
>> bold;
> I announce an end that shall lightly and joyfully
> meet its trans-
>> lation:
> I announce myriads of youths, gigantic, sweet-
>> blooded;
> I announce a race of splendid and savage old men
> ...

Theo was stunned. The Quaker was reciting the passages from Whitman's "So Long" as if he too had drunk suddenly the same word-springs as the poet and Elias Hicks yet the recognition was broken by another voice demanding, "Someone hang the son-of-a-bitch. Don't let one more squeak come outta'im."

And other similar yellings rose up at the same instant the wife and three children appeared at the place where Dr. Blanchard stood, and embraced him. None of the four made any sound at that joining.

Theo knew the mob knew then all four demanded to be killed, demanded they claim the nerve of the full evil of their original sneaking theft of this man who had at mid-day been summoned to their false emergency.

"Kill all four," one voice yelled and with that the mob began to move away from the surrounded "Friends". Began to disperse at the sight of the huddled, unwavering Quakers.

Theo walked through the slowly thinning unsure mob knowing this last voice. It was a local rancher, who had a daughter in the war, a nurse on a navy hospital ship who witnessed Pearl Harbor, and was somewhere witnessing more. She was a loved daughter and though Theo wanted to ask that father how the daughter would have felt over a demand to lynch a whole family who came among them peacefully, he did not.

Instead he found the rancher waiting for the crowd to clear. Theo saw he was holding a pistol. And Theo moved more cautiously, more slowly, the rank smell of dry cow shit and hay making his nostrils quiver as he maneuvered behind this other man whose honest, life-long struggle he thought to this point he knew. But this night was different and Theo understood this other man was ready to kill.

So the World War I veteran came up without notice and placed the muzzle of the .44 hard against the back of the other man's skull and cocked the hammer.

"Drop your gun, Alfred," Theo whispered. "Try to remember that daughter of yours."

Theo followed the demand by pushing the muzzle of the .44 harder against the other man's bones.

"I won't miss," Theo added.

The rancher's body shook and the pistol dropped to the floor.

The remnant crowd moved away as Theo kicked the fallen steel out of reach.

"Now Alfred I want you to walk straight to that family and undo that goddamned noose, since I know it's you who put it there."

The wife and children still clung to the Doctor. None of the four knew quite what to do and so they stood peculiarly amazed any of them were still alive.

When Theo and the other man came nearer the wife and children made a tighter knot and this enraged Theo and he almost killed the other man then, named "Alfred," and the other man named "Alfred" knew it.

"Un-do that knot now," Theo whispered. "When that's done you crawl yer ass outta' here and think about that daughter of yours and how you'll face her. And don't forget the pistol you dropped. Either empty it in your own mouth so's to clean the filth come out it. Or bury it."

Theo walked the family to their car and followed them to their home. Said as he helped the Quakers to the front door, "Anything you need."

He heard the next day that Mrs. Blanchard began screaming in the middle of the night and couldn't stop screaming.

# Moths Will Suck First

S he saw the volcanoes no matter how far she might travel. The smoking mountains above Mexico City had both stirred and reduced her according to the tides as she knew them to be in herself, not necessarily rising or falling, but like the scorpions she'd known her whole life, appearing under a pillow or in the fold of a gown, a thing detached suddenly from the surrounding transience.

Though small scorpions in her house could be lethal, they were rare. If she took precautions the creatures inevitably exposed were collected and dried in Zapotec and Aztec ceramic jars she collected. Such earthenware wonders served as a reminder about her painting methods and how she might continue to draw courage and intelligence from the previous women who she felt were masters of this art.

Erina Avilar Castro remembered a close childhood friend, who at the beginning of her eighteenth year was stung on her right breast readying herself for bed. By sunrise the girl was delirious. By the following mid-day, dead. No one paid Erina for her skills then. No one, including herself, knew she had such skills.

She was only fourteen herself at the time of this death and for many months was torn by her revulsion over the final color of that breast wound and the growth of her own breasts. She had been allowed to visit that friend, whose parents prayed the encounter deliver their daughter the crucial step away from death's still ambiguous grasp. In her final stages of suffering and thrashing astonishment the victim tore her sweat soaked gown and so revealed the site of the sting.

Erina was also repulsed more by an other fact which amazed her and which she thought both violated the friend and herself. The color of the wound. The cruel blackish gloss which fascinated Erina with its inert heaviness.

The painter was in her 60th year in 1768 and felt the paint on her fingers as she rode in a carriage with her companion/servant Rebecca through the hills beyond their city. Mixtec cornfields stood in furrows, but barely. A three-year drought had gradually intensified and each felt the dryness sear edges of lips and ears as a cara-cara circled over dead goats across one of the narrow valleys they knew so well. Adults had not yet started to die but carpenters were already busy with small coffins for the young, wearied by sadness of having to use their tools for these things.

Twilight was difficult for Erina and Rebecca. They heard dull sounds of a hammer carried over wilted fields. Funeral processions and meager feasts were to begin soon. People danced in their masks of the living and dead. The two populations locked in a dilapidated, tenderly helpless embrace. Erina and Rebecca felt the two worlds ran yellow as hanging datura in their gardens. It was their favorite primary color. They began mixing Erina's tones for each painting – yellow first and counting the hours, depending on the season, black beckoning with its various hues attended by journeys in their Oaxacan world to mountains, jungles, and seacoasts where they collected plants, birds, insects, and artifacts of pre-conquest worlds barely a scratch away from the thin veneer marking their own civilization. The veneer of Mary and Her Son with which Erina began her life.

The breast wound had changed it. After her friend's death Erina began walking the ruins in hills above her city escorted by one of her father's vaqueros and the then new servant girl, Rebecca, brought from her village by a nun to live in Erina's household. An ancient plaza with its huge pyramids, the silence of their climbs up steep eroded steps, swoop of vultures placidly veering and patient, surrounding dry hillocks which they knew were lesser pyramids, crumbled and scorched. Occasionally gold and silver things appeared; miniature spiders, birds, snakes, fish, frogs undefinably whimsical and luxuriant in their barbaric challenge. Once Rebecca found a pair of obsidian ear spools carved to so thin and masterful a transparency that both young women were left nearly breathless by its unearthing. These were the first objects they packed for their journeys. Neither felt without them they could even begin to mix the paints.

Many took note of these unusual motions, especially for a prominent, ready to emerge young lady like Erina. The sight of an old family carriage trudging toward a pre-Columbian ruin, along with Erina's unhid curiosities, was an affront to haciendidos and priests. How could the scandal of it be contained? There was talk of a nunnery, an arranged marriage with a distant cousin in Spain, either one a preferred exile, and for her parents, a way to let any possible humiliation slide away without residue. Perhaps most glaring was the rumor Erina became interested in Mixtec and Zapotec, lowest of languages. Worse, as gossip curled, the Mazatec of a servant girl brought from distant hills. "Tongues of the conquered," Erina's father said to her mother, "and better left to join the emptiness of the land" in anguish over this only one born to them late.

Her parents knew their child was quick, uneasily so, and worried over barely submerged whispers about a "girl" who seemed to listen too fiercely and hear too clearly.

"No, not dangerous," a powerful priest confided to her mother, "but still unsettling. And, of course, we wouldn't want this to go further than it has."

But it had.

Erina's mother heard her daughter speak one morning. Not Spanish. And she remembered an unwanted sensation "of water cooling a hand" and being lulled for a moment of soft horror by her daughter's audacities. Yet when she emerged from the shade of those always remarkably near yet alien sounds she was terrified, though she'd heard Indian languages spoken every day over peeling tomatoes, laundry, seasonal labors in which those unemerged women of her houseworld shifted almost imperceptibly, their hands and fingers and forearms and muscles used, as hers were not.

If not "dangerous" as the priest said, then what?

And how to hide it from a worrying father with his allergies and sun nausea in a climate that for months was more fire pit with unnerving winds and vaguely malevolent cypress or tule tree shade, old impenetrable things with trunks like shoulders of dead demons, petrified and gigantic. Irina's mother was further afraid of avocado and chocolate. Both seemed, after her favorite parrots died from eating these things, far too suggestive and reckless. But it was sunset that made this parent feel her civilization personally widen and drip into coiled darkness escorted as it was by small flocks of short-tailed bats flying for wild and domestic fruit. Their slurping of fruit meat, their nightly cycles of feeding and sated sleep was like a vision of lust by which the waiting decompositions, checked only partially by an ever vigilant Saviour, would begin their reversal and wreckage.

One early fall day Erina's parents noticed their daughter's hands and wrists. Her skin pigment was a

compelling intense scarlet. She delayed ridding herself
of the color  she and they knew was as an important
treasure to one world as it was to another. The great
Aztec monarch demanded as tribute from conquered
cities at least 2000 spectacularly decorated cotton
blankets representing the greatest achievements of
those peoples who produced them. Erina felt by
those losses one could stumble over the vast names of
sorrow, and a violence more withering than war each
year thriving as monumental destitution similar, she
thought, to being gored by one of the prized bulls her
father bred for bull fights in Ciudad de Mexico, City of
Volcanoes where there were still found in the higher
snow fields images carved from hardened lava. Two
recently in her fifteenth year—a kneeling goddess,
her fleshless face, empty eye sockets, hair of wound
intestines. The other; a coiled rattlesnake, forked
tongue hanging from an open mouth ready to strike.
Erina heard of these discoveries from a friend of her
parents, a deputy to the viceroy who told them over a
formal visit of the finds in a voice nearly hushed with
contemptuous fear, not quite sure, even after more
than two hundred years of Spanish domination, what
secrets or spells these things might hold.

"I suppose one can't be completely sure," Erina
heard her mother say in response to this information
as the three adults watched each other in confused
silence which inevitably rose up whenever any
repulsive reminder of the "Peril" as they called it,

surfaced and weighed them down in temporary, though sickly bewildered drift. Montezuma also demanded forty bags of the dried insect substance derived from feeding on pads of cactus and its delicious nopales fruit. Cochineal dye was prized above both silver and gold. Erina's parents, haciendidos who had held their wealth and position since 1570, regarded that pigment on their daughter's skin as a sign she would be childless.

They did not want their world to unravel any more than this. This and no further.

# II

Their daughter was whole and handsomely thinned boned with a complexion that gave her fair skin a transparent glow, unusual in this climate where so many skin afflictions brought disfigurement and unease to even the most richly enclosed daily life. Her lips were full and alert. A girl might have warts, chronic rotten breath from mouth ulcers, carry disturbances from a father infected with syphilis, paralysis of limb or face, the host of tropical infections none of which she had.

There was however one starkly obvious tinge of somber hesitancy before what could have been considered a comely maiden and coveted prize for any future qualified suitor. Erina had a wandering left eye, and its glance, which occasionally frightened Christian and non-Christian, could not be ignored. Her eye turned outward, but as a child its destination was not permanent. Her parents prayed she would outgrow the problem, but fearfully, in the months of transition between her tenth and eleventh year, her retina intermittently migrated and then became a fixed, hopeless continent with a white sea lapping at it edges.

No prayers, no lighted candles could undo it though Erina's mother never wholly gave up her own daily ceremonies. Erina became increasingly friendless and alone. Her peers, except for the one stung by a scorpion grew confused by the intensity and self-consciousness of any direct eye-to-eye exchange. A mark, not necessarily of Satan, they confessed among themselves, whose allotment was not, thankfully their own, and conclusion enough.

There was an exception, one Erina considered the central charm of a life that would otherwise have ended as a stupor of isolation and pity. Rebecca, the Mazatec servant who had attended her since her seventh year. She came from a poor village in the far mountains; initially did not want to speak Spanish, did not want those sounds emerging from her throat. Though barely a woman at that moment, she told her mother and grandmother about Erina when allowed the rare trek home. The older women who were masters of songs and secrets which could result in their murders if they were found out, listened carefully to this dearly missed daughter who brought them her "savings" and kept them and others not from cruel hunger, but from plain starvation.

And when Erina's eye lost its anchor Rebecca noted the changes of those days, how the life-breath of the house became unrooted and transitory. Would the girl, otherwise considered beautiful, in becoming a woman, survive? And if survival meant isolation or subdued ridicule; hers the mark of a sinister and intolerable visitor finally crushing the barely touched mortal girl, who, though innocent, would be forced to breathe her days in gathering repudiation? Those who previously knew the family were fascinated and repelled, then grew weary and angry of that burden, became something denser than strangers. Such deformity, though many openly felt themselves because of education and travel to Europe, to be superior to inflexible superstition, was considered a sign of not only an ever lurking dread, but the work of original fiends the Church could never completely crush despite its fiercest efforts.

There was no remove. The wife of another prominent local official, wanting a section of her garden redesigned, watched in shock as her peons unearthed the frightening effigy of a monkey carved in onyx, its physical expression so animated, the senora of that household took to her bed in a swoon, and as it was reported to Erina's parents, needed the local bishop's reassurances before so unexpected an experience in the intimacy of her own home. A sudden reminder of European fragility and its toil. Conversion and destruction for three centuries which offered so solid an assurance, suffered paralysis in these moments. Were there any consolations, Erina sometimes asked herself while painting in old age, to sustain even those simplest household acts which became unsuspected vocations luring the devil, or, more uneasily, his elf-children like this superbly carved monkey, who had to be granted, if only for a nightmare aroused evening, its blood rotting silence.

These things commanded such pitiless irritation, and those like the senora of the garden, felt herself slipping toward noises of witches and needed the ancient string to escape the maze and lurid sexuality of the onyx monkey's pose. Erina knew this friend of her parents partially shrank with the "sickness" of the unearthed savage object; withdrew in the twilight and rebirth of a new favored "Madonna" of the Church.

For herself, Erina came to quickly realize, after her iris stopped its wanderings, how firm and morose her position would be in this community of her birth. She, like the unearthed monkey, would also command a silence. No, not as curdling, but as spiteful in its precise exclusions.

The servant, Rebecca, learned what Spanish she needed, knowing any reluctance furnished her masters with a reason for exile, and to return penniless to her village, be the cause of further sufferings. Though homesickness tortured and often nauseated the Mazatec girl, she understood the one way to soften her own and Erina's misery was a friendship. If she wanted to do this she would have to appear even more an unloving creature than she already was to this and other great households of their valley joined irremediably as it was to the ruined pyramids and plazas of the Older People. So she watched, noting how Erina shrank as from a wasting disease, averting her face and head, letting her shoulders droop and shuffling her feet with moderation enough to let visitors know she was about to walk into a room—give them a preparatory moment to cover their embarrassment.

Those whom she once thought admired adults were now like dull and hesitant children, solemnly nervous whenever this "once lovely girl" made her courteous appearances, then retreated into the noiseless, faraway odors of the hacienda with its scents of dry air and fountains, and horse gear. Rebecca noted too, how upon excusing herself from further intrusion, this done as if she were already partially transparent, the graciousness and manners carefully ministered for each occasion and its visitors, Erina retuned to her privacy and isolation, suddenly stood erect, her walk not that of sickly ghosts, but a girl readying herself for the world without apology or hesitation.

During this period Rebecca's mother and aunt made the dangerous journey from the remote, and to families like Erina's, sinister hills of the Sierra Madre del Sur and its cloud forests. There was always the possibility of the many faces Death provides; hungry jaguars and lions, snakebite, heat exhaustion, murder, or the witches' Double fooling even the most wary with impersonations these women knew were spun from earliest cocoons of disintegration so attractive and handsome to a human eye, and yet morbidly swarming at the point where that creaturely eye lurches and tilts in memories of its seeing. A region Rebecca's mother and aunt knew a Double had to master or die, taking its human host with it. They were afraid for Rebecca and so walked and ran the hundred miles distance arriving under cover of the strident quietness that arose with the European belief they were only partially human. The quietness held its exorbitant prices, and for those, like Rebecca's aunt and mother, there was a boatman going from one shore to another, similar too, yet less concerned than Death about the colors of morning and the shadows cast by certain trees at twilight. Small differences but in the dissolutions of seeing that comes with night, the breakages became swifter, dryer, wider and no strength of mind or dream could call these things to restoration. Rebecca feeling their nearness prepared tortillas, picked oranges, but stingily so the hacienda's gardener took no notice nor count. When she rode with her mistress and Erina to the market day in Oaxaca she saw them standing before the great and small baskets of seeds smiling in pleasure at such rich accumulation. They were able to mix their smiles with the joy of seeing Rebecca without being found out.

Two nights later they came when Venus seemed hottest to them.

They ate the tortillas first, then oranges. The girl had included fresh cool water with pitcher and cups she made herself as a kitchen servant assigned to replace any of the breakages in that household center. She required only minor instruction. Her plates, saucers, pitchers, bowls of differing sizes and needs were sought by other haciendas in the district. Her mother and aunt praised her for the taste and texture of the tortillas, for the relief of the fruit, and her potter's skills. When done they asked about Erina.

"What changes are there?" her mother asked.

"She is one thing. Then another," Rebecca answered.

"Is it of her own choosing?" The aunt added.

"Yes."

The two older women drank the water in long silence. There was no outward perplexity as they each held an orange, gotten for them, they knew, at some peril. At last the mother whispered, "The girl has become lifeless to her own people. Be her friend."

"Is there more?" Rebecca wanted to know seeing their faces grow heavy and distant.

"Her lifelessness will become your own if you don't."

In the flood of Rebecca's tears the two women were gone. All three understood what lingering could bring; a beating from other more experienced servants, foodless days to be gotten through, small but lacerating punishments meant to further break Indians like Rebecca, who for two-hundred years had been molded to life-long household routines. There were many who came back to their villages crushed with age by their mid-thirties; many too who died in ruthless solitudes and were buried.

It was Rebecca's aunt who heard the three-year-old child singing one morning and saw she memorized ancient complicated songs of their village she heard as rituals and processions went by. She called the mother to hear as they sat on the bare earthen floor of their shared hut, one husband having been killed by thieves, a second dwindling with fever. They were frightened. A child so charmed like this could be taken by nuns hopelessly beyond them.

That same week they went to a local woman, one who lived similarly to themselves. They did not want priests and nuns of their district to know; the songs often referred to Gods other than the crucified Lamb, and though they loved the Jesus, there were visits and trouble from his emissaries. The woman was expert in herbs and teas and was, though gently somber in her ways, fearfully respected for her abilities to ease troubles and sufferings of hers and other villages and often did what the prayers of Christian officials could not. But it was a danger to come to her. To be too easily seen. So the sisters visited when the Pleiades began their descent.

They brought Rebecca with them.

The woman was slight, face still drawn with terrible childhood hunger. More than half the villagers of their mountain world vanished from famine and disease. Though there was some food now, she still moved with cautions of that misery and smallness, her fingers and wrists partially crippled from earlier ravages. She wanted only an egg for the consultation. One of her two chickens had been attacked and carried off by a cara-cara.

"A sign," she said, smiling shyly at her visitors. The smile holding no deadness or obliterating gloom that raged under indifferent shells of so many in these hills, which was often the only protection they had from prying priests and officials who wanted only to know there was no remnant pagan demon in their souls. They were never not listening for rumor or whisper. And they well enough understood Indian languages and dialects.

The sisters set the egg before her.

"Ah," she said, "I can't decide where to eat it or let it hatch for another cara-cara who needs it too. Both of you. I thank you for the egg."

The dilemma of this was said with such gentle regard and unexpected humor the sisters were put at ease.

The woman then unfolded a straw mat and laid it between them.

"For the child. Place her here."

She began by touching Rebecca's face, feeling her head, turning palms up, rubbing hands and feet.

"Intelligent, beautifully intelligent," she said in a supple whisper, the child laughing easily while this was done.

"Now we'll wait for the singing."

And wait they did. Through the night letting Rebecca have her time, exploring as children will, moon motes cutting darkness into criss-crossed lines, or a wayward moth coming to rest and flexing its wings. The elderly woman whispered twice near Rebecca's ear, her patience watchfully easy, nearly motionless in its soothing hush over those hours. The moon had begun its quickening descent when Rebecca began, her chant-like tones having an almost acrobatic quality in their rhythms:

> In the place of rain and mists
> We are made
> We are made
>
> In the place of rain and mists
> We are cobwebs

> In the place
> Where rain
> Tastes like honey

The song was old, the old woman knew. The song was age-bent as some of the remote old tress in their wild mountains, the ones approached in secret for dreams and curses where snakes and birds and scorpions and spiders seemed to have ruins older than mankind. The girl sang it without flare. She let her tongue come to singing as to ghost sounds in search of lingering shade, as was proper the curer knew, to how humans might approach such gifts. Rebecca repeated the old sinew of words three times in succession then resumed her fascinations with what were now in pre-sunlit darknesses, unseen childish lures.

"You must watch for the day she will leave," the elder woman said after nearly an hour of wordlessness between them, adding, "the day she will never come back. Otherwise they will brand her face and make her into one of their beautiful worms."

They knew what the old woman meant. Nuns searched villages for ones like this. Stole children. Carefully, slowly drained them of all that had been. Turned them to dressed-in-black things, singing songs in languages of another world on days of Christmas and Easter. They saw it too as a more ancient transformation. The mystery double of fate for mortals and immortals dressed in flayed skins of previous selfs, singing of the soul's multiple identities full of awe and sacred danger and heart ache, more compelling than the tender Carpenter's agony.

When they heard of Erina's wandering eye they understood the "Day" had come. And as Rebecca watched, Erina's isolation began to increase. The girl who was once considered so desirable a future bride, began to walk the halls of her parent's estate at night, and often refused to eat.

"A shroud," Rebecca heard visitors sometimes whisper, "falling into powder, and for how much longer?" The question also held their desire to see Erina mercifully exiled to a proper nunnery so the shame of her would leak no farther.

# III

A man arrived for the funeral of the scorpion stung girl, one Erina had seen on the streets of her small city, buying fruit or charms from local female Mixtec vendors, dressed in their white cotton dresses for market day. Erina noticed her parents and their company whenever they passed by him. They never nodded to this obvious gentleman. Their manners were mostly distant and vaguely wilted before this person; a sudden bonelessness she could almost smell and which framed the man in soft mistrust.

She wanted to know more but saw how carefully and exactly elders shut away the encounter, allowing no more of it to mar them. He was of their social class but it seemed they willed him to dissolve. And when he stood over the dead body of Erina's friend they greeted him with a quiet, "Welcome Senior" in tones of formal sanction nearly reverential  rippling through the sorrow of the house. They directed their servants to fetch his easel, paints, a canvas ready on its stretcher.

And so he painted the dead girl quickly, skillfully, as if, Erina thought, he were tracing a dragonfly. Nothing more than the motion attended to with proper payment; his colors flat and vacuous, his "skill" a thing dried up and feeble, in accompaniment to its gruesome necessity.

Erina only glanced at this man and his work. It was late winter and the days had not yet filled their valley with any consistent heat. She remembered he readied his palette, his brushes, fixed the cloth drape for the dead girl's head, adjusted the necklace around her neck, touched her hands. She saw his lips move, but the whisper was inaudible as he walked in a tight circle around the body watching, hovering, turning up the lid of a dead right eye, pausing, studying the sightless thing there.

Erina at that moment was called away from the scene by her father's urgent tone, yet she knew where her own wandering eye had come to rest, but told no one. If her exile was to be inevitable, and she knew it was, then how could she apply herself to its possible fortunes rather than the carefully charted bitterness that would sweep her away.

Her late night journeys through arcades and gardens of her parent's hacienda were no longer merged with despair over her transformation. Her "eye" seemed secondary, the unreality of its rule over her life less stark, and the exaltation her parent's friends secretly felt over the disfigurement grew more narrow.

But where to start? And who to tell?

The image of that "painter" opening her dead friend's eye. Its violation left Erina feeling as if she were scratching in a glare of helplessness for months. In her nights of futility she began to think of herself as this kind of painter, applying her whole breath to another kind of shadow beyond the shadow she was slowly becoming.

She ordered paper, ink, various pens knowing this first act of extraction could draw no overt attentions. She had been crushed once for her wandering eye. To be crushed as a woman wandering, she understood, into forbidden acts would be to be twice robbed, the second thievery borne of her own possible carelessness.

She waited months. Her mother found these things in a delivery of fine linens from Mexico City. Erina arranged the placement of the items to seem an accident.

"Erina," her mother said, a few days after examining

the expensive rare cloth she ordered, "there are some misplaced curios here. Do you want to see them?" The daughter was hesitant, knowing precisely how her life depended upon what her reply might attract.

"Yes. What is it?" Erina responded letting the edginess of her voice burn away into the heavier firmness of the gardens where she often sat.

"Some ink and paper. Oh, and some pens too." Her mother's surprise and tone offered the daughter a comfort that had lain dead for years.

"Could someone have sent them by mistake. Shouldn't it be sent back?" Erina asked.

"To whom. Or where? The loss is final." Her mother's words cold as a centipede, enveloping both of them in the riddle.

Erina waited. A season. It made no difference. Let the moment be nondescript, she thought; a mid-morning lull. In April the sun will fill and the artist's things be nearly forgotten in their preservation as her mother's store of clutter. Insects can flutter, lizards become curious and hungry. She knew the cupboard, the shelf.

## IV

Her first attempts at "drawing" were a misery for her. Nothing seemed to yield. Her fingers felt wrenched, wrists fused. Her eye "spineless"; the word matching her feelings of dry recoil against each gesture of labor. "The blood in my fingertips feels like swollen scabs," she wrote in her notebook, wondering how to hold these tools which further lamed and aroused her. How many hours? Years? She devised "lessons" for herself in a corner of her mother's large garden. Rather than drawing on paper, she drew directly on the ground with the sharpened edge of a twig she'd found, smoothed the dirt and concentrated on her immediate surroundings. What flew, grew, and died in that exact corner. Erasing, drawing, erasing with the palms of her hands, bulge of her forearms letting the coldness of the soil find her.

Weeks passed. Months. She noticed a beginning, as yet uncertain fact; she did not feel so condemned and ugly. Her hands were stronger, fingers no longer the ruins she thought they were. There was also an image in the dirt before her; a flower with its stem, a small lizard hiding under the umbrella of the petals. The tight instance recorded with a nervous line which didn't fill her with shame. It was spare, clear, a little ragged, but she couldn't remember having done it. "And what form of mockery is this?" Erina asked herself, stumbling upon this trick of mind, and letting it further inflame her.

Rebecca also watched. The Mazatec servant was told to water and weed, attend to the main adjacent kitchen, help prepare meals, gather herbs, observe the young "mistress" from a distance and report to the "cook." But report what of the apparently "broken" and miserable patrona who seemed to drift into unshrinkable increase, moving from an almost feeble twilight to a perch, as if a newly proportioned and hungry nestling.

In early afternoons Erina abandoned her corner for siesta, and migrated to household interiors. Rebecca waited, sometimes for hours, letting her labors dictate where and how she moved, pressing at Erina's corner lightly. The dirt was always smoothed over and Rebecca, though afraid to over-linger, drew water from the garden well, poured the nourishment onto the plants in that corner as if it were any other part of the garden. Erina in late afternoon hours of a September day in her mother's second storey sewing parlor turned toward her "Dirt Pile" as she called it, and watched the servant girl attend to the plants there and shyly look down at the erased ground. The girl's labor seemed ordinary. Erina turned away.

At the end of that month Erina saw the servant girl again. Saw her do the same things.

"Are these orders?" she asked herself, knowing what her parents wanted to know.

Each girl in her stealth began a watch.

Erina observed no visible patterns to Rebecca's visits. She listened for household rumors. There were none.

In a late twilight of the following July Rebecca filled ceramic jugs she made with water. The day's labors stranded her in exhaustion but she carried the heavy cool things to herbs and roses, careful not to wet leafs or expose tomatoes, peppers, various squashes to night rot. Orange, lemon, and fig trees demanded a similar care. She did not waste a single mid-summer drop. Though tired, she found in watering a sudden renewal. Birds came to watch and hover and she didn't have to dig far into garden dirt for insect larvae or worms she set out on garden walls for birds to eat. Her end of day moments provided a suspension and freshness that lingered for her even in the repetitive days of heat strain and blisters.

The temperature was heavy on this day. Night dissipated nothing of its hardness which also carried vagueries of a deep burning that comes when sun ravenously feeds on little edges, its odors tart and sharp and never to be ignored. Erina watched the thin girl, nearly breathless, but still lifting, pouring, managing yet a new pattern as she approached the "corner" and began to water there. She looked down, as always quickly, at the dirt, at an arrow drawn there pointing toward the house. Rebecca looked away, poured the remaining precious gallons of water, placed empty vessels on the ground below fine weeding and cultivating she'd done in each raised garden segment. She turned toward the arrow, toward the immediate wall of the house, and let her eyes move up to a second storey window where she saw a silhouette, then Erina's face.

Erina in those months watched too as Rebecca kept the garden, shaped it for birds and insects, light and air, saw this was not random or accidental; watched the servant concentrate on the small, the unnoticed and what began to emerge from those charmed, unhurried labors. She saw death was as everywhere in that garden as life. Rebecca took account of each dead thing and either left its space empty or brought chicken manure and mixed it with soil and let that place wait. Her care was not boisterous, drew no eye nor sucked breath of unwanted surprise.

"Whose corner is whose?" Erina asked herself, growing less weary.

On that day she drew the arrow. Nothing more. Knowing both their lives depended on it.

# V

There was no single event. Nothing for attention to gather and produce its frame of whispers in that world. Erina let a weightless, trimmed suggestion loose, indistinct as the flit of a lizard diving for shadows.

"Mother. Can we take the carriage to market one day next week?"

"For why?" her mother asked.

"For seeds and flowers. See vendors like we used to?"

The mother remembered these things fascinated this daughter. Indian women coming from their far mountains and valleys, carrying, beyond their goods, their ancient arts of bargaining, old excited intelligences uncovered for those hours which Erina's mother thought repulsive, but harmless as she considered earlier excursions with the Mazatec servant, the one confined to kitchen, to garden because of her apparent aptitude. But more. Her passivity and faintness pleased the mother who did not want the thick hopelessness of other servants making her feel suspended in her own household, "Like a lemon," she thought, "in a bat's mouth," and shuddering in her own sensations.

She knew her daughter admired beautifully woven baskets of varying sizes, color patterns. Wondered aloud if these women were mathematicians hoarding catagories of numbers so peculiar, so complete that their coldness would allow only these appearances. Blind seed women, wrinkled female twins who counted seed and seed weight with fingertips so parched they seemed to outrace the intricate fears and murder lurking in the countryside. Butcheresses deftly and gracefully breaking necks of chickens, the birds hovering headless, squirting blood there in the women's hands. Sellers of orange and green, purple and brown chocolate with flavors of river beds.

"Maybe older than water, eh Mama?" the imaginative girl speculated in wonders her mother hoped could be delicately crushed for her daughter's sake, for the sake of future nuns and priests who would surely, she felt, grow scornful of a too obvious intelligence not properly nipped by a mother such as herself.

A servant was ordered to clean and ready a simple black carriage, prepare horses, reigns, bridles, a vaquero for escort; Rebecca told she was to go with the Matron and her daughter. A Saturday, September of 1728. Erina, twenty years old. Her mother planned to place her in a convent by the age of twenty-five in Mexico or Spain. The trouble of it had licked the mother's flesh half away. The father desired an earlier beginning of exile. "To lessen sorrow. Let the bleeding begin so it can end," he proposed to his wife one night in their quarters. The mother stiffened. Said hardly a word for over a month. The marriage curdled.

There had been yet another plague in the villages. The countryside looked like a spit up bone. Crops and soil nothing more than scabbed combinations; "Mud to dust. Dust to mud. This trickle of words," Erina thought as she looked out, "as easily ready to dry up," catching herself in mid-thought, shamed over her own perceptions knowing partially the burdens she was to her mother who had to explain this curious daughter to herself, then to friends and visitors, feeling as if each word were covered with lice, the back of her throat brackish and cracked.

Children in small clumps wandering river and stream beds stared at the simple carriage. One boy threw a stone at the two overly groomed horses, then seemed to partially collapse from his exertions. The horses flinched, steadied themselves. The three women watched other children gather over their suddenly fallen companion. Yellow Fever. The *vomito negro*? None of them could see properly from their distance. Or rabies? They saw two staggering cows in a previous arroyo, no more than two miles from this village. Was it the dreaded stage of paralysis for the boy which might explain his behavior? A nun who came to see Erina at the request of the father brought news of a previous outbreak to their household. "Watch the horses," she warned. "And bulls. If they become docile. Some say a child can be bitten and for almost a year nothing will happen. In others it can only be days. I have seen both" as she touched her cross, sucked lightly at her astonishment, recalling her years of service among the poor.

Erina found herself at ease with this elder. Her disciplined yet humorous charm lingered in their home after the woman left. One hardly recalled her limp. Rather her manners and self assurance were a gentle stimulant. Erina's mother became even more silent knowing her husband's subtleties and arrangements. The visit of this nun made her seethe.

As they neared Oaxaca roads were nearly choked with Indians a-foot, their foreheads strapped, balancing weight of heavy sacks, both women and men bent forward in a lean, concentrating on each foot, one misstep could mean broken ankle or leg, though they held themselves in a moist watchfulness against dust, against exhaustion and seemed to nearly dissolve. Erina's mother pulled herself away from her momentary stare at these pobrecitos, crossed herself quickly for she had told her daughter "the Infant runs but Dread comes as a wide, slow river." There were other carriages in front and behind, carts, horsemen. Erina's mother pulled the curtains to avoid dust, human and animal waves. She checked and straightened Erina first, then herself, tidied Rebecca as nothing more than a barren afterthought. Noises outside were muffled, but one could hear clatter, creaks of loaded wagons, straining horses, snap of whips, press of muscles. Bells of the cathedral began their chimes as Erina's mother directed the driver toward outer precincts of the zocalo where she knew her husband waited. There were men from the great bull ring of Mexico City who came to see their hacienda's legendary fighting bulls and horses. Though between the parents there was little talk, Erina and her mother knew the family business and traditions, adored the bulls and horses. She wanted to surprise her daughter with the spectacle of a sale. Purchase of an animal meant great prestige for their ganadera. Fierce blood and hard malevolence attracted emissaries even from Spain.

All three heard the father's approaching footsteps as his strained, dim-faced wife drew back the curtains. Their exchange of syllables was done, Erina thought years later, as if each had scraped a partially swallowed spider.

The mother directed her driver to the southern edges of the city into a maze of corrals planted there for sale and inspection of animals once every three years. "Bulls, Mama?" Erina whispered.

"Yes, My child," her mother formally spoke, allowing her lips to change back from stone to flesh. Rebecca let her eyes fall on Erina's lap. The daughter let her fingers roll tight into small fists held forefinger to forefinger on her thighs. The servant bathed in anticipation and dark intensities of these matrons, felt herself begin to shudder. Might she be indentured to another household and if this were so, where? Vomit rose up and burned the back of her nostrils.

The older woman drew back the curtains once more. There were thunderheads rising behind the plateau of pyramids but the segment of sky above them was hard blue. As they approached the corrals they saw men riding savagely fine Andulusian mares, short tempered, fearsomely smart as their Arabian ancestors. The passage of their carriage made the horses stamp in near rage, the riders on them relaxed and superb, fingering reins as if those leathers were flexing/unflexing snakes born of necks, jaws, defiantly bulging horse eyes.

"Blood smell" Erina spoke almost involuntarily, leaning forward to see the graceful, bold fury of these horses bred for bull rings, ready to bite, ready to kick eternity itself to a pulp, Erina thought, and let her gaze fall on the young woman whose dark skin was drawn taut over temples and chin. The wide face stern with loneliness, but unbroken, jarred Erina as the other woman returned her gaze.

"Your father. There he is!" The mother could not hold her rush of language as she waited for the driver to open the carriage door, allow them to step down. The horses seemed like spilled fire, combed to a sheen, nostrils flaring with stinging hatred over scents of men and bulls. They were corner crazed and nearly lathered at hearing bellows of still unseen tethered bulls and bull piss caught in air made the horses swirl and kick. Vaqueros, including Erina's father, were gathered and relaxed in their silver braided saddles pulse to pulse with enraged rhythms of the beasts underneath them. There were puddles of horse piss to be stepped around. Rebecca was frightened by the streamlined, terrible bulk of the Andalusians, especially the wild blood-raw farts of a magnificent mare kicking and snorting not more than twenty feet from where they stood, the animal's malevolence and lust made Rebecca want to shrink in a current of abandonment.

The father refused to hide the world of the ganedera from either daughter or wife. The two women were composed and watchfully held their ground as riders and animals shredded air around them waiting for the appearance of the bulls. He felt helplessly proud as he watched the women stand, hard in their courage and full dresses, as the horses bit at each other, knowing their riders, wanting to feel the human rage in squeezing knees and thighs. To fight the bulls required this. No animal needed the spur, though metal there was to draw horse blood further, more elaborately. There would be no killing today. Only inspection and buying. Erina heard her father calling to his silver mare's temporary rider, saw him motion the vaquero to a corral built in the form of a bullring. The horse moving toward the enclosure spun, snapped its back and neck, eyes blared with cold murder, tail swishing, the grace of it sinister, viciously weightless, and as the animal and rider passed the threshold the horse's body flexed into a smooth, nearly awful prance, as if deliberately honing its own savageries, carrying the few spectators, vaqueros, and other horses with it, scouring the so far empty death arena as if it were no more than the tongue of hummingbird.

Erina noticed two well dressed strangers descend from a large carriage not far from her own. Both gone jowl heavy, were of medium height, and affected the latest fashion of Mexico City. They talked only to themselves, stood apart, had the accents of Madrienos, flaunted the syllables just enough to be heard as they moved toward the main corral to judge horse and bull flesh for possible inclusion either in the great arena of the Colonial capitol for the Viceroy's pleasure or to be seen in Spain as evidence of the limited but interesting breeding lines emerging out of the obscure provinces of the New World. But the three women and horsemen around them did notice, were alerted by the strained indifference of these visitors who wore their justacorps under the not yet too agressive sun, their dark grey coats narrow at shoulders and sleeves cut tight to arms. Erina's mother took a studied measure of the sleeve cuffs nearly folded to elbows; the hanging fabric of the coats descending as an open skirt to the knees. She looked even more carefully at the "gilet" or waistcoats buttoned down to waistline and there evenly flaring out as an inverted V extending around upper thighs and buttocks. She smirked at these too carefully polished meat buyers as she thought of others like them who came for the harvests her family had bred for nearly six generations and its traditions her husband married into. She appraised the flesh expertly; both the non-human and this other directing her gaze further to the buttonholes of the gilets embroidered with swirls of gold thread and the cravats of delicate lace studiedly twisted to emphasize male chins and necks, male skin pronounced as a complimentary frill which allowed her to snap open her fan, brush her face with just enough air. Both wore stockings, one pair blue, the other yellow, pulled over the hems of their knee-length breeches bordered at the folds by black silk hems.

Erina's father took his moment too to watch the strangers, so archly suave before piss puddle and horse shit, providing laughless comedy. They seemed like Inquisitors able to work a form of suffocation, so old after the piled decades. To him they were preening wasps cleaning their antennae as they stepped in their square toed high heels, but real.

And the mother moved her fan down over her breasts, fluttered the relieving wisps of air over her neck as she focused on the "allonge" of the heavier one, his large curly wig hanging below his shoulders with its two fattened wings rising nearly four inches above his hairline. She tightened her fingers with the increased motion of her fan. The other's wig was more in keeping with newest styles as she knew, distant as she was from the capitol. His was smaller, though equally curly, and hung just below ear-line. They both wore dark tricorn hats embroidered with expensive silver thread at the edges and assisted themselves with ivory and jade in-laid walking sticks. "Probably from China," the father mused to himself as he called for the vaquero, mounted his aging bull-killing mare, to better observe these men, who turned their eyes on the horseflesh underneath him which still had its taste for combat. The one missing and most announcable item: their swords which Erina and her mother knew would have been as the swirling gold threads of their waistcoats elaborately embroidered, advertising their importance. Neither one wore gloves, and as their audience knew, felt they had to.

One, who wore the larger allonge, stopped, turned in a haughty appraising circle and asked, "Senor Castro. Where is he?" He let the question and its varnished boredom drift, Erina thought, like a claw as she watched her father dismount from his dangerous mare, walk toward the visitors, and standing before them, wordlessly bowed.

The two, spent by mid-day heat, were taken to an open tent where they could more easily measure horses and bulls, be served refreshment. Fruit was brought to them on silver trays, oranges and grapes, cheese from the Castro ganadera; fresh baked bread, some water in a fine, hand-formed ceramic pitcher of Rebecca's to keep the water cool. The Mazatec, taking notice of the object, felt an involuntary chill of shame, folded her arms quickly over her breasts to still her alarm, then caught Erina watching her with so frank a reassuring gaze she nearly blushed.

At that moment three egrets swooped over their heads, startling men and horses; two cocks fighting for a hen, wing-grappled and luminous in their rigid bird angers and nearly crashed into the tent. The smaller more fashionable man in his surprised revulsion over the sudden taut-fleshed bird-storm fell over backwards in his chair and rose up sputtering in an over-elegant rage; waited for his friend to help straighten coat and wig and breeches, each flickering over the other in such smooth disgust Erina's mother had to check her own audible sneer.

Servants ran to the strangers, brushing crumbs and spilled food. The two waited sullenly for re-supplied trays in the harshening scents of the sun-grazed afternoon. In that narrow drift of scattered gazes and tensions Erina was able to stand next to Rebecca, take her hand. Both women grew breathless, their web of fingers tightened as they watched Senor Castro talk to the strangers, helping them with a thoughtful relieving ease to reclaim their possession of the afternoon, calling the least attention to himself. Senora Castro's lips flattened over her teeth in a fiery admiration for this man's natural gifts and both the younger women understood instantly how this mother and father had drawn themselves into each other's lives. And it was that moment, Erina knew, that freed her for Rebecca and the things to come, as the daughter knowingly eased her grip and stepped back to her mother's side.

The father signaled for his horse and an attendant vaquero. He spoke briefly, pointed, then remounted his silver mare and rode to the edge of the ring shaped corral, letting his horse rear and kick her front hoofs, its clutch of rage held to shoulders, curled ears, snort smoldered nostrils.

A bull bellowed. Both humans and horses turned

in the direction of the heavy, low threat. There were four. Each was let into a separate corral. One was white with light brown patches. The remaining, black. Erina knew by their almost iridescent nervousness they'd just been brought from the wild barancas and arroyos of her parent's lands where they'd learned to survive jaguars and lions; but also wolves and rattlesnakes, here, depending on the seasons, deadly for even animals this large. The other great peril; older more seasoned bulls, unpredictable, gruesomely mean. The range, exacting in its mercilessness, was managed and driven by the vaqueros, both Aztec mestizos and indentured Spaniards who could ride horses, Erina reckoned into her advanced age, as if Death had bit out their eyes and given an extra blind lifetime to carve out their vengeance as maniacal centaurs she had loved to watch as a girl baiting each other in contests of skill with their animals even the Ancient Shadow Itself might pause to admire.

The bulls, entering their separate enclosures, whirled and stamped, twisted their fanged heads in murderous, stiffened rage, blew a shower of drool from their nostrils, lifted their tails and let go a loathsome fringe of shit to register their intolerance of even the nearest moth. These were the gestures that made the visitors stand up, brush away the crumbs of their too elaborate meals. The animals stamped, circled their enclosures with a violence so contracted and hostile Erina felt both her fascination and nausea

rising to her shoulders. Each bull rose to a circling
fury goring air and lumber, then as suddenly sank into
a heavy, smothering stupidity. The blunted glare of it,
Erina knew, made an animal even more dangerous, its
savagery narrow and focused in an oblivion no one
could afford to ignore.

Her mother had read to her, the story of the
creature/beast, the one breathing in a labyrinth.
Prison monster filled with madness and lust, stuck
in some twilight between identities, dressing itself in
murder, and scrupulously sensual lifelessness as she
came to articulate it through her painting. She knew
it wasn't the exact story, but she knew too she had to
trick herself out of her own childhood and that her
recurring dream about a bull filled her with more
distant terror than the old story and what boiled in
it. The dream had come early to her, maybe her sixth
or seventh year after riding with her father for an
inspection of the hacienda's lands. The journey had
taken four days, though the father had wished it to
be longer. She saw hills and rivers, arroyos and small
flowered plains where bulls grazed for most of their
lives in the wild. They were escorted by vaqueros and
at night they stopped and she heard their stories and
ate the feasts of meat cooked on open fires. On one
leg of the "inspection" as her father called it, a wild
horseman appeared in a mid-afternoon and there was
a conference between her father and this man whose

first words were "How beautiful the day." The whispers between the two lasted no more than a minute. She stared after him as he rode away, as if being swallowed by the land mysteries and so unlike anyone she'd ever seen.

After this she noticed the carriage moved faster as if now there was a destination, though her father ordered a halt and walked with her over bluffs, or through meadows, explaining where they were and how it related to their lives. She never saw and would never see her father again so happy. Toward twilight she saw a campfire on a distant knoll. There was the smell of smoke and burning meat. There were the drum-like sounds of Tule trees carried on early evening winds.

"Ah. The Noche Triste goes walking," her father said, smiling over the beat in the leaves. He told his daughter too, the great water resistant wood of the "Noche Triste" was used as piers to hold up Tenochtitlan; one of the first words she learned and loved all of her life to feel its syllables rise and fall away from her palette, as if in whispering, the Aztec city might be pulled back to life from either its own sound or a brush stroke.

Though the sun was at least an hour from setting the horseman waited. Their carriage followed him slowly into a wide ravine filled with "Little Skulls." The beautiful cactus whose seeds, Erina knew, were used for rattles and dancing. She thought it a lucky day to hear the drums of the old trees, to be in this ravine where the delicate skulls grow out of hidden twilight dust, and to see her father so happy. She recalled how the horseman climbed the slope of a bluff enshrouded with smells of chocolate from the tree with white flowers, "Rose of Funerals" as her father called it, the lush enwrinkled white of its petals so swollen in the falling sun of that afternoon.

When the horseman signaled a halt father and daughter walked to the top of the small rise. There were two bodies knotted there, their eyes locked in rage; a jaguar and a bull. The great cat had crushed the bull's throat, caught an eye with a claw, left it to dangle venomously at the edge of its socket. But still the bull had grown more precise in its fury, gored the jaguar in the chest, at the moment the great "Tigre," the horseman said, "Smelled its triumph." Both lay in the small lake of blood that had not yet been absorbed into soil. Erina remembered staring at the animals, then at the two men whose faces seemed to go almost corpse-smooth before the dilated final concentrations of the beasts. "Moths will suck first," the horseman said to Erina's father, not really caring, Erina knew, who in that emptiness heard, "then the others."

The aroma of chocolate reminded her of her single trip to Spain, as passengers with her mother and Rebecca, allowed a berth on the "Silver Fleet" from the New World. Seville, City of Jasmine, gardens, veiled women, and Velazques, master, as she came to know, of a nearly terrifying indifferent suspense of ordinary life caught in the "bodengon" as it was called. Rendering people and objects in the sudden plainness of their being alive and penetrated by nothing more than light. She was deeply awed by the artist's "Christ in the House of Martha and Mary." A kitchen scene presented as if it were nothing more than an old wives tale. Cloves of garlic, two eggs, a jug of olive oil, a single curling pepper. The young girl with her muscled, flexed hands, large peasant forearms, work-weary face. The old woman whispering from behind, touching the girl's large shoulder, heavy cloth of her drab brown dress, sparse and bereft, its creases and folds painted as if to catch living motions of the tired body crushing garlic cloves and the reflection in the upper right segment of the painting—Jesus and two females listening carefully to his preaching in a vacant room, light motionless and cold. The young, forlorn girl, seemed to Erina, unsure of the story and its lore, that her life of constant numbing labor will fulfill her as the act of worldly worship of the Son. Her eyes, her cheeks swollen with exhaustion hold a millenniums long skepticism each girl must bear or not, Erina noted for herself, as she stared at the artist's work full of lures and wincing anguish she recognized would re-shape her own life and could not escape.

Erina could not release herself from feeling the tale of the brutal repetition was held in the image of the four fish who in their deaths stare at the viewer as if their four aloof and inaccessible eyes are the trespass belonging to the sensualities of grief and delusion.

She knew this version of still-life. Its open evocation of spare, hidden dignities with their background of murderous seventeenth century Spanish melancholy ravaged her world. The haunted decay, plague, and starvation gave this King's painter a way to tell stories so unwanted in their unsuspected disruptions that they caused a seizure of murmurous curiosity, otherwise they might have been too unbearable. Erina was also deeply fascinated by the fact that this master made no preliminary sketches and had to create from nothing a looseness of brush strokes that made it possible to build up thin layers of light and contour never seen before. These things she studied. And she listened, enraptured by the madness of the Spanish Kings and their courts and how Velazquez was able to suggest the delusions of those worlds through a single red pepper lying on the table of "Christ in the House of Martha and Mary" and the two eggs in their white repose holding what intolerable weights of virginity and chastity?

And she wondered over the cracked cloves of garlic.

What did they invoke as she thought of the final hours of Philip III lying in his death chamber with piled desiccate bodies of dead saints whispering to him of the waiting graces or further horrors in the next world?

Both she and Rebecca marveled over the pearl worn by Queen Isabel as Velazquez painted her. The great bell-shaped jewel hanging from a long necklace which for them held uncomprehending motions of another story about the Americas; this seething thing found by an Indian slave in a miniscule oyster and nearly tossed back in to its American depths, yet saved for Spanish Queens from the 1550s onward as each successive ruling generation presided over more fevered disasters and impoverishments as if the luminosities of the gem exacted a cold putrescence from the conqueror who unknowing covered his royal off-spring in magical charms and wards against evil without once suspecting the beautiful little American comet which dangled from the necks of its Queens. This consort of Philip IV also wears the pearl. Her cruel, tight, yet attractive face, Erina remembered, betrayed her need for elaborate spiderish feedings. Her joys as she watched snakes being released onto the unsuspecting aristocratic audiences of the King's theaters, causing panic and tramplings, as the two young women shuddered beneath the painter's image.

But it was Court dwarfs who reminded these Oaxacan visitors most closely of their American valleys. Erina, as she was accustomed, spent time at a neighboring hacienda. The estate's patrona collected and kept ancient ceramic figurines in a separate room with stacked shelves for this purpose. There were things there which had frightened her—an urn with the head of a lascivious beast, part bat, part jaguar, its face contorted with leering rabidity, tongue distended, head arched with ancient insolence and ruin—the unspeakable revulsions that attend those who might be stolen and ravished. The "Murcielago" God of Night and Death who hears heartbeats of creatures, a small thing no larger than a knuckle, watching everyone and everything, panting. Or the human face she picked up, half flesh, half bone with still clinging but rotted skin, left eye about to burst with writhing maggots. The object rendered with such assured quietude over the fact of a human face, this fellow artist, as Erina had to, worked against death's appraisal, splitting what reality might hold, into this disinterestedly staring double. There was an acrobat too, more, a contortionist, body bent so that soles of feet press on head crown, elbows spread to exact body width, forearms extended as angled pillars holding a face which to her later shock resembled Velazquez's portrait of Francisco Lezcano, the mentally stunted dwarf, reading Tarot for amusements of the Royal Court, his smile holding invitations of broken prophecies and worlds, the one she understood who was a sex toy cobbling his secrets to the arch of his head, his lips, his hands distended with soft fat, bemused hopeless knowledge weighing his eyelids.

Surrounded by starvation and plague the Spanish Court amused itself with wigs, elaborate fashions and feasts, hunting expeditions, theatric spectacles and collections of cretins, dwarfs, hydrocephalics who were given as presents from one European Court to another. Erina saw their portraits as a kind of signal to herself; that painting be done quickly, allowing for the space of suggestion and tender animation not removed from the meticulous brutalities held so precariously in the artist's fingertips and registering the hovering disintegrations. The one painting which stung her, gave her nerve before the about-to-rot corpses that waited for she and Rebecca's attentions was of the court jester, Pablo de Valladolid. She studied the solitary figure that for her inhabited no reference to any world attached to any known fate she could discern. There was no suggestion of a defining space either up or down, or the recession of depth that might hold the eye or mind to its assurances. The hands of the figure were large, strong, repulsively flexed, and held nothing. The face stiff, impassive, coldly creaturely in its stare. The body held no form other than its intricate drapery of loose dark linens. Its feet were spread and the only support for the figure's weight or being was its own awkwardly grotesque shadow that appeared for Erina and Rebecca to be at once the projection of the body or a probing spider's legs searching for and stumbling in this abyss upon its prey. The sorrow of it so measured and precise she felt as breathless as the corpses she knew one day she would paint. The image's hands gesture in the same direction carrying the weight of the nothing which clusters, sinisterly or not, as the two women appraised those ambiguities, over fingers and wrists. The central bulk of the figure is captured in a flotation, its barren and nearly botanical purity reminded Rebecca of the Five Days of Bad Luck that leapt out of her own people's ancient calendar even to this "Madonna" who to her seemed, with his extended hand, to be pointing toward the early morning flowers his King picked to freshen those hours while half his city died of thirst and prostitution.

In the portrait of the King's personal dwarf, "El Primo" or Don Diego de Acedo, Erina and Rebecca wondered how Velazquez was able to hold this person's deep intelligence and the sense of possible shattered belief in either Creation or God haunting the sitter's eyes and mouth. He was very small and the two women were unsure of what pain his limbs might have given him, or the increasingly limited functions brought about by a dwarf's afflictions that they saw in the markets and rural villages of their native Oaxaca. The men and women who were never saved as "presents" with their skeletons festering, faces upheaved by too much warp of bone, limping or crawling because of leprosy, yaws, or nameless infection, each one as marked as Erina knew herself to be with molestations swarming and transitory. "Is this what Velazquez notes in this painting?" Erina recorded in her sketchbook. "This King's secretary: is he holding the Book of Flippant Negations or Evils in his lap as he stares up from a passage that stings him with an even more austere separateness and despondency?"

Neither Erina's mother nor Rebecca wanted her to see "Calabazas": the cross-eyed. But the daughter knew more tightly what kindled in her; what she belonged to. She studied the jester's collar and cuffs. The loose peculiar brush work, its contrast with the more disciplined modeling of the face created an enriched glare Erina had never seen, even a comment on the most hostile depths of mortality so quiescent and unmocking Erina felt herself without insulation. The phosphorescent expressive energy of the collar and cuffs gave the details of this drunkard's face and hands, his enrapt debauchery and breakage working his Queen and King for their cruel laughter, a tensely hesitant dignity resistant to the ridicule and bondage which ensnared his life. She was astonished too by the painter's command over the dwarf's hands; the left held palm up and relaxedly open on top of the bent right knee, fingers loosely splayed, and the right hand partially closed, laid to rest there as if unknowingly stuffed in a coffin. The presence of these hands, Erina thought, telling more than face or pose of body, as if these were foundlings, uneasy, semi-neglected, pretending to sleep; little phantoms resting from their browse among the living. "How will I," Erina recorded in her sketchbook, "portray the hands of the dead, edge of face or nose, place them in state, and then proceed to give them an intense a story as the one here; the freshly dead flesh, wetly cool and inscrutable, frozenly transparent as some ivory from an as yet unnamed and unrevealed creature?"

Erina's mother was able to glance only once at the painter's picture of Queen Mariana. She turned from the image, broke into tears and walked away spreading her fan over her face to hide, keep her quivering in check. Erina and Rebecca however, let their own eyes drift and be caught. The Queen with all her regalia, her fortune of birth, normality of limb and blessings of girlhood comeliness was the most powerless, and cruelly fate-ravished of any of the figures they were invited to or allowed to see. A poisoned, anvil-cold emptiness and boredom drowned her by the age of nineteen when the painting was executed. She was already five years into marriage. Her face at that moment lacerated in haggard resentment, sexual disgust and disappointment. Her magnificently voluminous hair and dress, the artist's invention of new brush strokes and hand-work to vivify the innermost extremes that adhere to the girl's collapsed lips, the dip of her nose. Erina knew in this Velazquez's dangerous poise and wondered how these persons of the Court trapped in the twilight of their riches could have ever allowed their precariousness to be so fiercely recorded.

"Who was Velazquez?" Erina asked. "to record these royal beings in their most remote helplessness and who showered him with rewards?"

# VI

It was the jaguar-slashed bull that re-occurred in Erina's dream. She was often frozen in the starkness of the image, hoping her own wandering eye would not accidentally settle in this region, the bull trapped too in the stifling dispossession of the dream, trying to gore its own never entirely disattached taunting eye and stalking her through wild ravines. The visitors from Mexico City had tossed their silver plates full of food on the ground, wiped their faces with silken handkerchiefs as they walked quickly to the corrals studying the bulls that coiled themselves in even tighter circles, the two men greedy for the rage-heavy animals.

The bulls in their separate spaces shook their heads, stamped the perimeters of their enclosures goring the air, eyes partially rolled back in hot panic. The air stunk of their sharp/luring musk, tongues dangling with froth, testicles weighted, swaying; their anger monotonous and sweet. Erina looked at her mother. Her mother's lips trembled. The truest daughter of the "ganadera" breeding bulls for the Plaza in Mexico City, each flank carrying the brand of their family; the head of a swan in simple outline, its eye a snake's rattle, the image it was said, drawn by one of the surviving Aztec sons brought to the legendary College of Tlatelolco, and who lived to be over a 100.

Erina watched as the two men appraised the flesh. One stood too close to the ring and was sprayed with flying drool. He shrieked, explosively wiped his face and chest, stammered in a display of gloating nausea. Erina and her mother touched hands, compelled themselves to make no overt gestures of contempt or to even partially smile as the father looked toward them, assuring himself their faces registered nothing but stone. He was proud of their careful self-mastery. It was his first attraction to Erina's mother, and in this second took his eyes off his mare, let the reins slide from his hands. The horse always testing, always blindly fierce, lurched away, stumbled for a second in its freedom, bucked the father into the dirt, then whirled, tried to shake the gorgeous saddle and leatherwork from its skull and body. It trotted, looked for an escape, and seeing none stared at the corral of the nearest bull. Men rushed to assist the father, but he was up, calling the horse's name, walking carefully toward his animal which at that point glared only at him as it backed up, nervously moving its head up and down in warning, even to this master, to come no nearer. Erina's father walked more carefully and the horse lowered her ears, stamped the ground with her right hoof, swished her tail, the pitch of horse rage sleek and vicious.

Erina, recalling the scene, couldn't remember her father's small gestures; his horse charged and the man was able to jump away, but not without injury. He broke his wrist. The horse stopped over the fallen body, shook its head from side to side, reared halfway on its hind legs as if to further mangle and ruin Erina's father. But the mare stopped, turned toward the small arena of the nearest bull, broke into a run and jumped the fence. Her father ignored his broken bones and ran after the animal as it steadied itself. The bull wasn't immediately aware of its sudden intruder. Its back was turned when the horse took flight and when it landed the bull was temporarily startled. It lifted its head, sniffed, focused for one deadly moment, then trotted in wayward circles before its visitor.

The two creatures let their hate grow.

The bull was first. It charged with its head down, horns ready to slash. The horse spun, jumped away, caught the bull in the face with a crushing kick from its back hoofs. The bovid shook itself as blood gushed from its nose and hanging lower jaw. The two visitors screeched a vulgar "Olay" at the combat as Erina and Rebecca followed the mother to the side of the injured husband who was watching the spectacle in hopeless pain; bones protruding from skin. The mother glanced down, turned away, could not stop a rush of anguish, though both felt the rupturous angers toward each other over their daughter; anger which had no names, destroyed their courage, and caused each to go narrow, as Erina realized in old age, in loneliness.

The horse watched its victim carefully now, having

been trained by its master for this violence. The bull bellowed in agony and disbelief as it tried to corner the horse for a second charge. The horse waited, and in the final instance exploded over the bull's back and nearly tumbled on its side. Unable to check its momentum, the bull fell face first into the lumber of the ring. Its high pitched bellow was gaudy and grotesque as the injured beast turned toward its tormentor, this time with its jaw hanging by barely a thread, and flapping. But Erina could see the bull shaking blood and drool off of itself, watching her father's horse. It seemed to draw itself into a sturdy, certain lunacy, and though dazed, stood composed and untroubled as it watched the horse circling, trying to gain enough speed to jump the barrier once more, leave the victim aswim in its own wreckage.

Erina knew her father let this horse run their lands, but just enough to give it "the smell of the horizon" as he said "and the jaguars to give her permanent rage." The bull stared, scraped its front hoofs. Then it lunged for the horse who had also made its decision to jump, and nearly did, except for its right front hoof, which caught the edge of a board, caused the animal to flip back on the bull's waiting horns. The horse screamed as the bull twisted its head, the violence of the impact bursting guts all over the bull as it dropped to its front knees.

Erina's mother gathered herself as if she were the rightful daughter of this ferocity; its bravery and revulsion the exact business of her heritage. The two animals were breathing. Stench of exposed viscera flared up, knotted the air. She walked toward her husband through the nauseous sting, leaned down and helped him rise from where he'd fallen in a sudden despair. His mare was lurching against the throes of her death biting at the bull, blood gurgling from both their nostrils. The two visitors rushed to Erina's mother and asked it they could have both heads as a momento of the combat. "Both animals," they stammered, "a wonder." She whispered to her husband who was unable to concentrate on anything at that moment but the final waves of blood coming from his horse's nostrils and eyes. The animal was struggling to stand and somehow called out of itself a last surge, balanced on all fours, guts dangling, then it collapsed. And both animals were terrible and soft in their heap, their violence still dense with its purity, their bodies not yet completely settled in death.

"Vive Caballo" the two visitors clottedly yelled, not able to check themselves.

Erina's father turned to them. "The heads. They are yours."

He looked down then, focused on his injury. Understood for the first time his whole body was trembling.

"Erina. Make sure we have the ears and hoofs. Don't forget her saddle and reins."

Her father did not pass out as they thought he

might. He ordered another horse, mounted it and rode the many miles back to his estate.

With the help of the horseman the daughter did as she was told. He cut flesh and leather while the two buyers hovered, not hiding their impatience, then handed the daughter his obsidian knife with its straight oak handle and walked away.

No one could have anticipated the impact of this combat. The visitors presented a contract to the ganadera, to supply the family's bulls to the Plaza in MexicoCity. "As to the horse," they said, "none like it have we seen. None like will draw breath again."

To these words the mother sneered, remembering the priggish eagerness of these men for the violence, nearly shivering with glee over the sufferings, faces flushed and craning like their words.


Erina's father struggled. A doctor, one of the buyers sent from the capitol, examined his injury, pronounced it very dangerous and ripe for gangrene.

He could set it, "But wrist and hand can only wither and cripple."

He could amputate.

The father had become feverish. The deadness spreading up.

"There is little time" the physician told Erina and her mother.

It took months to recover. Intermittent fevers and nausea needed hourly attentions and the one most capable both in stamina and skill was Rebecca. Accompanied by Erina she collected and boiled herbs, cast a tone of gentle care and assurance and gradually the two women became companions, holding their secret, and the beginning of Erina's skills. The severed hand of her own father. She took it. Drew it carefully. Cast herself into the immediate study and labor. The theft done with Rebecca's help. The limb returned quickly without a cast of suspicion.

It was their life together and Erina became known in her world for painting bodies as if their last breath had not yet wholly been summoned into the exile.

# Up
# Fish
# Creek
# Road

**H**er name was Pearl probably not called that for either the oyster or its jewel but something starker and saltier in the flesh. His name was Jim. You could think of Jim Thorpe. The one who said "Thanks King" to the delighted Swedish monarch who handed the Oklahoman his Olympic gold. Jim Steals Horse, the magic thief of the plains, or Jim the Steel Man who worked the magnet cranes of a certain mill whose once spewing smoke stacks rose downgrade from Primal Cucamonga Peak into a polluted California Sky.

It was said up and down Fish Creek Road she was the last of the Esopus. Not Chingachcook of the Mohicans but one who wore the land on her shoulders with some bluntness knowing that a rock accompanied every seed.

Or was it her brother, Sy, who everyone thought a little slow.

Both of them traced their blood directly back to Kaelcop, chief of the Amorgarickakan in that far away line of the Esopus who had a village called Sagiers, mostly for summer fishing. And though the annals omit it, courting too, as the edges of the great Ice Age stream run into long sweet meadows full of fertile swamp marigolds and eggs whether turtle, fish, or human ready for tidal winds and summer fog.

Pearl's ancestors, the Esopus, were known for their distrust of the Colonial Dutch. Looked upon those intruders wearily as cheats and liars. She could name the conflicts from the moment Pieter Miniut bought Manahatta from the Metoacs. "Beaver War ate three-quarters of the seventeenth century," she'd say, delivering a handful of rhubarb. "Isn't enough for an immediate pie, but for lunchtime cookies it'll serve up a cure."

There was the "Pig War." "Whiskey War." The "Peach War" with its fruits of murderous rage and cannibalism. Her ancestors during those summer festivals may even have visited Shodac, the great Mahican capitol that lay for centuries opposite the first moorings of Fort Orange. One would have thought too, far into the nineteen eighties, the common ways of twentieth century men were close, the tides of New York City pulled as much by the Moon as the tides of Paumanoc, though their wash might contain the gamble of more recent immigrants ready to lose their fortunes against four acres of the sorriest soil ever tilled by human breath and hand rather than sea urchins and starfish come to till the sapphires and rubies at the core of dying far distant suns.

If politics ever reached these heights and hollows it came with the tinges of corruption quickening neither blood nor bone, but flowed at the bottom of it remorseless as a hundred centuries as if all that time were already owned and had. Women could come and go, secret lagoons of sturgeon, the herds of Mastodon chewing their delicious forests, Clovis People come to strike it rich with the fatal details of their precocious, eerie arrowheads gutting the old flows of the land. Every river shoulder, pool of greasy, radon stung water filled with jealousy, retribution; some rage, some thirst, a love of unease, and if not a fear of death, then a suspicious eye as to where that Old Pine Cone might wander according to its notions and lures, neither tardy, on time, or nervous.

Who's to say those Clovis People weren't the same kind of miners as the Dutch or French come into the country for beaver, the strike of elephant marvelous as the strike of big watery rodents, even the rumor of diggings enough for the rages of ten wars and better not to ask for change least the good turn instantly to the worst, the simple request blasting away the insulations of luck whether already rotted or streaked through with skinned and tanned gorgeous coin. Get drunk on Mastodon meat or beaver fur who'll account for the whisperings of feasts or riches and who'll quit such hoardings and spendings where they stand for love or hate then turn toward home without conviction?

There was always the acrid need of money. No jeers from poverty since poverty accompanied birth and its convulsions, such as they were, and became kin, adjusting the trysts of its relations, loved or unloved, there was no end to the affair. One could say its footprint was invisible, come to a cousin or aunt like pregnancy or the touch of a lover who causes instant wrinkles that chill the winter and stillborn the mind but never to be told out of household no matter what persuasion, and speak with triple tongue knowing the best parts of kindness might be too cautious for the long visit.

Present Pearl with a vase-full of wild lilacs and black-eyed susans from Inge Rolfson's meadow and she'd tell you the story of the Half Moon and Henry Hudson's crew of 20 and how things got to be on the afternoon of September 12, 1609. The weather in those distant hours was hot and windy one moment and the next filled with thunder and rain and those Dutch People seemed adrift both on the River and in a blindness as to what was actually before their eyes. Seems they couldn't dredge up hardly a word about what they did see other than the place was "pleasant" to look at and there were some high hills adrift as themselves somewhere on the northern horizon. "Think if they could sound a fathom they could'a sounded the goddamned land." And with that she'd pour some pure maple syrup directly into a glass of well water that smelled and tasted like a wild rose petal, mix it with a wooden spoon her grandmother carved out of Linden wood, and hope you hadn't already grown too thirsty from the medium haul of a story that ought, at the least end of its barest soundings, get a proper start.

"Sy," the brother, "Should'a been President," his sister would say at such moments over a swill of maple syrup poured into a favorite shot glass, her words spiced with a look out the back window to make sure no ravens were eating her apples. "Least his brains dropped to the well bottom seventy years ago and they're waiting like the day after tomorrow not exactly like the dead but not exactly like the living either." Wasn't none of it said with intentional humiliation or vacant swells of meanness. Just a fact, matter of fact, synched to the fondness over a brother who periodically wandered off into the near wilderness for a day or two, then return, as if he'd found a three pound ruby someplace yonder, and would never, no matter how much ice-cream and ruhbarb pie you'd stick before'im, tell the location.

There was no disappointment in such things as lilacs and their sumptuous perfumes, a ripe tangle of black caps and their thorns swelling in the humid afternoon sun. If these were not miracles then they were a miracle's first cousins, and the remove, though slight, was cause for an enriched fondness of such austere materializations held to the recordings of daily facts and their enterprise so as to avoid any ostentations other than the phrased "BEEUTAFOOL" which might of occasion slip out and wander between neighbors, even a copperhead hunting frogs in a pond recently emerged from winter layers of ice. There was also the possibility of coming to her back porch, thirsty from afternoon chores for a glass of lemonade and a peanut butter and banana sandwich, which after seven hours war with humidity and mosquitoes that seemed more related to wasps, tasted gloriously of summer flowers and meadows emerging in their newly wind thrushed waves.

If there was a time to consider or re-consider the trailings of this story it would be between the slightest whispers of spring with the snow drops appearing under a thinned grainy snow bank with the first sun heated hints of air here and there subtracting the wandering left-over scorches of cold for half a morning and the smell of winter rot surging over the still leafless forest when the dead leafs are froze stiff in heating noon shadow and a giant pileated woodpecker can be heard for at least a mile through the stark tree-gloom pounding a last-year-of-its-life oak like some terrible ax-man forming the hours if not of bad news then the return of snow flurry and the stiff sealed ice enfolding a rotted swamp maple trunk collapsed from it roots a year or two previous with the onset of August frosts. The woodpecker seemed to have the flight of a hawk, a kind of slow, scouring grace holding the tree generations from the glacial floods forward on the graze of its wing tips. There weren't many left and they appeared in their wild seclusions and hungers to be more like the Mastodon or ice age javelina that once browsed here. The bird patient in its carnivorous relations but for tree trunks and their holds of larvae meat and it felt in hearing the bird at its work on a fog slurried late afternoon when the trees had had done with their shedding, that it could be a glacier suffering the poundings, or, note, if the huge woodpecker

crossed your path three or four times of a wayward
hour, about the hard winter ahead; who'd get through
who wouldn't. That kind of news, lost its anchor, and
set out on a spectral journey, so's to say, not full of
dread or treachery, but full of what can't be helped
and come "sooner than expected" as Jim might have
said, readying he and Pearl's seasondone gardens with
manure and hay and that Poor Man's Fertilizer called
Snow pitchforked down as a sunk underskin worth
the rot and the labor, the extra deft tillage rounding
off the autumn.

"Many salmons" were sighted on September third
and fourth 1609 and "great mullets" of such proportion
as to reap some ailing exhaustion from four good
crewmen hauling it aboard. The night drew a "hard
wind." On the fourth the People of the country came
aboard "us" and they, according the Juet's Journal,
seemed very glad of "our coming." The "people of
the country" traded tobacco for knives and beads
and the crew of the Half Moon were impressed by the
"loose" deer skin the Indians wore. And if one were
to translate Juet's phrase "well dressed" marking that
initial moment, the Indians were probably wearing
fine quill-worked garments, elegant moccasins, their
bodies strong and healthy from summer harvest and
communal works of drying meat and fruit and storing
corn. Enhancements of copper jewelry caught the
author's spare, reticent eye. He saw the Indians loved

fashion—they themselves noticed and desired the strangers' clothes, and having the heart of beautiful manners, invited the crew ashore to share in the village larder of maize and wheat, along with a "great store" of bread generously given. The country the Dutchmen saw was full of huge old growth oak, maple, pine, beech, sycamore, linden, birch, walnut, cherry, hickory, and numerous other in-waiting lumber along with wild turkey whose oil restored lost bodies and body parts, whisperers who made the heads of humans burst, owls eyes for games of dice with ghosts who couldn't stop ageing beyond mortality, beyond the wandering skins of Lost Sisters, beyond the cannibal voices of nameless lakes. Many of the trees would, at that moment, have reached, depending on the species, maximum age, from two hundred to six hundred years old—those oldest showing their sprout sometime around 950AD. Some of the white and rock oak off of Fish Creek and Clint Finger Roads were at least five feet in diameter and a hundred fifty feet tall indicating a dimension of awe not yet broken or evaporated at the moment Juet tested his flattened syllables, and rimmed with both comeliness and toll, each to each, tipped with their own voiceless pulverizations the Dutchmen were unkowingly setting to wheel and secret declaration.

Around 1930 early 31' Jim said the Depression hit Fish Creek and the surrounding swamps "Like as to a skeleton'd run from it if it could." Only winter job available was with an axe down on Mount Marion.

"'Bout a five mile walk into the snow out of the snow. Had to trudge home past dark. Work at ten above zero slowed it down some and five cents an hour near enough to warm your fingers" and a man's steep lasting wince over that deepfreeze. Hand labor that killed some end-of-the-line nerves in finger tips and lips, got part of an eyelid, scraped a brow. That graze of frostbite over knuckles and wrists, not set too hard, but set. The skin there still sore, sun and snow weary, and not a complaint, though he'd never made, even as a fine carpenter, more than $3.50 an hour's wage. And dignity enough, given what a man might know to help his neighbors when needed; refurbish some tractors, old 32' flatheads, patch a roof mid-January when the temperature goes bad, come around once in a while to fill up the wood heap with a cord not saying one word about children gone sick from it and either dead by twelve or took to stealing and other trouble out of desperations that wouldn't ever go away. Some of those children off to prison, froze to death binges, car wrecks not more than a mile from home, shot by girlfriends, stolen by religion and taken to Tongues and trances. "Some even got the rabies. Poor devils," he'd say with a shudder.

The other job in that time was in the quarries. There's a local museum full of tools; wedges, sleds, hammers, drills, chisels, horsegear, hand-powered booms, chains, hoists, saws. Much of it hand forged, and the forms apart from the original utility, have the inutility of eccentric design, attractive proportion, awkward and strained decoration marking their solemn exile from daily need. One might say the tools are "beautiful" but try one of the objects on for eight to ten hours of the exacting days intended for them and see how "beauty's" pronunciation can be re-cast in the new spelling bees of experience. The thick slabbed sidewalks of Manhattan and Brooklyn originate in these Catskill ravines and six generations of local hands worked the rocks.

Jim had another, perhaps more intimate inventory. The men who split the cliffs here were veterans in their generations of the Mexican, Civil, Plains, Phillipine, First World War and a couple of Cheyenne who rode up the Hudson after a stint in Buffalo Bill's Wild Show, liked the girls in the local bars and stayed a few seasons; were veterans themselves, dare it be said, of the Little Big Horn—that American afternoon mysteriously finding its ways into the dance halls of Kingston and Saugerties. The work, if you took your eyes off it for even a second, had a proclivity for certain kinds of theft—mix stone and stone weight and torn muscles. Everyone bore the mark of that thievery. Missing fingers and hands caught between four-ton slabs headed for Fifth Avenue or Brooklyn Heights. One or both eyes the unfortunate targets of slate splinters or chips. Broken backs, legs, arms, hips, a mean rupture turned to gangrene, the side of a skull rammed just enough to make the victim permanently silly. And the different, not always mentioned hazards, black powder, and later, dynamite. Some of those men were so refined with the explosives they could split a ten ton rectangle with nearly perfect proportions from its three hundred million year-old roots. Up to the Civil War the majority of the North's powder supply was produced in a mill just down a sparrow's maiden flight from Fish Creek Road. The hill people knew it as their intimate familiar until 1862/63 when the explosion of the Powder Mill could be heard far as Albany and Water Vliet one hundred and more miles. But if the edge of slab didn't steal your hand then it was the black powder. Men came drunk to work and by the end of the day, dead, wishing they were dead, or swearing off the mean labor and wages gone five years mining gold in the Sierras, signed on to hunt Apache, somehow wandered back, as if crushed hands, wrecked shoulders and elbows was a lover, and drift as you might, one day there'd you'd be with a sledge hammer and wedge, a flask of hard cider to get through the smaller, leaner injuries that was love's habit.

September 5th. The morning, Juet saw was "light" supposing that to mean a sky, cloudless and still and the stillness weighing on the land and its creatures without strain as can happen in an early Hudson Valley autumn; the odors of summer flowers hanging, not heavily on the nostrils, but as a waning frill hovering between the last wisps of a declining summer heat and the on-set of a not-far-off killing frost. There might have been clouds of insects massing for the noon day sun, bees and wasps and gnats death set as they were and searching for the brands of carrion; fallen apples, left over pollen from wind cracked flower, a ripe with maggots wolf, to feast there until the lick of an iced-air came for them, came for everything in them. A "flood came." Was the river awash in sea-tide or fall torrentials from the Adirondacks heaved south, fronted with thick wavechop and ocean pull? The water would have been fresh, the river wide, its shallows filled with grasses, rotting trees, sturgeon, otter, beaver, nesting eagle and osprey, flocks of North American parakeets and an occasional peregrine falcon diving for choice mid-air snacks of passenger pigeon. The crew "went on land there." The phrasing still droops with the footprints of that moment, the weight of bodies European and Europe standing wandlike in the glare of the four-word parch. There would have been the smell of water and land and rotted trees bursting from various creeks and swamps. Tangs of autumn, hard and dry, flocks of birds gathering, wild animals nervous over the odors of about to descend chill; a stray crinkle of ice edging pond shore making deer blow their nostrils with warning. The "Journal" does not record the presence of flying squirrels gliding the forest canopy from tree to tree as if that riverine world were a jungle, not full of monkeys, but air-borne rodents gracefully a-flight as gliders spreading the flaps of their bodies, gone to air and shadows of oak and maple, fabulous as griffons and the still partially wet sunlight nearly vaporing the land, the great annual tropical surge of the northern river withering, the whole succulence of it turning to desiccation and full aridities and desertions within no more than a week as if it were the breath of a Sphinx making a twilight sinew of its scouring respirations inviting the more fierce and wavering lights of winter.

"So" the sentence begins in this same recording, the trailing vowel of the adverb hovering with its rounded miniature ocean of menace and depth of peril, the vowel shore swaying as "they went into the woods" and saw another store there, the shelf life and stage methods of that super market aisle servicing the "Half Moon's" immediate hungers, a foreshadow of shopping habits and individual consumer trends for the "goodly oaks" and, to a lesser, speculative projection, "some currants." One of the Indians brought the berries as a sign of friendship to get past the immediate surveillance and on board, pouring, one suspects, a personal handful for the author, who thought them "sweet and good." Those "goodly oaks" and "good" currants; the adjective's diphthongs are oceans too in the repositories which remain unexplained or unexplored as geography, are even, to the moment of this commentary in the opening eighth year of the twenty first century as remote still as the methane seas of Saturn's Titan. And even here one wonders about our means as the possible carriers of language, how to dare language to reveal itself through these fossils as one thinks of Mary Smith Jones, the "Last Eyak"; last Full Blood to be fluent in her language which will go extinct recalling in the eighth year of the twenty first century that ninth year of the seventeenth where the Half Moon swayed and dripped with the new tides, the sky climbing to black curd of thunder and a never before experienced flocculence in wind and Land's Breath for the visitors.

The Indians were obviously expert with these humans, foreign as they were, knowing the truth of their, at that point, already fermented more than one hundred year lure and not what temptations necessarily beget, but what unnecessarily renders astonishment and forms a high sea's elegance as it took place on that September Five of the Ninth Year of said century nine days into the journey. Had they come to the approximate point of Poughkeepsie and seen the Shawangunks in the enhazed distances to the west? The five hundred million year-old Cliff Country full of spires and lures and year-round cave ice that make the local forest cool as a twenty thousand year old glade with musk ox and mastodon and caribou pale there in the shimmering gloom. Would they have seen the small herds of forest buffalo come to stare with their remnant scents of unpredictable indfference?

Was the gift of "currants" a deluge of the "many who came aboard"? They, it seems, who were as "sweet" as their offerings of fruit wore "mantles of feathers"

"and some in skins of divers sorts of good furs."
When one recalls various chronicled descriptions of
feather works from Peru to the Georgian Bay there are
a number of startling preservations; the featherworks
themselves, to Codexes, to archived "on-the-spot"
watercolors and drawings. The fashion would have
been elaborate and complex; fitted and cut shell work,
frilled and painted rawhide, startling tattoos, necklaces
of bear claw, wolf teeth, deer and moose hoof, long
greased hair enhanced by nearly silken fur of weasel,
otter, beaver, bobcat; moccasins embroidered with
porcupine quill and alluring tails of wolf, fox, cougar,
sewed to heels and shoulders, handsomely cured fur
of bear and buffalo. The craft heading backwards deep
thousands of years, rich and sexy having an eccentric
splendor derived from perilous, lonely dream added
to the most homely overlooked arts of daily labors;
what was got from mother to great aunt—sewing and
curing techniques, clashing colors to startle mind
and eye, a smear of purple on cheek or neck looking
like the wandering throat of a star. Juet says nothing
about the arts of body painting, the allures of face
covered with black and yellow dyes mixed with oil
of bear. Perhaps one of the guests wore a ceremonial
cloak of turkey and hawk feathers in honor of the
invitation—a warrior's chin dyed red, one eye circled
in black holding a fan of hummingbird or parakeet
feathers, head and beak protruding out of that bird
mass. The young brave flexibly alert, gaudy with

shadows and vindictive summonings he had been born into measured and wrenched as the ready to murder, suspicious Europeans.

The women "came to us" the recording states, "with hemp." Does that mean nets of different sorts thrown to water or air for bird or fish? Did those nets, when fully spread resemble webs of spider, webs of mind. And what sorts of knots were conceived for each usage. Was some of the hemp used for carrying children, injured hunters and warriors, loads of apples, butchered meat, wood, squash and corn. Was it to be used, as the crew may have suspected, for their own corpses?

The "They" in the next sentence were the women who had red copper tobacco pipes and "other" copper they wore around their necks. That copper tradition and its "trade", the expert and attractive metal craft extended to the remote and mysterious "Copper People" who may have been the first great metalurgists of the species mining the shore worlds of the Great Lakes over five thousand years ago. No one knows to this day who those "People" were other than the signatures they left behind: tangs, ear-rings, simple, yet firmly beautiful spear points accompanying haphazardly discovered burials, the bodies interred when their earth was still rebounding from weight of Ice. The "...other things..." of copper they (the women) did wear around their necks were items which piqued the crew's notice. There is in the diction an impression of arousal and longing but what to do with the robust male escorts and were the sexual favors and trinkets hovering over the Half Moon on that day worth the ineptitude? And was it the Evil which kept their eyes in check or the Eye of Evil they feared to over-attract and in being lured, enfeeble and cast them into spells? The citing ends: "At night they went on land again, so we rode very quiet, but durst not trust them..." as if revealing whisper, slap of water on ship's bow could have ignited fears of being eaten alive, throats phantasmagorically crushed in sleep. The solemnly rendered "...so we rode very quiet ..." and its withered, estranged anguish. And floating here, another vessel composed of more distant vapors. Hawthorne's "Miasmatic Conscience" with its timbers of depletion/corruption equal in its tresspasses to the still oozing Pequod?

The Mount Marion outcrop lies about two miles south of the Saugerties exit. Various pine, oak, birch, and scrub (meaning thick patches of poison ivy, knotted brambles of wild berry) define its lower slopes. Its edge is a kind of thick dull blade of layered deposits so old the words "ancestral" "origins" "primordial" or even Old Doom with its fossil diphthongs don't quite come to the borders of explanation. Most of that "Mountain" is formed of shale and sandstone laid down four hundred million years ago, during the Age of Fish. I don't know if Fish Creek Road offers a direct journey to the far distant shadows which sometimes do emerge out of a snow bank or ice fall, but if you walk the crest and dips of this piece of ground why you might trip over a stone like the one I'm just now holding in the palm of my hand, indented with the nearly perfect impression of four hundred million year old brachiopods, and shell fragments. One fossil imprint looks like a far flung initial insect experiment:

up for a skittish flight before any order of fish knew about flying food, elegantly held in the metamorphosis, not necessarily gone beyond dreams, but a dream's remotest perchings, not yet quite full of the smell of things, or the smell of worlds and their endurances; a sea-shell print hardly larger than half a human thumb. Turn the rock over and there are sand ripples caught and held in their flight and coming upon a hand-held tale of wonders when half the thing called "America" was a shallow sea from the west shore of the Hudson to undisdained Iowa and from shoreline to bottom no more than six hundred feet deep. Sharks were there and heavily armored fish and bits of coral stick up from tree roots and part froze mud. Encrusted in poison ivy and crushed as fill for a local rural "driveway" all that four hundred million years gone to another, perhaps even fancier crumble under the wheels of station wagons, pick-ups, children stomping their cold feet waiting to be hauled off to Halloween. And it would have been like a tropical Hudson's Bay, bigger, fish-new, full of lightning, hurricanes, waterspouts, whirlpools, fish shadows hovering as underwater clouds in that freshly costumed deluge. Its eastern horizon between four hundred fifty and two hundred fifty million years ago held the appearances and disintegrations of three mountain chains extending from what is now northern Greenland to southern Alabama, each uplift equal at least to the Himalayas. Maybe old William Blake himself saw the shadows of those mountainous sunsets washing over "The Marriage of Heaven & Hell" or "America A Prophecy" and the visionary threshold of his unmapped trusts lying as molten sediments under the furnace of soul and being and giant forms he awakened? Walk a ten mile circuit in the opening weeks of spring and those black fly bites will sting and itch a Hudson Valley month yet no matter how many Silurian rocks you turn up for your pocket magnifying glass you'll find not one firebrat, no dragonflies, no antennae licking the immediate air for the already then too complicated and weirdly staggering fates.

The "Mountain", really a small mesa-like glacially crushed protrusion, is old enough to hold the first record of terrestrial plants and their appearance. Those ancestors had no separate leafs or stems. Millipedes came later, to sup that earliest green, and carnivores; namely spiders, to envenom the centipedes and worms, and fungus (another late arrivor as one considers the untraceable not yets and haven't ever beens the juries of these sediments enfold) to decompose that music, recompose it. So if you hold this stone I found on Mount Marion somewhere in 1981/82 of the twentieth century's last decades, stick it close to your human flesh you may hear the symphonies of those killers and eaters and their parleys over who gets what flesh and when; what fancy armor, scales, hair, fangs, wings, mandibles, lovers with antennae lovers with fifty eyes. Was Death a Child, astonished, unhurried, spreading the Peril, trying its smoothness on for size? Walking over those shales I didn't want to ever have the kind of naked luck to run across the preserved footsteps of that Infant. Let the Mystery reside among the swamp marigolds, yellow as a pre-Cambrian Day.

Jawless fish were the swimmers. There were trilobites, nautiloids ten to twelve feet long which must have been spectacular riding the shallows with their elaborately marked elongated funneled shells, and multi-tentacled heads (were they toxic as the blue-ringed octopus?). And fish that seem still part crab crudely finned and tailed, some having the aspect of slithering spoons no thoroughbred sailfish would turn an eye for nor spread the beautiful sex accordion riding its spine. Scorpion-like Eurypterids stuffed face up in these Silurian shields look like ghost kites gone once up for orbit, its poisonous eternity unhinged by an accidental human footstep four hundred million years into a holocene or anthropocene future, ephemeral as a mix of hot Catskill autumn shade or the Frederick Church miniature landscapes I often think about, their lines and masses and hand work holding the wonders of the cunningly beautiful hostilities and so indifferently watchful as a first human eye to witness the glacial terminations and hungry and starved and uncertain.

As to the fate of those shales? In the mid-1980s I had a job; an investigative reporter, thinking then, as I still do, about Democracy, and the tradition of the small town newspaper—its worth for a community; the powerless, those who have power, and what information might provide as a central inclusion of daily life from gossip, to obituaries, to arrests, family feuds, school board meetings, and the clamor of waiting unknowns. Rumors began their local swirl. People came down with skin and lung infections. I'd attempted to hone my nose for a story by going to town zoning board meetings, PTA gatherings, church functions, town hall picnics, country fairs. I did interviews with farmers, housewives, biologists, geologists, women who started shelters for abused women, women who founded a workshop and experimental studio space for other women artists, local authors, a college president, and the hosts inhabiting the rural outback of the central Hudson Valley. I met a woman who I have admired since that time, the head of a town zoning board about to be overwhelmed by developers and lawyers from downstream New York City who were very smart; heavily educated, heavily financed. This woman, a housewife, decided she'd stand in their way. By "standing" I mean she did her homework and research. Spent over a year traveling around America, talking to zoning boards in Seattle, North Dakota, Texas, South Carolina. To anyone who'd help her learn. She became one of the most thorough scholars and historians of zoning laws and regulations in the nation. I saw her almost spellbindingly unravel a highly paid lawyer's presentation one night, a presentation for a development worth what she knew to be dangerous millions and a threat to her town's well-being. The lawyer was shocked by her control of the details and expressive clarity; he was stunned by the questions and their application to legal precedents he had neither considered or known. I was astounded too and thought (and still do) that if she had run for higher office, those abilities might have influenced issues of development and tragic land misuses at a national level. But as she said, her biggest concern was for her kids and her town. She was compassionate, courageous and rose up out of her own Italian kitchen and household to a civic awareness I've never forgotten. She was responsible for not only saving her community but guiding it to a vision of its future it would never have had without the luck of her being at home. I found out more about Democracy reporting for a small town newspaper: Democracy and its wasting impediments and farces along with its generative capacities to excite common recognitions and communal sharings than I had ever learned before.

I thought about that single democratic voice as I considered the rumors of exotic skin infections and sores that appeared on my side of the River. One obscure July Monday night the Town of Saugerties called a Board meeting. The reason: a Mount Marion-based mining operation, Northeast Solite, made a request to dump some of its "waste" chemicals into the Town's central sewer system. The company, in support of its application, submitted a list of thirty-seven compounds it intended to filter in the form of wastewater through the sewers. Nothing more in the "notice."

The "list" included a witch's brew of industrial chemicals associated with leukemia, neurological injury, birth defects, and a cauldron of other potential disfigurement. The company stored these industrial wastes for its burning processes. In October and November of 1982 Northeast Solite illegally incinerated PCBs and was forced by the State of New York to burn coal instead. The company wanted to resume burning these fuels though the protocols and standards for such a process were at that time at best vague and undetermined. The ground adjacent to the mine revealed the presence of heavy metals; lead, cadmium, zinc, and copper in drinking water concentrations that exceeded by ten times what is thought to be a safe standard. There was at that time a margin of safety involved in incineration technology. Northeast Solite's product was aggregate rather than cement. To avoid being overly technical Solite submitted the Mount Marion shales to an extreme heating process to separate the ancient rock from the liquids which accumulated in the geologic formation over the ages. The final product was an aggregate which could be further crushed and used for fill in road construction as well as other building processes and road grading techniques; by the ton relatively cheap and easy to transport. The major problem: kiln protocols and filtration systems. Northeast Solite had no satisfactory system to prevent the usual chemical transformations that can occur during the incineration of toxic wastes. Chlorine and chlorinated organic chemical wastes can transform into much more toxic forms of organic chemicals under high temperatures such as dioxin and its sister related compounds, dibenzofurans. There is no safe dose for dioxin exposure. It is a carcinogen linked to birth defects, immune system supression, skin diseases, diabetes, and heart malfunction. These are some of the most toxic substances known to science. In the case of Northeast Solite's burning protocol there was no effective control, and emissions vaporized into what can be characterized, in the ancient sense, "monstrocities"; omens and warnings of threat and looming deformity. Northeast Solite's illegal PCB burns of October and November of 1982 ignited a potentially very dangerous incineration and Saugerties area residents contracted skin sores that, in some cases, did not heal for two years.

These and other issues at the core of the Mount Marion company's illegal toxic burn resulted in new requirements and guidelines to be adhered to without exception in New York State. In the shadows of Northeast Solite's illegal activity lay the Love Canal crisis. I continued for a time to pursue the company's origins. I traced its ownership to a Virginia mining operation. One of the partners was a man named William Casey who was then head of the CIA under the Reagan Administration. The other origin was a New Jersey based environmental "service"; a supplier of toxic waste solvents with organized crime connections involved with landfill schemes and price fixing of garbage. Those origins made me pause and I decided to call the New York State Crime Commission, not for advice necessarily, but for conformation of various facts I'd dug up and wanted to investigate. As I was asking questions the person I was talking to suddenly interrupted. He asked me if I had a wife and kids. I confirmed I had both, but asked in turn what his question had to do with our present business. He said then:

"You really want to know what you're uncovering?
Why don't you have your wife and kid go out
and start your car in the morning for you."

I have never forgotten the madness of that
conversation nor the abyss which continues to whisper
out of it. A small pile of those rocks from the Mount
Marion Formation still sits on a shelf reminding me
of the quiet wet sun light of a mid-summer Hudson
River afternoon when I, then a young father, and my
son turned over a drive way full of luring fossils that
came in a dump truck.

The forces of light fall on canyons of granite
smoothed to semi-nubbed hills and twisted slabs. As
one climbs and grabs for a hold, insect-like wings
of granite peel off with barest touch of finger, so
primordially rotten has the old rock become. Was the
whole of this cliff country swathed in final oceans of
asteroidal fire; some geologic infection come to speed
up the otherwise unnoticed mortal goings-on of such
isolate canyon places and the gradations of shadow
and hot light come as torturous contraries to these
surfaces? I suppose as a Californian coming from the
alluvial outcrops of the San Gabriels and the river
bluffs of the Santa Ana these are some of the native
questions I seem to carry. There are more, especially for
those children like myself who knew early the legends
of murder that haunt the California landscape. When

I lived in the Catskills these questions seemed to be part of the weight of an old family suitcase homely and cracked as some too exposed leather that clung around even when I walked the shores of the Esopus Creek following flight and perch of early spring bald eagles or climbed the mysterious and sometimes dangerously enraptured back country of Panther Mountain and Shandaken discovering with my eyes (and thinking of the way the generations of my grandfathers and grandmothers thought of the huge spaces of their struggles—"eye reach" and what that settler vocabulary revealed about their minds and the hazard to their minds if they let that reach wander too far from the company of others) not easily recognizing the smaller room for time so often hid and subtle in these mountains as opposed to the room for time in the desert world of my upbringing that can hollow and sear without your knowing till later; an hour, a year, a decade. These mountains are the deposits from a river delta draining the huge Acadians with heights of thirty thousand and possibly more feet. Their raging torrents are held in the stillness and higher reaches as formations of pebbles mixed in sandstone, gravel it is said from crushing, dilated rapids glazing the four hundred million year-old riverscapes preserved in these smoothed on the their way to dust pebbles in the unimaginable remoteness of those indifferent, mutilate, and hill slurping cascades.

In the more sever elevations of my wanderings

I'd come upon groves of black cherry trees, startling outriders rooted beyond chainsaw and axe and filtering as beautiful a sunshine and wind as the most forsaken Panamint Dudleya, both of them coveting a preference for rock. If my "eye-reach" moved toward the fossil horizons of the Catskill hollows and forest my ear-reach didn't drift far from what was underfoot. A field bite from a "Crotalus horridus" seven wilderness miles from home would have meant at worst, an agonized death, at best, loss of leg or arm. The timber rattlesnakes of those hollows and ledges loomed up in the valley where I lived, some said to be a gorgeous jet black. The one I saw of an early mid-summer morning had a russet white thick body and an orange stripe running the whole of its length. It reared up at my approach, threw itself down a small poison ivy enshrouded slope, each of us stung by our mutual surprise. The serpent was strong, alert, so impersonally beautiful I felt like the standing numb. And I was glad neither me nor the rattler was forced to hold a ground. That scholar of the woods and the Southern Cane Break rattler are the same species. Their venom is made up of hemotoxins and neurotoxins meaning if the rattler don't kill'ya then the cobra will. The pit vipers, though they hadn't rejected their oldest mustiest food locker, seemed untraceably to find preference and longing in the neighborhood lore of our often summer- cold hollows, for the local flying meat. I don't quite know what that preference does to the rules of natural selection and environmental pressure. Far as I can tell a thirst for hot bird's blood can never be underestimated, especially if sharpened by a million year longing, and how such protracted watchfulnesses turn a headfull of death into a new vintage, fine as the rarest winter rainbow.

Those thoughts of bird hunters turned to my own native pit viper, "Crotalus scutulatus", the Mojave rattler. Quick, ugly tempered, bad as a torpedo. A night slider from February to late October. Prefers open mesquite and creosote country and has a defensive pose that reminds the victim of a miniature sandstone rock arch. Its rattle sound is a penetrant, continuously jaggedy piece of desertion that gets cupped right under your nostrils, so close does the warning come to smell. And it probably should for the suspecting and unsuspecting. Its venom has its own name, "Mojave toxin"; so unlike and more potent than any of its cousins. It is the cobra of the deserts where I come from. "Pick that son'abitch up" like my father might've said, "and son, you jest spilled your cards."

In 1981 Fish Creek and all the roads for countless square miles around suffered an infestation. I'm still not sure "infestation", after nearly thirty years, is a piece of vocabulary, though I've chewed it enough, which does attest to the vulgarity and distrust of days that business caused. We'd purchased a small clapboard farmhouse built in 1859-1860. Two storeys, low ceilinged, no insulation; window weights and all. A thing in, I don't know what kind of need; there were so many, for twenty seven thousand dollars and about a good spit over an acre. And it took some work to be in it since we were used to a huge New York City factory loft space and didn't know quite how to gauge the cramped rooms, corners, walls, and a single bathroom more appropriately fitted to a thirty pound mouse. The house and its land occupied the next nine years inside/outside. I was tearing down old horsehair plaster (still stinking of horse through the peculiar American decades since), examining the, at least, one hundred twenty year old carpentry; saw and hammer marks, chiseled joints. Obviously hand-work crude and durable from timber milled locally before the Civil War. It was a hot (nasty-humid) early summer morning. Not a cloud. I'd taken a break from the work. Looked out the back window of the crude dining room with a cast iron wood stove which I worried might be susceptible to chimney fire, sitting empty as it was, and so easily beckoning my new fears about Northeast country winters. There was no wind either I could discern. The humidity was so dense it formed a haze over the canopy, air almost spongy with it. And damned if it didn't sound like a rainstorm outside. Coming from the desert makes anyone who stays the secret "one second too long" in the blur of an emptiness a little distrustful. "See enough mirages out there boy and look at your soul in the palm of your hand turn to the most peculiar dust the angels ever seen." I remembered that warning, with its pinch, for a child, of immense finalities as I looked out the window once more, trying to get hold of that rainstorm. I had a lot of work to do but decided I'd go outside for a close inspection of the terrain, you might say, feeling at that point like a pilgrim to the Catskills, so foreign were they to me and irritating, knowing nothing of the hid and subtle one astir leaf might invite. I walked down the slope of our back yard, stood under a huge rock oak, looked up to the cloudless sky, and still heard those raindrops. If I'd still smoked I'd have set down, rolled me one, and took a deep breath. Make me feel better. At least that was some protection from the goddamned truth of the thing. It was still raining. And there were some of the hairiest, ugliest caterpillars I ever saw everywhere, all over that and the other oaks I could see eating the canopy as if they'd heard from the asteroid itself about the next visit and better to get the Last Feast in, leave one leaf and invite the truly unlikable demons. I was bare-headed too when I did figure out I was standing under a rain of gypsy moth caterpillar shit. That scared me. Can't say I've seen scarier things than other women and men. Everyone does get delivered. But the sight of the eating and the sound of its immediate rain; even the richest, most apocalypsed breathed Southern California Miracle Mile Preacher couldn't have rubbed this up. The thought of it, as I realized how stripped the mountains and hillsides had so quickly become, was so morbid I didn't know if I could go outside. And night time. The hard rainfall never stopped for nearly a month.

Pearl might have said the Saints had made certain things as they were, but things as they were, snow and wind, summer tilled thunderheads had moved beyond the Christian Paradise. Whether a foot or two, she didn't know, but suspected it might be a mile, as less is more under the veil of such suspicions. And speculation wouldn't abide since some garden hoeing or pruning waited, and she may as well get there first before the moths laid their worms. Otherwise "Things" had been about the same since the Crash of 29'. People being Creatures such as they are might still appreciate a fresh baked cherry pie with some lemonade on a sweltered July afternoon come what the stockmarket, in its legend, may or may not do as to the arts of envy or a deer too maggot ridden for proper dressing and consideration no matter how hungry you're invited to be. Of a sundown on the Fourth of July she recited the smaller lists of the boys killed in 1917, 1942, 51', 67' from the hollows around Fish Creek. The boys, edging the list too, came home a little shaggy, taken to mumbling and brawls up in the bars of Hudson and Columbiaville, froze tight to a car in Oliveria, bottle of whiskey untouched, pictures of some young Germans in a wallet, the ones killed somewhere out there. Even worse, pestering a son back from Vietnam, breathless and ravaged, tell'im to his face the death fever leaking out of him wasn't exactly "a real war." That son of Ernest and Lucy Jane felling lumber last year. "Say he let a tree take him. Men on his crew refused to touch the harvest for any pay. Say he fought to the roots of his eyes in 68'. Went on a personal rampage. Imagine that. Kid could sing before he left. Return back, silent. Wasn't like something scary. Went and evaporated is all. Everyone tried to do right by'im. Give'im a new pair of oars. My God he had the prettiest skin a girl ever saw. The well his father dug in 47'. Water was said to taste like a diamond, smoothed the skin of him and his sisters. Depends on the dowser. Jays were the first to look over the body. Lumberjacks put a freshly sharp axe in his coffin. A seemingly thing to do since every tooth in his head was broke by the tree blast. He wasn't touched by one twig."

Sunday September 6, 1609. Ship and crew were under some "fair weather." Fall was approaching and the average temperatures for this time of year, the low seventies. Nights going slowly cooler, and some days, as they can, reach the low to mid-eighties with minimal humidity. The days are stunning in these early autumn weeks and often a scavenging calm settles over the land with scented winds carrying the perfumes of water, over-ripe apples and oaks in early transformation along with the odors of hills drying, smell of ageing forest canopy picked over by constantly, subtly churning winds doing away with all previous tropical spillage. The overflow of forest and river life going taut in desertion, straying, quick fermentations, as if everything dipped in some hard, merciless small talk. The light of the Hudson Valley changes from wet-softness in the extremes of variation and luscious nearly dripping half lights and shades of yellow/greens to crisp hardness with tints of grey, depleted blue, sky riven and wraithlike with dehydrations, every color having a colder depth and sheen. In the dry occasionally parched light of an eighty degree early September afternoon one can feel the faint tinges of irreversible frost hovering, bee and wasp corpses underfoot, squirrels in a more manic last forage, cardinals billowing their feathers, deer going grey, some emaciated, tick wasted, to be dead by mid-January thaw, easy then for coyotes, buzzards, foxes. John Colman, "Englishman" with four crewmen, took a boat into a "land ... were as pleasant with grass and flowers, and goodly trees, as ever they have seen, and very sweet smells came from them ..." Often, during these weeks one can be startled and pricked by the luxuriant washes of warmed, dry air, the dying grasses heaved by thrush of hot breeze, red-winged blackbirds foraging, a lone cardinal resting on a stump next to a pair of yellow and black vereos, their flames of color plunging the observer into the mysteries of painless, gentle loneliness for that second, before all three flit into the invisibles and the sounds of Canadian geese in migratory formation glinted by swarms of gnats and flies. The gathering toward killing frost and winter has not yet exacted its increase of touchy apprehensions. On the return foray the men "... were set upon by two canoes ..."; twelve warriors in one, fourteen in the other. Juet's passage says nothing about the desperations of the fight. Was it better to smother the words, keep them distant and buried for the sake of a more definite caution against the subscripts of panic and horror? The warriors, having sung their Death Songs, prepared themselves with sweat bath and paint, then stripped for the deadly relentlessness required of their Visions. The exultance in the crafts of violence would not have been unspeakable to other brave men no matter how distant or strange their worlds. The Half Moon crew wandering in defiance of safety, were as unyielding, though the constricted passage, "The night came on and it began to rain so that their match went out ..." does convey a sense of powerlessness and thickening horror not trivial or superficial.

The "... one man slain ..." in the incident, the "Englishman" named John Colman "... with arrow shot into his throat, and two more hurt ..." (the names and extent of the injuries not given). First hemorrhage. Little blood lake of the "Englishman" teeming there. The frenzies and writhing held already and close in the syllables of disintegration "So their match went out ..." For the Indians. Try such fools on for size. Go ankle deep. Drink little. Eat that part of sky which most resembles the snowflakes of fall.

When, outside of admittance, in the earliest hours of spring scrolled with fog, the previous hard cold of deep winter goes heavy with melt, those earliest moments of grey with the leafless oaks and maples dripping, spring reads like a withering of hours. Cabin fever still steals over hands and face. The half cord in the woodpile lies semi-soaked in rotted ice from slash rain. You need a hammer to break some of it. Wait for morning sun. By late March wood and wood burning and stove stocking suck at you especially at dawn with last coals still their transparent red; glowering smell of hot chimney tars enough to vaporize the soak. Wood hiss and stench of wood hiss, open the flu, bash the wood in. Wait for flame and tinder smoke. Spring seems at that beginning rigidest corpse and hoax with another storm building. A late March blizzard potent and climbing to the tips of surrounding hills turning the new red sap surge of the forest and forest glow of sap sinking to burnt grey again. The smell of the blizzard almost stabs you and though sun blooms in cloudless sky titmouse hover and groom for the afternoon in preparation, watchful, nervous. A newly arrived, thin from migration heron stares at ice-locked pond, swings its beak at clumps of cattails. There are abandoned year-old robins' nests in the apple trees exposed in risen spring light no longer hid by shades of silver grey and thinned browns of meadow grasses wracked by snow. Some hold nearly weightless, yolkless blue eggs, the throb all compact and dead, thumb-thick and no longer than the tip of my middle finger. The frank scantness holding nothing strident or amiss. Raven or jay will find it. Smell of blizzard rises from glare of ice drops at stream edge, thrush of glinted pine needles. A quick wetness tilting down from cloudless air cakes nostrils with smudge and gossip of it at noon of a fifty degree day, the seep of warmth having no room to grow, become fifty-five or sixty degree things shoulder deep. The scent of it throat hard. A kind of rubbing stubble moving over the eyebrows as chipmunks bark in the distance.

I remember the first time Jim introduced me to the scale of the land, how it rises from the River from one ancient rock ledge to another. He'd show me a huge slab of limestone covered with ripple marks of rivers, shallow sea bottoms, prints of rain drops from storms old as the light from colliding galaxies, the glacial striations scoured into the rocks in our own backyard. The thought of continental glacial scratches I stood on directly made the land seem a complex shadow I could neither touch nor properly assemble.

Jim led me to a ridge of thin laminated sandstone sheets. Layers from river bottoms and fast currents, the formation tightly elegant in its fixed stack; luxuriant, startling in its symmetry. And was the river an Amazon born out of the huge Acadians, or a Ganges? From that rise off of Fish Creek one could better see the

northern and northwest horizons. In fall the sweep
of sky colors told a more direct story. The variations
of blue indicated   weather to come, storms and
temperatures. "How to stay put inside a week, a day.
Let the guesswork settle." I thought it simple advice,
not knowing the cloak of humor dispensed, nor until
later, the long years of bloodshot, often cruel work that
had not broken these people as it might others. They
were kind, tolerant, alert, witty, mindful and lively and
had no use in calling attention to themselves. Their
accents and phrases remind me still of my childhood
and the elders who inhabited the California valleys of
my remote memories. Men and women born in the
70s and 80s of the nineteenth century whose talk
and accentual banter held the currents of those older
American speech rhythms and sounds. Their appraisal
of a horse, color of alfalfa in frailest sprout, those
pronunciations and locutions still catching the web of
my ear. The way my mother's father, born in the 1870s,
asked for a hammer or complimented my mother, held
a tonality and hesitation, the voices and what they
contained so differenciated, including the way they
held their bodies, paused in their motions. Jim and
Pearl brought me to these sensations long after my
grandmothers and grandfathers died. Their talk and
gesture held too their lifetime isolation on Fish Creek
and it gave them a clarity I've rarely known walking
the immediate eskers, drumlins, meadows and creeks
as they did for more than eighty years knowing the

sites of nesting birds and bird generations, deer and wild turkey paths, the motions of air and storm. There were the neighborhood boys gone to Saipan, Iwo Jima, girls married, moved off the Nebraska, "Down Texas way," each departing hollowed by the increasing girth and height of trees. Their intimacy, humor, and sorrow held close but would condone no unrespectable strain, "and don't forget to attend to the manure, air it out some. Keep it trim."

One late March day an unusual thaw began to wash over our valley. A series of blizzards had erupted the previous three weeks tracking from the West with grinding fury about every four and a half days. The blizzard and partial blindness followed by a relieving warmth of forty and fifty degree interludes. Every separate storm delivered about three feet of snow. Total winter's payload: a hundred fifty-five inches until our entrance road looked like a luge, the shoulder of snow on each side half again the height of our car and the road shrunk to a width not tolerant of another storm, not to say any possible ingress of ourselves. We had a snow blower. It was a good machine designed for suburban blacktop smooth driveways. Our road, composed of crushed gravel, imposed a further labor. In the midst of heavy continuous wind-stabbing snow fall gravel got caught in spinning blades and snow chute; the pin which engaged the blades and fed snow into chute broke or bent so badly we'd have to replace it, stop the machine, dig out ice-crusted gravel and blades, dig out impacted snow and pound in a new pin. May not sound awkward but a forty mile per hour wind pushing snow and cold and some inch of misery swallowing your voice and sometimes your blood turned the labor into a relentless stifling toll. I can still hear that machine grinding, stalling, see Gail standing bravely next to me, as we watched the blades spinning out nothing but some cold air. I searched my pockets for a pin, and remembered at those passages Lawrence Olivier's last frenzies in his Richard III movie, squeezing out Shakespeare's most frightening revelations of madness and life mockery, the satyr lure of the dictator marooning whole societies in decomposition, the corpse making "bottled spider" writhing and spinning his last syllables. I hammered out those mangled pins in wind-factor temperatures of ten below zero and more. Under thirty degrees and nearly fourteen years separation from those storms my fingers go numb, skin aches from nerve damage. We bought a tractor too, "a big son-of-a-bitch" as my father might've said. Had it outfitted with a plough blade and bucket, interchangeable for the season depending on need. And I loved that machine. Used it for hauling rock, trees I chained sawed down, doing land-scape work for Gail. I loved its smell. Loved to service it, check the hydraulics. Make sure it wouldn't kill me.

The last of that season's serial blizzards came in scattered thin then more thickened flurries. Little wind at the beginning coming from the west and air still mixed with pockets of warmth to be pounded away and blue of sky draining as if sucked carrion riven to faintness or faintness half parting for the radiant veils of long thin clouds topping the horizon, stripping sun of its sunflesh and that narrowing of the eye adjusting to cross-patterns of dry light. Watching deer eat faster, hearing coyotes howl on the farther ridges, no extravagance in the sound, and knowing in it, they are watching me, looking for signs, their clockwork wound to killing. Nothing careless, left to stir as they study the shadows too, passing over the hills. Quaking aspen shiver under a blast of whitish grey light, the stranded soft clumpings of their leaf mass gathering to the ear like water torn by a mallard's feet. There is a large gosse hawk tightening its last hunting circle then swerving into the slate grey tree haze full speed, flight bold, not brushing a twig. "An hour. Twenty minutes," I ask myself in the still nearly delicate twilight of whitening air the blizzard carries, trees creaking, the softening undercurrents of undefinable noises sending me to check the wood, tighten ropes and stakes holding canvas cover, carry in enough supply to feed the stove for the night. Watch sundown horizon turn a washed out pinkish red. No sailors to take warning because warning's come and gone.

A wind began to howl, and by "howl" I mean a prolonged high pitched whine that went down mind into my stomach, curled around my balls and I never got used to it. A clotted witch's shriek I've only heard in that valley, and though I can't speak for Gail, I do know that fury twisting around our home made her run colder, and neither of us wanted to finger the trouble vibrating our windows. That sound went from murmur to unraveled scream and its ferocity left a corrosive halo in our throats and there was no defense from it, one of the most truly spoken things I've ever heard. It got in your body and crawled to the top of your neck as clouds of snow and ice mist convulsed over the land. The last things to be checked before sleep: make sure boots were ready, snow blower oiled, tires chained, multiple pairs of gloves dried. Sun up. Seething snow flurries cutting eyebrows. Clear basement entrance accumulation with shovel. Nuthatches and chickadees at work on oak trunks. Sun unexpectedly warm. A sign to hurry before snow curdles, turns to stark weight. Gear up snow blower, rev the steel, let release down slowly through fingers. It'll be at least four miles up and down the access road and four hours. When I look up at the hills at end of morning there's five, nearly six feet of snow. Wind's gotten strangely warm. Temperature at sun up about twelve degrees. Temperature at noon when we've done with clearing; forty to forty-two degrees. Rill of running water and melt heard everywhere. You want the warmth to be a pleasure and relief, admit it in. Let it be fine over the skin as you watch the forest churn with running sap. But it's late January, and though a

minor thaw can occur, this one makes you shiver as the
heating softness of air sets in. You take off your coat,
head gear, try to escape your own small cloud of vapor.
Sunset comes, brings the Milky Way. Temperatures
risen to forty-five degrees. Sound of running water
growing fills ear and mind is nearly a smolder  of
weighings and loosenings shedding pronouncement
as it calls for another load of night time wood.

Morning sunny, almost sixty degrees. The
bordering stream has swollen. We can hear boulders.
Dumb breathless weight of them pressing, fermenting
our attentions. No birds in air. No signs of deer. Wing
of bird. Wing of storm. Which tells more and what
as land under cloudless sky becomes insidious with
swarm sounds of water, almost sickly melt lurchings
of tree line. Stream advancing to cascade proportions.
Temperature at 1:30pm nearly seventy degrees. We
decide to have lunch in our loosened but undeclared
confusions, make sandwiches. As we look out our
windows the huge snow mass on the mountain slopes
begins to move, hesitant of its own tremendousness at
first, then lurching, jiggling, gaining speed, knocking
down trees, splashing over rocks and gullies. It slides
toward our house. A kind of spasmodic, engorged
sheet pushing a cool wind before it. And we are frozen;
ourselves, our son, our dogs. I still, even today, want
to say "in horror" yet the stumble of any utterance is
stale. It was horror, if one wants to rummage through
a vocabulary. But more, it was desertion and paralysis

and it was tumbling at its own suffocating murderous speed at everything we knew. The weight of it. The advance of it. The swelling odor of it almost desolates me. If the images rise up after years I can barely separate myself from the spell of that watching. Its gathering. Its intoxication.

The wave somehow deflected, smashed against our car, over our gardens and backyard, moved upslope toward the stream roar. In a spasm there, it settled, died of its own weight. And we stared. At the denuded slopes, broken trees. The noiseless, stark fact of it fanned over everything we could see, squeezing us in a barrenness. We looked at each other. I suppose to see if we were alive, if we and the avalanche were hallucinations. The stupefaction and imprisonment so new and bruising. What could we know or know how to do or where to begin speech that would hold us together, hold to what needed to be done? We were miles from help. I opened the front door, the dread in us thick as the cold thing covering the valley, covering what we knew. Sun had loosened the huge snow thing from its root, sent it down scalding and ripping. We could hear the sun heating and churning it and water beginning to hollow it. The way it lay reminded me of a snail's enveloping foot, the image of sea and sea shore gathering more incongruity as I walked down the porch steps, let myself sink into the body of it as Gail and Clay watched.

I didn't know what tool to use, to name, that might

help me as I walked thigh deep into the going to slush snow mass which had settled, begun to leak. The sound of water curling and running and simmering; the misting snow sheet under sun's heat, the tangle of bitter astonishment over the devastation; violence unraveling into an immoveable bursted isolation made me ache with wordlessness. If I turned in a slow circle maybe a thought would come, the name of a tool. I looked at our basement entrance, the outside shower where we found late night summer relief soaking ourselves and watching meteors and the Milky Way in near rapture as fireflies rose and descended in their rhythms at the forest edge I'd cleared with my chain saw. The first words I was able to speak, "unlock the basement door." Not too fancy. But at least I got it up and out of my throat. Something to give courage as Clay descended into the cellar and Gail watched me, I knew, calmly running through her own gears. There were only three of us. It was two in the afternoon as the dogs observed from the sliding window doors, afraid, no barking.

Clay managed to shove the door open. He was fifteen at that point as I attempted to gauge his strength, stamina; what could be done without injury.

"Let's try to shovel this slush out, son."

We started. The weight and work was manageably light, not easy. With each gesture of labor we gained more confidence. Dug out some paths. Dug out the equipment. Realized the huge mass was in melt though barely a murmur from this muffled, sealed thing. There were also drainage gullies we had excavated for summer deluges churning up the Catskills. Clay and I moved from point to point as Gail suggested. She wanted to work at our sides. But we told her "no", her back, her spinal fusion wasn't worth the possible agony. So she did the instant mapping. We followed, letting ourselves be three together. In the first hour and a half the temperature fell from seventy to thirty-seven. The front of the valley remained untouched by the slide. There was good radio reception and warning: the temperatures in our area were to fall from their mid-day seventy to a next morning ten degrees and lower. It was two forty-five. Darkness set in at the latest; four-twenty. The mountain ridges would go from red to purple to blue gray to black. Our labor became more like irrigation; clearing paths for slush gone three-quarters water. We were wrenched practically out of our fingers and wrists. Of light left. An hour and thirty minutes. The car and pickup were parked in puddles of water. Easy to forget. I asked Gail to move the machinery (cars and tractor) down the drive. The expanding puddles once frozen would lock the vehicles in a two month and more grip.

As I struggled beside Clay I remembered a preceding July afternoon. I'd worked the morning clearing land, taking down trees for winter wood. The chainsaw is the most dangerous machine I've used. No room for smallest error either with steel or tree. Lose your concentration, end up maimed or dead. "Some goddamned bad cards," the gambling Jewish farmers I knew might say, as they shuffled, drank whiskey, and planned for their millions. Trees can twist, chain saws can buck into your face, the forces don't have applicable equations, just injuries and stories of expert woodsmen having to crawl, if they didn't die, for miles to get help. So I took the safety manual seriously. Wore goggles, gloves, chaps, steel-toed boots, and long sleeve shirt. Still don't know what the shirt was for; keep me from being beamed up, chased by the horrible forest shrimp my mother-in-law thought might be out there? I was in my forties, strong as I was ever going to be, had stamina, was ably stubborn for the work. And with first signs of fatigue I set the machine down walked away. I don't want and still don't want to chance the other side second I know was waiting. It's the only store bought thing that can butcher you like a piece of melted butter and I haven't even described how a fully branched new felled oak or maple can kick back twenty feet like some piece of let loose rabies, a hostility to feed on the mysteries. It was time to quit anyway. A full solar eclipse was a half hour from starting. The blue of sky had already subtly darkened, cast a wing over our valley. There was no wind and every tree in the forest around and above us slightly swayed as the moon's shadow approached the edge of the sun along with a halo of light red light. I don't recall the exact time of the sequence but it took approximately forty-five minutes for the moon to move completely over the face of the sun. The mountains, forest, and air turned a light, shimmering, silvery pink. A wind rose up out of that color soaking the whole valley in its mist. At the same time every leaf in the forest began to shudder, not violently, but in a held uniform rhythm. We could almost smell the color, the wind, sound of the forest shaking. As the moon continued its passage the silvery-pink haze transformed to reddish green, then gradually to a familiar blue as the eclipse accompanied wind dissipated and died. The silence as the face of the sun began to re-emerge was also unlike any silence we've undergone. It was thick, nearly silken, and cast all that we saw into momentary suspension. I don't know what the word "wild" means exactly. I too have my nostalgias over a previous America lying indeterminably in some canyon of my Westerner's dreams. But for those seconds we were immersed in a wildness so total, ruthlessly beautiful, unknowably strange; there can never be shelter nor safety from it.

"I don't know how much longer I can do this, Pop," Clay said. It was about ten to four by then. We'd cleared around the house, cut access paths to wood and other necessities. Somehow shoveled and pushed most of the immediate discouragement where it could drain downgrade. At four thirty Clay and me were worn to a thread, still fatigued with shock, and Gail undressed us both; Clay to his shower, me to a tub. In the morning the temperature fell to almost five below zero.

From September 7th to September 16th Juet says there was "fair" and "hot weather." The great lightning and thunder storms usually pass over the Catskills by this time. Summer thunder heads and their chaotic air masses can be dangerous at ground level; anything above tree line gets re-routed and thunder in our valley was often so convulsive and complex our house shook under the vibratory roar of air descending down the surrounding slopes breaking and uprooting trees. The crack of tree trunks, the living wood-laid-bare-sound of the rippage still drenches my ear and makes my skin waver. The highest Catskill peak is no more than forty-one hundred feet elevation yet summer storm air currents build to a violence so wrenching it kindles the ghosts of those Acadians and their flaring wonders. I did not want to be outside in those moments of storm pressing and growing. On one summer journey we tried to get home from back country where the animals we saw never experienced human beings. It is almost impossible today to undergo this mutual shock of first species encounter. To be eyed and studied by chipmunk or turkey or grouse, your image marked before the barely repressed draining panic of the other creature so spellweaved for that moment by what must be the unbearable pungence of what you are, the piercing germination of your appearance, the other being calling its warnings. What have you dared by your trespass at the end of the twentieth century committed to this other creaturely memory as you are and is your distance/nearness the coming of salt, the dripping of salt?

A storm had built for over an hour as we descended. The humidity accumulated in knots to be walked through and forest steamed under thunder shell, accelerating wind-whip preceding downpour, small heavy drops to tell you the gale had arrived, its beak and body soon to follow with slowly bellowing blasts of lightning that can scald and explode the largest oaks. We made it to about the edge of a neighboring meadow, to the bear clawed cabin. And no further. It was the equivalent of a suddenly rampaged stream; not water but wind flattening summer grass and lightning crackled and venomous, prickling the skin between your fingers to let you know how hungry it was. So we waited as mid-day dark pulsed and thickened, for lightning to pile and explode watch fireflies spread their heaps of pulsing insect meat rising and falling at meadow's edge from ground to tree tops, one form of living light to be heaved by another.

"People" came aboard during this run of days the diary says. "They offered" "no violence" in those autumn quietudes. Instead they wanted to exchange Indian wheat and tobacco for "knives and beads."

September 9th. Two great canoes full of men came aboard showily wanting to buy knives. The crew, alert and perched, took two hostages. The other warriors apparently went on land to decide what to do. They sent another canoe with two new hostages for exchange. The Half Moon took one of those and let the other go but "...he which we had taken, got up and leaped overboard ..."

September 11th. Though perhaps every person of the country was escape prone and therefore doubly untrustworthy, they did on this day make a "... show of love ..." offering tobacco and Indian wheat, then left for the night. The end-phrase of the passage "... but we durst not trust them ..." Cut was the throat. The Fatherless. The Motherless. Fattening the Face. Fattening the foot. A little?

Did they want to be fattened by "Indian wheat" or by a "show of love" and could that have meant handfuls of wild figs or smoked passenger pigeons, some deliciously stirred peril, sumptuous as a welling fountain of never experienced minutes calling to them to unexpectedly wander before their suppositions. Something subtly nervous as Love's allure, gently cajoling as the scents of drying fern washing over the ripples of the river?

September 12th. They appeared with twenty-eight canoes. It was early morning. Their vessels full of women and men and now "children." Was it an addition more frightening and perverse yet encountered? The crew suffered no one to come aboard though the visitors brought with them oysters and beans which were purchased. The Indians also brought "... great tobacco pipes of yellow copper ..." and "... pots of earth to dress their meat in ..." Were those low fired ceramic storage jugs and what spices were used to dress that meat and how ceremonially attractive were the Indians, dressed as they may have been and accompanied by their children, in regalia, painted, tattooed, their  effulgence ripe as parakeets in marshes, kingfishers preening at river's bank. And which meat was which in the reference? The last line of the passage reads as a Mystery from the Tomb or the Hour of the Tomb striking the Perils of Love in the moistness of a sewing bee among dangerous Elves: "... It floweth south-east by south within ... " as if it will be further of the poisons and it will be a good road. They will have sweets. They will die. The Chorus of Love gathers as a Moon Flower Partridge.

September 13th. Early morning winds from the north accompanied by a flood and "four canoes" with a "... great store of very good oysters ..." Was the simple lure of good food the germ of a more quickened Satanism. The thrall, expectancy, the sap undoing the earnest "... and none of them to come aboard us ..." The whole of Europe therein returning the weakest shadow of heaven and who claims authorship in the name of prophecy? In the name of "... It floweth ... " as an opened oyster?

September 14th. Again, fair weather, "very fine" and by that does the author mean the luxuriant weightless air that sweeps over land and water during these days of shifting light and wind, nights still warm but tinged with coil of winter, glut to come of leafless trees, ash-grey skies, the world burnt with frost, eyes tearing with it unexpectedly on a hot afternoon with no longer pollinated breezes. The ship sailed twelve leagues where the River expanded to at least a mile's width. Here "...the land grew...": the diction in this instance holding some beat of awe in the syllables. The Alien trees. Alien People. Alien sky. Were they served stews of oyster mixed with meat of pumpkin, cuts of venison, salmon, sprinkles of trout and corn, bear fat thrown in for lushness and sensuality. And what spices to call a man's throat to blossom in secret over the unquenchable comings of possible hoar-frost. No Persephone would have been there but the vases were often inscribed with shadow presences and wandering faces, half-formed beings pushing at membranous veils, earthenware pipes with ten-eyed dream faces floating in and out of each other's skin ready to lick the world of seeing with foot long eyelashes, the intolerable vulgairty of seeing's rage and gluttony.

The land. It "...grew very high and mountainous..." as if some squirming heap risen from the roots of the cannibal Man/Flea whose fresh killed heart flies around the inside of a kettle looking for escape.

Last rendering for this mid-September day: "The river is full of fish." But what could this mean? Did the People intend to bring the Story of the Woman Who Becomes a Snake to the crew and infect them with this Dream of a fearful, even sore-hearted swallowing? The newly wedded Girl while awaiting her husband's return decided to catch fish in her water basket. She cooks, eats half the catch, and saves the rest for her lover. But she becomes thirsty from the feast and goes back to the stream and drinks and can't stop drinking, and with each slurp becomes more thirsty and begins in the midst of that thirst to transform into a snake. What is the firmness of seeing, its lingering invitation or trespass upon the unknown. Was it the impersonation of fish sent swimming that day. And what world will be full of fish with hairy feet who can make all men's dreams of food into ants, the cousins of ants who decorate themselves with the heads of men?

September 15th-September 16th. The morning was "...misty until sun arose." The River's depth "very good" with a "...great store of salmon..." as they passed the "high mountains." Was it the face of Overlook Mountain and its surrounding peaks which come to the eye with a radiance at this time of year of changing leaf and sky, the brightness of light smitten with stillness, its having lived for the season and now also dying so emphatically with the toll of an increasingly shallow warmth.

Ship's crew while under "full sail" realized the two hostage "savages" escaped through a "port" and called to the Europeans as they swam "in scorn." Is it the scorn of the Kept who know the Keepers are demented. Can such "Orenda" happen in an hour, a second. And the "scorn": is it like the cannibal who in its seance of Love devours mercy back to the earliest dawns when mercy was bitterest poison, its crumbs transparent as jellyfish?

Here also ship's crew found "...very loving people, and very old men..." If this is an appraisal then of what sort of "loving"? Was it fragile, tender, subtly unpromising, proudfully reluctant as it itself appraised the Strangers. The "old men": were they both fresh and frail and utterly new in their persons. Were they of the Hell that rises up and pursues each man, disenfranchises the Sailor, catches him by the hair, sells him for being toad-cold and unwakeful? This is the place, where they, ship's crew "...were well used." The advantage of the well fucked, fucked dark on the fringes of "very good fish." Did they have tails and sun themselves next to those fires, their whiskers fibril, voluptuous, and later, sun of sunrise in slit of sky, shafts of light growing to fans inaccessible with the propensities of wolves. Did they come to the Europeans as the Peregrine, folded in their dive, impassive, cracking the sailors open. No bewitchments, dismantlings? The hardly noticeable rent like the rotten chick of an eagle, fore-ordaining, drawing a nation-to-come, to come and taste it.

When I recall Pearl I also remember the earliest settlement story of an old friend from Texas, her great-grandmother who came into the Palo Duro Country when the Comanche and Kiowa still roamed the southern plains. Those horse-born warriors rode their animals as if they'd waited the whole fifteen thousand years of the extinction, wanting to smother the disappearances with their own defiance. And when Equus sniffed and kicked once more on the horizon they rode the animals as if they themselves were sparrow hawks weaving a prankish geography over the horses' bodies, stinking of the glaciers, gone hawk boned as they threaded themselves into those fresh storms of horse blood.

That grandmother came into the Palisaded Plains or Llano Estacado of Eastern New Mexico and West Texas. This southern-most extension of the high plains is the uneroded remains of fifty million year old river sediments and sand storms endlessly blown over this huge slab about half as old as old Mount Marion herself. Some of those sediments might include Coronado's nightmares about this great waterlessness, and where he, with his Cibola thirsts, let the first horses escape into the hallowing world of their origins. When she came to the edges of the Palo

Duro Canyon, my friend told me she wandered into a graveyard where the bones of sabre-toothed tigers, rhinoceros, mastodons, horses, and borophagines lay on the exposed escarpments, some bits of slag from the repulsive furnaces of demons. She came to know those borophagines, the hyena/dogs and scavengers that sniffed that air for forty million years, some big as lions, others crafty as raccoons and climbed trees to test up the ripe dead. She knew what those ancients could do to Mastodon femurs, shred them like a hyena chomping some accidental snowball. The goddamned thought of those goblins over an elephant carcass with condors swooping overhead was an affair of carrion the most wandering mind might want to avoid. Go a light knee deep into that stink and no telling what the country round might want to teach you.

She was also at the southern-most end of what the soil of the plains allowed her at that crossroads of forbearance she entered: the sod house and its mysteries dug up, stacked in raw cubes, an interior trenched four, five foot deep, hold heat in winter, escape the ninety degree summer nights. Moved in some furniture, a whale oil lamp, nothin cozy, but nothin bitter either compared to the possible shambles waiting at the edges. That first night she Germanically set herself to a tidying things up and when she lit the lamp she noticed the walls of sod enclosing her seemed to have a motion of their own. It was rattlesnakes pushing at the burrows she'd broken, waking from their hibernations.

One big serpent jammed itself through, fell into its coils, snapped its rattles, and she killed it. For the rest of the night my friend's grandmother chose not to abandon her handmade sod-works. Instead she found a hatchet and everytime a snake's head appeared, she chopped it off until by morning a good chunk of her sod-house floor was smothered in snakes' blood and severed heads. Next night it was nearly the same thing until the old ground ran out of serpents. I've never known really what to think about this story. It holds to itself all the aloofest roots of dark-crossed American mythologies, along with the willful, determined young Queen of a Hell so small, so sinister, and so primordial in the spell of sacrifice that no American home has ever been the same for me, as that young woman, alone in her otherworldly stillness and concentration made the vastness of what she was doing into the what-you-had-to-do-story of bare hands, some ghoulish witchery, and the semblances of fertility and evaporation circling wand-like over voiceless arrangements shaded as Fedallah in the hold of the Pequod sharpening his harpoon for what Corpses of Doom?

Pearl and Jim sometimes wandered their countryside with what might be called wands. They were witches too, though to themselves what they did encompassed the necessities of the everyday. Any thoughts given over to superstition were of the catagory of incertitudes, not to give offense, but part of unreliable leisures and unsober indulgences having nothing to do with the obligements of neighbors or the proper sightings of a rifle the week before deer season.

Dowsers, water-witches, diviners. None of the three was really acceptable, but on occasion someone's well ran dry and Jim's equation grew lean and sharp:

NO  WATER
NO   LIFE

Not an evil mathematics, more it was somber as a dove's call and had an unfretted stillness to it neither consolable nor inconsolable, as the unaccounted winged visitor who watches the goings and struggles of men and women. A dried up well meant possible abandonment of one's home. A richer man and a poorer man staggered by the sight of his dribbled up, ailing faucets could also rent a "Pounder" for a negociated price whether money, labor, or if the woman of the house a fine quiltmaker, then a homely high masterpiece to warm a body from toes to nose. "Pounder": a drilling rig that slowly pounded through and broke the layers of rock until it reached a functional water vein, and, if lucky, an acquifir. The process was painstaking, demanded skill and lore. A good pounder not only knew his equipment but knew the sounds, the ones he was told about, the ones he accumulated. Some pounders were local legends. They'd come, spend days, were loners avoiding the faster boarers and drillers who went through rock with no sense of what the life of water is. One pounder we knew, who pounded our well, spent nearly a week and found an ice-age deposit rising up at a hundred gallons per minute. The water he found tasted and smelled like some favorite flower of mammoths waiting for the now extinct spring blooms, and which made their trunks curl with pleasure. He'd smoke, read his paper, lean over for an hour, listen, then get up to adjust the equipment, sit down again and resume listening. It was, outside of Jim and Pearl, as close to divination as anything I've seen, and the voices that spilled up were full of life. Yet, in the case of this one man, who was always private and noiseless in his way, no one knows what whisperings he heard during those years of listening. One afternoon after finding water he went home and committed suicide. No signals, no indications of despair. People didn't talk much of it, outside of bewildered sorrow, didn't say too much either other than to remark on the fine blue of his eyes, knowing how long he'd stuck his ear to the ground. Must'a been the loneliness of the occupation they said, recollecting he was as good at what he did as the bees foraging for pollen, a true honey maker, never one better to come and do such an intimate thing.

We were told the area of the western Catskills where we later settled was too haunted for the Delaware Indians who entered the high meadows and

hollows for ritual purposes only. Gail loved this land
and one section near the top southern crest of the hills
which surrounded our home, she walked by herself,
thought of that high ridge as a cathedral of huge trees
joined to spectral shades of light she could study and
be touched by. The light often was dispersed so that it
fell as veils or mists, depending on motion of clouds,
funnels or shafts, a rainlight bursting blues of sky and
falling in mixtures of yellows, greens, shades of purple.
Winds of light mixed with winds of air. There were
also cairns gathered under this tree cathedral touched
by that light. The rocks were stacked approximately
waist high, forming organized circular mounds. The
cairns had   settled into their weight and no one knew
the exact age of these objects said to be works of the
Red Paint People, ancient swordfish hunters who
sailed the waves of land inward this far. No artifacts or
burials. The dates: four to six thousand BP. A skilled,
advanced maritime culture coming to earlier groves of
maple and wild cherry, doing swordfish dances then
walking from here to the "Hudson" and their ocean
going canoes? No one has an answer and some of the
night screams we thought confirmation of this void.
Once when doe were birthing fawns we listened as the
coyotes ate the still enwrapped newborns. We could
hear the savage gluttony and an occasional coyote
howl along with   screams of creatures we couldn't
identify, whether bobcats, owls, gosse-hawks, foxes
or ghosts impatiently gathered, we didn't know. But

such incidents seemed to come from a still unfinished Earth when there were monsters and cannibals who could conjure ghastly diseases and conjure the rites of drastic cure; the old contests about who would be the living, who the dead, who the monster dancers and whisperers banishing sicknesses for an hour, a day, make each circle the Rim of the World as impatiently as those screaming beings we heard recasting the small valley where we lived into pathless spells, possessions, and greetings; Haqoonde:s, Old Longnose Himself come to bewitch us, steal our child?

Pearl and Jim were both Water Witches. A rare untalked-of-thing in one house. No children. Respect for each other born, I often thought, of their knowing no help ever did arrive. Theirs was an erased whereabouts and they were not pulverized, but made of it an arrangement of gentle fortitudes having lived to be fluent in their constraints and full of interest over what comes to the back and front doors. Pearl had suffered an early womanhood maiming. A surface infection on her breast grew to a proportion where a doctor to finally protect himself, cut off both her breasts. It was in the mid-30s and they were poor and by that I mean there was no room and they were harnessed; had to live it, be scoured by it, take what breaths came to them and barrennesses perpetually tracing the heights; man height, woman height, the curtailed height of night stamping the soil hard in sterility and prowling all the clock-work. She told Gail over tea and talking of spring flowers and lilacs one day she had the most beautiful breasts and the next day they were lopped away as she looked across Fish Creek Road and the curve where our houses stood across each other, at Jim chopping wood in the tireless rhythms he'd come to at seventy-five years old, clop of ax and split oak sounding like the everlasting invitation of heartsease, earthy and true and fleeting as the meanest winter on the first sun-curled heat waves of spring.

When Waterwitching they walked the land, an inch-by-inch substance of care with cherry branches. What they took seriously was a house lying thirsty and unbearable, and the thing they were doing, they couldn't help, didn't ask questions of it, nor were they shamed by it, let others talk in to and out of. By holding a Y-shaped cherry rod firmly, both arms relaxedly stretched from mid-chest outward, our two neighbors walked the perimeter around the house of a needful family, the tail of the Y extending outward from both hands. "Pick cherry, hickory, quaking aspen," they advised, "doesn't matter." The two diviners holding the freshly cut branches walked slowly in circles until the rod physically, visibly bent downwards on the exact spot where water lay underground, the actual "attraction" "divination" exerting enough force to bend the two dowsers' wrists and arms. "Oh hell," they'd say in comment offering us a beautiful tomato from their garden. Jim showed us the technique, walked the perimeter of our house and found the well, pronounced it "slow"; no more than two gallon per minute, "but enough" and a "here you try it." Both Gail and I took the exact rod and realized if we walked from there to Omaha, stood over the under-Prairie Oglala Fresh Water Sea, the only use we'd come to: to provide Jim and Pearl a shake-of-the-head smile over their young neighbors. Who can tell what will come of hearing the Whistlers of the Woods whispering their ancient contract not to molest human beings, is fading with age, and that the underground remnants of the Chicadee who brings the Dead back to life are shredded.

Wakener of the Land
Deadener of the Land

if these too
are your names
Come
use up our words

Come
be the Thief
the Collector

Remind us
How free Speech once was
How free Speech
once is

September 17th through September 26th. Juet says of the 17th: "...fair sun-shining weather, and very hot..." The mid-fall heat wave was accompanied by stiff, gale-like winds as the Half Moon sailed south. The winds drain the land of its tropical remnants. Canadian geese, red-winged blackbirds, robins, herons will not test the encroaching barreness. See them gather singly; in twos and threes for an afternoon meadow forage. Watch closely as they hop, dry bath themselves in a bowl of dust, preen, snap up into the southward turning thermals, and whether flight, stately as with herons in their slow orderly rhythms, long necks and legs telling of the ancient vocations of endurance drifting from one geologic age to another; the robin more taut, hostage to its smaller body having to work the air constantly. Each day you feel and see the depletions until there are no more of these visitors who in leaving make you feel on those hot afternoons dull and abandoned.

The recording on September 19th. "...people of the country came flocking aboard, and brought us grapes and pompions, which we bought for trifles..." Were they bird-like in their curiosities, keen and nervous as they moved over ship's deck, their heads turning, hands and shoulders flexed. Did they pry and squawk as ravens. Were they as falcons, semi-extinguished in folded watchfulness, a vein of fury, vitally talkless? The earliest chronicles of European settlement report the delight of wild grapes. For the non-human inhabitants grapes were a favorite forage along with enough blue berries as compliment to transform the wild seasons into ripe vineyards stretching to the horizon, a wealthfull topping for fluencies of joy accorded to all. "Pompions": If those are pumpkins, then were they dried, sweetened with maple syrup. Did the "people" bring pumpkins filled with honey and fruit for roasting? The other lucre brought aboard: "...beavers' skins and otters' skins..." which unfolded as treasures hot as gold. The Indians were given in exchange "...beads, knives, and hatchets..." How else explain the temperature of these syllables and sudden omission of self-protective coiling and caution. The Indians studying the hard malignant skull of the greed, palpitant as they were, had not enough quickness before the witchery, no seasoning.

The 21st. Ship's carpenter "...went on land and made a foreyard..." The labor would have taken some hours to cut down, not a sapling, but at least a fifty-year-old oak grown to a good twenty-five feet. Whittle it down with able, well arranged ax work and chisels to support a fore-sail and braces while ship's master, wanting to test for "treachery" brought the "...chiefmen of the country..." aboard, got them drunk. One, whose wife accompanied him, they, the crew, admired for her modesty, compared her to their own women.

September 22nd. At 3:00 in the afternoon "savages" were once again welcomed aboard. They "...

made all oration..." Were they dressed in ritual finery of glistening fur and hide, tattooed and painted. What featherwork did they carry for blessings? As to "...and made all oration...": how did the Speakers gesture. Were tobacco offerings given, feathered fans used to sweep breath away from lips, cleanse the racing blood and land forms left by the defeated cannibal sorcerers who were attracted to the planet by the scent of human meat? There is no mention of the quality of the feast, nor of the "platter"—whether it was carved of wood, had incised designs, or engraved ceramic with the outline of living waters decorating its edges:

They found the water to be "inconstant"; no verifiable or sure soundings of depth.

September 24th. Went on land "...gathered good store of chestnuts..." found "...deep water and anchored..."

September 25th. Crew and officers walked west side of river, discovered "...good ground for corn and other garden herbs..." Included in this hoard of

fertile soil "...sweet wood in great abundance..."; "...
great store of slate for houses..." and other stone for
construction needs. Oak, chestnut, yew, walnut. These
are cities the geese will stare at. Their wild eyes will
see the fathomless seas and mists of men.

September 26th. Returned to the site of "loving
people." There were two "old men." One, the one
they tested previously for "treachery." The other,
an elder stranger who "showed" Henry Hudson "...
all the country thereabout, as though it were at his
command..." Hudson bade them to "...dine with
him..." The guests brought "...two old women and two
young maidens..." sixteen or seventeen, Juet estimates,
"...who behaved themselves very modestly..." Hudson
gave the old men a knife. They returned the courtesy
with a gift of tobacco. When they departed "...down
the river..." they made signs "...boat and crew should
come down with them..." This passage reads as a Ghost
Story and the Journey of Time before certain Ghosts
become visible again. Are the two old men luring them
toward the Blood Clot who can't lay still and crawls up
the sleeping bodies of visitors. Were the two "old men"
the two "old women" and the two "young maidens"
mixed with water by wave working feathered sorcerers
of the river who summoned them, sent them to show
the strangers "...all the country thereabout..."?

Honey Stirers
who buy the Dearest Words
Talk Buyers

The word designating "Awareness" is also a blood stain.
The dream of the vocabulary in this instance
is volitant with rumor of the mind planted and bearing
its forms as one explanation of the elusive Word
that does not and will not settle as men do
or as a man will be likely to do
at some point in his life and be abandoned
by his unsettled words.
The one word set to sailing and polluting the trachea.


As to serpents. We had a large station wagon able to haul tools, sheet rock, needed lumber (primarily 2 X 4s) bought at a local mill. My father-in-law at that time gave me a shovel, my favorite, and one I still have. A light, well-balanced, stable scoop, with shallow hull. Easy to handle under full load. Affords minimal muscle tear, back strain, the host of small injuries one can expect with labor; count on the visit. I've cleared manure, snow; cleaned ditches for pipe, spread rock and soil. That shovel and me have accompanied each other through tons of labor. I can't think of a better, more trusted companion for those chores that had to be done, and on occasion, though we live in a city now, will be waiting in the morning. It hangs ready in our tool shed.

But the strangest labor between myself and that object started with a trifle (to bring Juet's word forward). I'd gone to the town dump. Hauled broken sheet rock, construction debris, rotted board, asbestos shingles. Took my shovel and cleared the deep bay of the car. Threw the tool into the empty space and decided, before going home to work that loomed over me in those years, to take a small journey through the back country of Saugerties, explore and savor the Hudson Valley spring surge of new life. I'd never seen, really, the first flower blooms of the Valley, walked its swamps, small stream-beds, the ravines and gullies of hidden light, so cunning and vaporous in their multitude of moods. The land around us was defined by water and water surge and there were ponds of various sizes everywhere over land and marsh country. Islands of water full of their own living expression of insects, amphibians, small mammals, birds, reptiles and plants. Those ponds were also full of close-shrouded and briered wilds. First sightings of snowdrops often sprouting out of the final, meanest uncertainties of a hard winter are most near to me; there a quick cluster in a snowbank, peculiar and daintily white, reaching for sun in early spring hours when sun seems to want to burrow and continue dying. The other wonder: Sound of the initial one or two peepers, shouldering all the hostilities that might smother them for a whispy frog song, then to be shut down by temporary freeze; one more. But the messengers have come, feintly, foolishly, and yes, hungrily too. Charmed glottons risen from the quagmires.

I drove over a rise, looking at the horizon, wondering if the billowing clouds meant another late March/early April blizzard. Wasn't paying attention and when I fronted my eyes, saw an undefined grey clump at the bottom of the hill. And it was moving. And what the hell could it be? I coasted, pulled over to the thin shoulder of an isolate country road, shut the station wagon down, got out for a close range sniff. The thing was still moving. It had claws, goddamnit, and whether it could pick up some speed from a Silurian event invisibly lurking in the local shale, I didn't know. And not knowing what else to do I walked closer, the chain of Southern California Cold War teenage horror movies I know by heart, crawling up my spine. The thing was like some still hot piece of Cretaceous shrapnel come through the veil somewhere. It took time out from its painful land motions to watch me. It was a large snapping turtle migrating, as I later learned, from one pond to another. Must have weighed sixty pounds. Well armed and armored. When I came nearer it turned and shit just to let me know. It had the tail of an alligator with fleshy crests, smelled of spicy pond slime and rot. I found out this was a smoothed shelled old one. Its head was disproportionately large, and though it had small eyes, I knew they were fixed on me, ready for business. It couldn't retract its head or tail. Didn't try. I put the shovel handle a couple of feet in front of the reptile to make sure once again of I didn't know what. Head with its nasty beak missed the mark I'd laid for it, set itself to its previous stillness like as to that God who just created Man, wanted to taste test the results. I was shocked by the speed of the strike and glad it wasn't my hand, my wrist. It didn't apologize and wouldn't have minded the takings; food comes as it may from the willing idiotic Adam brooding among the Temptations. This one was a fellow carnivore who took birds, small mammals, snakes, fish and is a piece of fury. The turtle can stretch its head over its back, reach far to its side for finger, thumb, steer a web of cartilage toward permanent disassembly. Was it migrating because of pollution, starvation, to lay eggs? Terrestrial travel was obviously workable for this hobo but it was dolorous and might take miles. My lady or gentleman was halfway across the road so I gave it a quick air-borne ride on my shovel, walked a good twenty feet beyond the road edge and let the serpent down. That became a yearly ritual to see if I could outrace some of the locals who thought sport to run over these wild, near wonderfully loathsome, smolderingly hostile beings who weren't always killed, but nearly always maimed and left to torturous death. Their turtle weight still hangs on my wrists and forearms. Their turtle stench sets me to dreaming over the earliest Catskill Jack-in-the Pulpits.

During that summer when I dug out individual trenches, raised concrete block piers for Gail's new studio, I'd take a late-morning break. The temperatures made it impossible to work mid-day. Eighty-five to ninety degree heat with ninety-five percent humidity. I'd do the digging from 7 to 10am, then from 5 to

8:30pm; watch the days recede while working pick, digging bar, shovel, a basic inch-by-inch gouging that, under the flap of thin top soil lay nothing but resistance. The work was slow, measured, and in those years of the eighties I was a "House Husband" finding occasional employment while Gail earned the money doing fashion catalogues in New York. She was gone five days a week. My other real job was to take care of our son, Clay. That phase of "fatherhood" absorbed me for eight years. It meant shopping, cooking, organizing, washing and hanging laundry, telling stories, and what often painfully stunned me; the re-imagining of self and ambitions. Included in daily ritual; visiting doctors, hearing the good and bad news. I taught Clay the ceremonies and rituals of eating, to think about good manners, to be watchful of others. These smallest acts forced me to wholly re-appraise my sense of "manhood" and what I discovered to be vague and often destructive assumptions about women, my own "male" expectations, and the most basic daily activities of sharing in a relationship (the questions that arose then, and continue to re-arise now have not lessened in their surprises nor their edgyness). The other things; holding himself ethically in a world, listening, being quiet, inventing courage and compassion; can these life-giving words be taught and can they ever speak to the possible living actions that are their mysterious twins?

He saw me restoring a house, washing dishes,

building and landscaping, cooking, stumbling and trying not to. He ate my cooking. I am not a good cook as are most of my male friends, many of them writers and artists who are excellent improvisors, steady and inventive at the flame. I will, if no one's around, settle for a peanut butter and jelly sandwich, bad chili, an iceberg lettuce salad with store-bought ranch dressing. I made fresh dinners every night, some, a part of Gail's preparations for the week ahead, some my own. I took Clay to his day camps, readied him for bed, taught him how to bathe, read him children's books, fairy tales, the worlds of dinosaurs and snakes. When his mother came home he'd ask her about Gaboon vipers, mambas, bush-masters over breakfast.

I learned to think about Clay and Gail, to anticipate. In the summer late afternoon breezes I threw him endless whiffle balls and he endlessly swung at them, hit them; I chased them. I had to transform my way of thinking, hearing, seeing. Be ready. Listen as I had never listened before. Those hours and years lay wholly outside anything I had ever known. I am sure now the absorption and isolation I know as a writer helped me in this process. I am used to being alone, have spent much of my life doing hard labor (including writing) of one kind or another. We did not have money so Gail and I became skilled at carpentry, house construction, gardening, home restoration. Gail is also one of the best carpenters and craftswomen I know. On any construction site she is always at least ten steps ahead.

Give her a hammer, a welder's helmet and she's on home-ground and will transfer that information directly over to the processes necessary to make art. I'd take Clay for hikes, talk to him of the terrain, count the number of birds and mammals and names, show him how to dig up and prepare gardens, set and spread manure, plant vegetables, see it through to maturity and seasonal dying. I let him play with tools, make mud pies, dressed his cuts, insect bites, watched over him as he hunted for snake's and bird's nests. There were always snakes: copperheads in swamps, timber rattlers on higher slopes, bad-tempered, fast, brown water snakes, garter snakes, milk snakes. Can't predict when a venomous one will appear so we taught Clay to be weary, call if he saw a serpent. If it were non-venomous I often picked it up, let it coil around wrist and arm, let Clay touch, examine, wonder (as I did), then let the visitor disappear into edging brambles. One of the most beautiful serpents was the stunning black racer which grows to nearly eight feet in length. This snake hunts by sight, is agile, extremely alert, will eat rodents, frogs, other snakes, birds, and insects. I looked forward to sightings of these very shy serpents. They are sleek, dark flamed, luxuriantly attractive when seen in the soar of their motions, or at rest in the branches of tall brush. Clay and I were walking toward our garden to check on ripening tomatoes. I saw ground movement about twenty feet ahead, picked up Clay immediately, not knowing at that moment what it was. I stood still, pointed so he could see. The grasses were mid-ankle high and moving. It was a big snake that emerged at the foot of a huge rock oak, a black racer. It hesitated for a moment then began to climb the trunk of that oak, flexing itself up, a stealthy black unrelenting chord over the tides of oak bark at once alarming and hypnotic as the line of it sensuously strained and dilated upward searching for birds. As I think of it now, was it Pan, the Fatal, the Wonderful who casts us in spells of living awe; was the mistletoe cut at such moments, to call the Druid God, the Terrible, when dangerous visitors inched their way up the trunks of World Trees invoking prophecy and mystical dread; did the poisonous Disease Killers of the forests let themselves be seen as the snakes glistened in their smooth finalities?

House Husband. It took. It ate time. Twenty four hours a day. The preciousness that oriented me as a male, the bastions so easily assumed and taken, began to swirl down some nameless drain. Once, prior to our move from New York City, I took care of Clay for many weeks. He was almost two at that point. I made his breakfasts. Read to him. Dressed him. Carried him downstairs with carriage, water, lunch. I was one of the first fathers among our group of friends. I thought it an adventure, son strapped to father, a picture of joy as people smiled and walked by. Then the "adventure" began to grind in. There was a playground at the end of Thompson Street, a few blocks from our loft. I found myself pushing Clay and other kids on swings every morning around 10:00am. I was the only male. The others parents on duty were females. I talked absorbedly with them about their new children and mine. They joked, chatted, kept up a banter among themselves. Had an ancient lore. I did not. Sometimes I'd ask if they'd mind watching while I went to the corner bodega for a snack. At first it was soda and chips. After a few weeks, a beer. Hell, it was usually eleven-thirty. Have a beer, eat a sandwich. Watch the kid. Figure how to regard the huge six hours till sundown. That nap. While he's sleeping I'll get some writing done. But when he slept I slept. Or sat and stared. When I finished one of those beers I felt like I'd entered the tenth ring of melancholy. Alone with a nearly two-year-old child, who, if I didn't watch every second might either eat a dog turd, step into the street. And if I forgot the teddy bear woe unto me. There were hours that rubbed so hard I thought it might be better to go give some blood; don't stop with a quart, just empty the container, please. Another couple, close friends, invited us for dinner. They'd had a boy, a year prior to ours. Michael and Clay were crib mates who have become life-long friends. During the evening I described what I thought was the hole my days had crawled into. As I moved my small story forward, our friend, Kitty, smiled. She has a very graceful Irish smile, the kind that registers its humor over any permutation of bullshit no matter how long it's been deep froze. She looked at me, straight at me. "Why Honey", she said, "you have the housewife blues," and asked whether I'd like some brandy with desert. I thought too, well women have been doing this for what, six million years, and here I am after five weeks ready for mummification.

There was also a small playground at Independence Plaza where I often took Clay for the company of other parents and kids we knew, and often, their and our friends joined for late afternoons. An early summer day around 8:00am I decided to take Clay, let him teeter-totter, explore the sand pit. No one but Clay, myself, a neighborhood office worker and life-long bachelor named Vinnie, a gentle, kindly man who lifted weights, lived with his unmarried sister and elderly mother. He'd shyly do push-ups, help with various children. I remember him, a body-builder image from a late forties comic book advertisement, modest in his accomplishment, tightly cut at 58, handsome, well-ironed, about five-seven, Italian from Downtown with gentle voice. I liked Vinnie. Admired his quietness, his loyalty to mother and sister. I was playing with Clay in the large sandbox watching him touch and explore. Vinnie was doing various loosening exercises, hand stands for Clay who was delighted. "Watch me, Clay!" Vinnie said, as he climbed, set himself for the jungle gym, hung and reached from one bar to another with an almost youthful ease. He made it, maybe three quarters, suddenly paused, began swaying back and forth, first two hands, then one, the swaying motion growing more heavy and strange.

"Look at Vinnie, Dad. Why's Vinnie doing that?" Clay asked. And I was watching too as Vinnie swung, the fingers of his one hand loosening their grip as Vinnie's eyes rolled back in his head, the body dropped. "What's wrong with Vinnie, Dad?" Clay asked once more as I watched his face turn a shade of purple, lips seize back to expose teeth mouth gone agape with death rattle. I picked up Clay and ran, yelled loud as I could for help. Artists were in their surrounding lofts. I looked back. Vinnie hadn't moved. And I waited for nearly half an hour. The rescue ambulance came with two medics. "What happened?" they asked as we looked across the field at Vinnie lying under the jungle gym. All four of us walked toward the body. Clay and me stopped about half way as the medics applied the paddles. I held Clay, watched Vinnie bounce once, twice as the medics got up to get the gurney.

When Clay was eight to ten months old I'd strap him to my chest, walk lower Manhattan from Tribeca to thirtieth street, Christopher street to Avenue C; from the Lower East Side to Chelsea. On certain afternoons the wanderings took up book stores, walks on the River, smells of spices, trips to get fresh mozzarella, fruit, prosciutto bread still hot from the baker's oven. Those afternoons also took up sad purpose. In those months a child of young neighbors, not dissimilar to ourselves, disappeared. His image was on every wall, corner, window. That disappearance sometimes mars me thirty years later. For the first forty-eight crucial hours after Etan Patz vanished many of the residents of our neighborhood scoured the shadows hoping to find any trace. Then the days set in with a reward, and the months. We'd see his parents in local markets accompanied initially by their families, then alone, the thing, the thought of it unbearable. They'd shifted their perception for only that second, and he was gone. So I, and I know there were other fathers, searched for Etan Patz, with and without Clay haunted by the thought of that possibility. He was never found.

And with that too the rupture of the civilization in the form of "3 Mile Island" the Pennsylvania nuclear power plant that nearly went to "meltdown." We watched in numbed astonishment as preparations and warnings were given for the evacuation of New York, Philadelphia, and vital sections of the Northeast. New parents at the end of the twentieth century and Gail asked on one of those evenings, "Have we let ourselves bring a son into this evil a world?" as we discussed what to pack, what to leave, where exactly to go. Fatherhood. Motherhood.

Gail came home one weekend and Clay called his mother "Dad." After putting him to bed she came downstairs and cried. That was one of a number of goddamned hard moments. And we also needed new electrical lines just then. The last installed nineteen twenty-five, nineteen thirty? Wire strung through pine studs, not dry rotted, but resin varnished, so old were the basics. And if set fire what sudden tinder would they be. Would the thing engulf us like some sun-stroked bale of hay? What questions could I ask about a bottomed up old house, myself, a young father, attempting this alchemy. What was safety, what potential endangerment. I took down one slab of horse hair plaster in the kitchen; found the biggest hornet's nest I'd ever seen. Lucky too, it was a cold early summer night. One unlucky afternoon Gail cut through a wasps' nest while trimming some lilacs. Got stung so bad on lips and cheek; though nearly in shock she refused to go to hospital. The numbness in her face from those toxins lasted more than a week. Clearing out space for insulation in the second storey I came across powdered debris. What the possible fuck could this be I whispered, a new consternation swelling in my throat. So I got a scoop for this material embedded between studs. I looked closely, hesitated as I readied the tool for extraction, saw skeletal debris, a couple of skulls, small femurs. I called Gail first. Then across Fish Creek for Jim who generously came over as always, asked to see a skull. He looked at it. Looked at the pre-Civil War framing I'd exposed.

"Dave," he said, "I think it's bats. Come and gone."

"Bats!" I answered. "You mean a bat roost?"

"Yup," he answered. "Looks like good insulation or good manure for Gail's garden."

I was left up on the roof to consider, to grapple

with this fact of houseguests, what kind of house exactly was this one, we'd bought along with a secret pile, not exactly caprolites but close; color of white washed grey, weird as the ashes of Nineveh, as I dug it out and found more bones.

I also dug ditches for electrical lines through the front yard. Three. Needed to be two foot wide two foot deep. Each about thirty feet long. Got a reference for a good local electrician. Andreissen the name. Came up one afternoon to check over the job site, offer an estimate. Got out of his truck. Don't know to this day how since he was bigger than his own vehicle. Hair over seven feet. Weighed in at about four hundred pounds. Hands big as desk tops. Thought he'd break through the front porch, and when he got inside thought he'd either collapse the floor or push through the ceiling. So huge he had to enter sideways through the doors. First thing Clay wanted was a ride.

"Daddy. He's really big!"

"That's right, son," Mr. Andreissen said, the inflection of that tone not a reprimand, but an assertion, bare-faced as it was, that people as they do, stared at him since the cradle. When he and Clay had done with their mutual estimations and introductions Mr. Andreissen gave Clay a ride on his shoulders. Our son was so scared/delighted I was afraid he might puke on Mr. Andreissen's head, but he thankfully just stared up there, uphigh at all the world, some true amazements writ across his face, some bewilderment when he looked down from that mountain.

"Will I be that big, Dad?"

"Don't know, Son."

"That man coming back?"

"Says he is, in about a week."

Clay wasn't sure what a "week" exactly is. Every day he'd go out and wait. Look down Fish Creek Road ask again "How big?" and wonder when the "Viking" (I told him I thought Mr. Andreissen was a Viking), was going to come back.

I didn't tell him about the "Berserkers" but I did tell him who the Vikings and Scralings were. About Leif Erikson, Columbus, Magellan, Cortez, Henry the Navigator, Marco Polo. We didn't have television so stories had to be told, rhymes made up. It was an occasion to go to the Woodstock public library which had an excellent collection of children's material. I found, in reading to my son, the stories traveled both ways and I was educating myself from the toes up. I know too he looked for the sail, the row of shields ribbing the hull, wanted the raiders to carry him directly to a fjord; one way ticket, no questions asked.

"What's a fjord, Dad? Tell me again," he'd ask while making mud pies next to the ditch I was digging at sunset. I'd draw Norway, Sweden, Denmark in the dirt, tell'im a fjord is made of deep water and high cliffs and big shadows where the Viking Gods lived. By the time Mr. Andreissen came back Clay was ready; volunteer for captivity, be transformed into a fish's breath, find the River that is "The Twilight of the Gods"- it didn't matter.

Poor Mr. Andreissen. His truck was full of wire, pipe, the mess of previous jobs, and he'd brought one of his sons who was an inch shorter at six-eleven-and-three-quarters. And poor Clay. He was stole in wordless awe over these apparitions. It was almost the same for me. When the job was half done he told me he had eleven kids. Shortest were the girls who averaged six-four, six-five.

"Eleven, huh," I commented, trying to make it sound normal. There were two of'em far as I could tell wandering the yard.

If Clay and I were both taken captive, how'd I explain that to Gail?

Late afternoon on one of those days I needed to lay pipe and wire. Ditches were ready, fill piled up. I told Clay to stay away from the holes. They were too deep. I gave him a ball with string to play with, pointed him down slope of the yard to a fresh mowed space of grass where he could play and be watched turned my head then, began laying pipe and heard a child's scream. There was Clay lying in one of the ditches and rising up, hands, shoulders entwined in the string, blood gushing from the area of his right eye (the thought of it twenty-seven years later still fills me with looming sorrow). He was angry, hog tied, seared. Mr. Andreissen and I looked at each other, then at Clay. As I ran toward him I tried to gauge what I saw, thought, as I gently lifted him, he'd punctured out his eye, and I tried to avoid shaking, vomiting. When I looked more closely, I knew it wasn't the eye, it was a bad gash above his eyebrow. Wound enough to scare him, me, and two huge Vikings. I took him to the bathroom, cleaned the gash with hot water, soap (still scared, knowing the worst was only an ugly nearness away), got some moment of calm and looked at the rest of our son's face. The eye was fine. I put some peroxide on the cut (he'd tripped, fallen face first on a sharp rock), found a good band-aid, carried him downstairs.

"Looked bad for a moment," Mr. Andreissen said, waiting for Clay to get out of earshot.

"It did," I offered, still unable to find breath or relief.

"Had eleven," he said. "Boy'll heal up in no time."

What the hell did I know, a new father. I'd had rock fights as a boy. Played cowboys and Indians with real .22s, got into fights, broke bones. Didn't get through it unscathed and wasn't dead. After the Andriessens left I gave Clay some milk and cookies. Thought about stitches, then thought about electricity the house needed. It was Monday. Gail came home from New York on Fridays. I cleaned the wound twice a day, changed band-aids. On the third day it looked better. Friday we went down to Kingston to greet Clay's Mom as she got off the bus.

"What's that band-aid over his eye?" was the first thing she asked.

"A cut," I said.

"How?" she asked back.

"Fell in a ditch."

"Bad?"

"Thought it was. Thought at first he'd put out his eye. Cut's just over the eyebrow. Bled pretty bad. Scared hell out of me and the Andreissens."

"He's OK though?" She looked closer at Clay, at me.

She picked Clay up, kissed him, said, "Let's go out to dinner."

Nothing else till we got home.

"Let's have a look at that cut," Gail said when we sat down.

She gently lifted the bandage. Sucked in her breath.

"David!" she tried to whisper my name, not wanting to startle our son.

She got him ready for bed. Put a new bandage on. Read a story. Sang a lullaby. That done she came into our room, asked what happened. I told her. Told her about the string. The blood all over his face. She knew I was still terrified by the thought of that moment. I could see her wavering over the two males in her life. The one, not exactly trying to be a mother, but trying to be a father. The other, fallen asleep, glad his mother was home.

"Why didn't you get stitches?" she asked.

"Stitches?" I answered, filled with unworthiness and stupidity.

"He'll have a scar," she said as tears welled up.

I hadn't thought about it the way I should have; was just glad for that eye. During this eight year period too, we found out Clay had a learning disability. I took him for tests. Results mixed. Advanced language and vocabulary skills but a "borderline dyslexia." I was crushed when I left that office. I had "learning disabilities" as a child. The experience angered me, made me feel shame and bewilderment. I was lucky. My parents were wealthy at that point in my childhood and were able to get me help. I didn't know and still don't know what would have happened to me given the kind of angers I carry. The thought of my own son burdened and outraged by similar frustrations caused me to go silent and a little nauseous.

We called around and were given the name of a local fifth grade teacher who sometimes tutored kids like Clay, depending on the extent of the "disability." We took our son for an initial interview and evaluation. Mrs. Wasserman decided to try to help Clay and Clay ended up adoring his teacher. She gave him courage. Mrs. Wasserman was also a small woman with a hunched back and gentle but demanding in ways that filled Clay with reassurance and desire to learn. She was a significant influence on our son's development. I picked him up from those sessions, watched how he hugged his teacher, how she hugged him, marked his progress each night, and recalled my own childhood struggle. I've never forgotten that time I shared with Clay. I never learned so much about what life and love means as I did during those years concentrating on the immediate issues of daily life. How to listen, watch, stand, answer a child's questions and reform my own questions. I have never gone through so much surprise nor through so much painful personal reappraisal. I had for years been composing compact lyrics, finding their melodies, and singing them acappella, not publicly, but privately to our son and his mother. The issues and mysteries of private life always hovered. As well too, the issues of the artist (Gail) and the writer (me) having children and how find proper regard before all that weighed and still weighs there. What is tenderness, vulnerability, the ability to stand inside one's own terrible embarrassments and find not only the desolations but the reservoirs of recoverable dignities hovering and waiting.

> Sleep
> Sleep Little Son
> Sleep Sleep
> Dreams will come.
>
> Where are you going
> Where have you
> come from
>
> Oh Little
> Little Son
>
> My Baby Boy

September 27th through September 30th: The weather for these days was "fair", Juet remarks, yet

there came "much wind" and "dry close weather."
Does this mean the often moistureless early fall
air gave them ill-humor and nameless anxieties
as they sailed back down the great river? Crew's
company "...went on land to fish..." but found no
"good place" though they "...took four or five and
twenty mullets, breams, basses and barbills..." in less
than an hour. They let the Half Moon drift south day
and night.

On the 29th "...there came certain Indians in
a canoe to us..." Is it proper to affix meaning to the
adjective "certain" and the underlying mood the
diction summons. Was there a certainty or anticipation
of dread over the canoe's appearance or others similar
to it as they passed the Catskills and Shawangunks?
Though "after dinner" Indians did board to sell
"Indian Wheat" the ship sending them away "...rode
quietly all night in seven fathoms water..." Was it those
hours of September 15th and the "very loving people"
Juet remembered. Had some crew members raped
the women and some boys "...where we were well
used..."? The entry reads as a kind of maimed noise
and tangle of things partially ailing, held to harness.
Sailoric compensation and spoils must inhabit which
twilights of certainty's invasion. Was the Paddler of
that canoe the Noah of another Flood Hudson and
crew may have seen. The sudden unveiling of the
Sickly/Marvelous Towers their civilization would
become as the Medicine Dreamer let the Corn Dwarfs

appear among the skyscrapers and poisoned horizons on his water drenched paddle. Let the play grow and fade there, be another bewitched mist language or eye could not hold or find truce for?

Fair weather for the 30th. Juet refers to a "...stiff gale between the mountains..." People came aboard with "small skins" to trade. The place of this anchorage "...very pleasant to build a town on..." may refer to the present site of Newburgh. The record states the mountains "...look as if some metal or mineral were in them..." noting the trees "were all blasted" and some slopes apparently treeless. Was it disease, the rare tornado which leaves all that it touches "barren." "The People brought a stone aboard like emery..."Juet speculates it might "cut iron or steel" and "yet" when put to water "...it made a color like black lead glistening..." And here the most heightened phrase of the "Journal." The wording fresh, has conviction, a differenciated volume. It is not edgy with dullness much of the "Journal" evokes.

Was it only a stone they presented. Was it more, from their Legends. The sound of burying violence out of their world and the things of violence. The sound of the end of the slaughter. Will there ever be time enough to let the blood dry?

> Who holds a grown Woman
> A grown Man?

A spine holds them.

And can it be abandoned?

Only as the thumb is abandoned
or the throat
in its marriage to food
and the words for food.

And what is Corn?

A very beautiful young girl.
And I myself
am going to remove her skirt
and clothes.

Should one perhaps smell her fragrance first?

Then, I'll take off her clothes.

And what is the eye of the spider
that sees the men and women
grow into the turtles of the sea
and are denied shelter?
Time has relatives
and in each of their footprints
are born the Day  the Month  the Sky
Earth and Pyramids of Water and Land.

I want to eat Heaven
slice the feet of its angels in half
dream of handless ghosts.

Son, bring me the left eye of a dragonfly.

And who then
are the earliest
Two-By-Two People

What was their madness
their lust?

Mother of Mother of Priests
it is embroidered on the soles of your feet

Your blossoms and their riddles
Egrets broken in flight

As Sun withers even the most prolonged Words.

And where the Word is not settled
Does it become the "Strong Hum"

And is it the Blue Bird
that makes Cities breathe

Teething in the Throat
Planted as Wild Teeth there

Hungry/Gulped
Gulped and Gulped?

I planted a row of pine trees in the front yard. Each needed at least a three foot deep pit. Gail wanted it to block the kitchen window view of a neighbor. We'd spent nine years restoring an old house. Flower gardens for the freshened bouquets Gail made at least twice a week in season, vegetable gardens we'd nurtured; fences constructed. I'd gotten a load of wood. The seasonal ritual of wood chopping was contained and intimate. I could watch the flight of birds and insects. Spot deer in the woods. Hear woodpeckers and discern by the sound of beak against wood which species was at work, sight hawks and buzzards, listen to Canadian geese honking in preparatory flight. Having grown up too in earthquake country I thought of this as a larder. My parents canned food and stored containers of water "in case." An earthquake held the same barefaced unknowns as an atomic bomb air raid drill. And I enjoyed the physical labor; axe, wedge, sledge hammer, rhythms I had to master over eight to ten cords, how to gather myself, not be injured, not wander, know what was enough. An axe is a beautiful, singular tool. You have to be ready with it, balanced. It demands proportion from you, coordination. It crystalizes a form of human motion and its twin for me is the throw of a discuss, a motion equally incisive and compact. There was also the calm of repetition and the desire to mix sweat with the perfect arc of an axe, arms, hands in flight attached to nothing more than a thin handle.

I was at the end of a day. I'd set a chunk to be split and heard a new female neighbor yell "There goes Jew Man." I stopped. Wasn't sure what I'd heard. Wanted to let it wander off and disappear. I set my feet again and the voice spread up into a "There's Jew Man." It sliced right through, felt like the downpour of a sewer. Hadn't experienced anything like that since I was a kid. I walked into the kitchen, poured a glass of water.

"Fuck me," I thought, "What the hell do I do now. How do I even begin to tell Gail or anybody?"

I tried to tell Clay about the Nazis. Couldn't explain that worth a goddamned. We tried to live it out for nearly a year. I mowed the lawn adjacent to her property and on another afternoon ran over shards of broken bottles thrown over the fence. And I got mad. Gail during those months heard that voice and began a pitch into illness. It reached such level of dread she could hardly go to her studio. I called the police, explained what was taking place. They could do nothing. "Legally our hands are tied," one officer told us. And I started going over my choices. "Stay put," I told Gail one night, "they'll leave." That neighbor was good. She knew how to invade, ease up, let things cool, then let her voice float and poison our lives. I thought if I heard her say "Jew Man" one more time I'd initiate my own invasion. But I had a family and went from my family into prisons where I saw what violence does, and what happens once you start moving toward the one mistake that gets anyone a ticket, anyone. If it weren't for those prisons and what I saw I might have moved toward that catastrophe. I was sliding into a bad rage.

One day I woke up, announced to Gail and Clay, "We're going to look for land. If we can't find any we'll move back to the desert." We told Jim and Pearl. They'd heard the neighbor too. Hated it.

"Can't shoot'em, Dave," he said, knowing. "Fish Creek'll be here when you visit."

We found an isolated nearly thirty-seven acres. On the way home a Cooper's hawk flew right into my driver's side window bay, knocked itself out. I could have been mauled by the hawk but wasn't. We knew of a Hawk Woman in Saugerties who specialized in rehabilitating injured raptors. Gail wrapped the bird in a blanket, covered its eyes, kept it calm on her lap. The bird, we learned, was later set free. The hawk incident began a new phase of our lives, however we interpreted it: a sign, an oracular conjunction, a hawk's miscalculation?

October 1st through October 5th. Juet announces a "wild variable" of "fair weather." The phrased astonishment over the Hudson Valley fall with its spectacular dramas of sky, cloud, migrating bird flocks through vast sun-rayed surfaces and plumes. The Half Moon was at this point "...below the mountains..." yet "..the people of the mountains..." wondered at ship and its weapons, were allowed aboard to trade "some small skins." In the afternoon Juet wrote a single man in a canoe "...kept hanging under our stern..." They could not keep him "from thence." In his insistence, the man "...got up by our rudder to the cabin window..." and "stole out" Juet's "...pillow, two shirts, two bandeleers..." They shot him in the heart. The other Indians, panic struck, leapt from their canoes and swam. Juet with crew members manned a small ship's boat and retrieved the stolen objects. Another man "got hold" of Juet's boat, attempted to capsize, but ship's cook cut off one of the man's hands with a sword "...and he was drowned..." Ebb came by "that time." They weighed anchor and "rode well."

"Fair Weather" recorded for October 2nd. One of the Indians who previously escaped captivity reappeared accompanied by "... two canoes full of men..." who unleashed arrows at ship's stern. The Half Moon's crew "...discharged six muskets..." killing

"...two or three of them..." "From a point of land..." adjacent to anchorage a hundred came and shot more arrows. Juet shot cannon, "killed two." The others fled "into the woods..." Another canoe with "nine or ten" men came to fight. Juet "shot it through" with cannon, killed one. Crew with muskets killed "three or four."

"So they went away" the recording states.

Ship casts off, "with in a while" floated down two leagues "beyond"—anchored in a bay "...clear from all danger of them" "...on other side of river..." They saw a "...very good piece of ground..." and what they thought might be a mine of silver or copper on "...that side of the river that is called Manna-hata..." Only thing to trouble them was "...much wind and rain..."

Though this is the first recording of the legendary name of the Island World "Manna-hata" where are we to go who come after, after hearing "So they went away"? Was it "They" rather who would have nothing more to do with such ugly creatures? They who entered oak puffballs and flew wind-born over the waters. And in entering such puffballs who will sup on the Stranger there in the earliest part of the night collecting remnant suppositions of time, wandering time, the welling fountain of minutes phrasing the disposals of the dead?

October 3rd. Very strong gusts of wind, rain, ship driven to oozy ground. But wind continued to come, drove the ship all night into "Thick weather. So we rode..." The adverb full of pragmatic squanderings and rations, even as to a suffering from the teeth begetting the stinging vowel as it yawns and grafts itself to the Journal, the initial "So" which begins the journey "into the woods..."

October 4th. "Fair Weather" once more taking ship and crew out to the "...the great mouth of the great river..." Then they took their boat "...set ...main sail and spritsail, and...topsails, and steered away...into the main...sea..."

October 5th. Also "fair weather." The wind "variable". "Course toward England..."

Can these last passages be equated to a primordial blister, a blister perhaps, of time, or the blister of the wife, in the ancient story, got from the spark of a fire. A blister on her hand which she rubbed, rubbed until she tasted her own blood. And loved it. Craved the taste of her personal sea and with a knife began at her own flesh until her meat was gone from legs and arms. The woman knowing how dangerous she was warned her dog. "You better go," she said. And with those words ate the rest of herself. Hungrier then, she used small sticks to get at her bone marrow. Loving that she stuffed her fresh hollowed bones with pebbles and hearing her skeleton rattle she danced and she rattled and thought the new found sound fine.

"So they went away"
"You better go"

may serve as either a glyph or a fraction for man infested agony loved passed the blunt twitching of a lip.

"...and on the seventh day of November, stilo novo, being Saturday, by the Grace of God, we safely arrived in the range of Dartmouth in Devonshire in the year 1609."

And I want to think of Persephone
but She, Her Image
will not hold

Her share
is too chaste

Hollow with the Lore
of flowers and ghosts

Loosened further
from the morsels of healing
left to the Living

I, calling on You
the Older Mistress
become more stunted

You, Your Shadow
cannot receive Us

And though I would lift a rose
from its blossoms to find You

You, Your Faceless Hell and its Wonder
can You know Death as It Is now

Who utters and sells It
advances Its Tides

Belongs to It as You cannot and will never?

# Rooster
# &
# Leroy

I t was twenty-eight degrees. Sun predicted that morning, with afternoon temperatures rising to the 40s. Lonyo Street had a string of nasty factories, vacant lots, chain-link fences, abandoned cars along with a home-grown wind made out of ice, some pain, the recipe so far restrained. Dogs were barking in the near distance. "Didn't git a chance to git breakfast," Terry mumbled to himself, "bet they'll wanna finish the meal."

The extra-high fence he was looking for was topped with razor wire to administer some surgery to the snow flurries. When he got to the front gates two men were waiting along with those two dogs he'd just heard, big German shepherds with hard eyes, unkempt and graveyard nervous after night sentry in a lot full of cars.

Terry could see some cop cruisers, too. Three to be exact. Detectives and street officers havin some coffee, doughnuts, morning smokes. There was also a guest in one of the backseats; a hooker. They'd brought her a coffee too. Her top lip was badly split. Some pimp Terry figured, who didn't want to give his instructions twice. Or by the cops themselves just to show a Lady of the Night the real shades come summer, winter, heroin or high heels.

Terry needed a job. Down to a last $100.00. Interviewed the day before with an insurance company and they'd told him to be here at 7:30 am next morning to start his "training." One of the men gave Terry the down and up look, not slow, not fast, just the seconds necessary to hollow out the object with its alert, stealthy indifference. The two were set heavy in their shoes, wore trenchcoats, "pinkies" on little fingers, had the look of hardcore insurance adjustors who'd seen a half-continent of wrecked cars and their cargos.

One, the adjustor named Bradley, pulled out a *Lucky Strike* from a clear plastic cigarette humidifier. "Keep'em fresh and chained-up for any emergencies," he said right then and there, as his partner, Lynn, fished a thick ring of keys from his coat pocket, asked to see "sum identification there, son. Gotta make sure, cause even though it don't give off smell, the whole fuckin lots'a gole mine."

Terry dug for a wallet, as one of the cops opened a door, threw some still smoking coffee onto a patch of sidewalk ice, stamped his feet, applied a forefinger to his left nostril, and blew some sun-rise snot out into the frost-charred air, then looked at the hooker, who seemed to get the instant melancholy chills.

"Wanna see that too." The cop ordered loud enough to curl the lips of the two dogs."Keep yer billfold right there so's we cin all have a little check."

The cop said it, meant it, even though his voice wasn't streaked yet with any of the dry meanness that might be waiting at the other end of the day for someone else. Terry let his eye fall on the hooker as the cop leaned into his inspection, turned the driver's license over once or twice, then headed for his cruiser radio to check background. The hooker, nineteen or twenty, "pretty" whatever that meant, with her drained West Virginia or Tennessee country-girl face, gave Terry a precise stare as the cop radioed in, breathed out the information as if each letter and number was a kind of circling vulture, riding the currents in those circles of theirs, letting the inventory sink in. There was static, but not enough to interfere with the female voice at the other end who sounded like she'd been on a three-pound a day diet, lost twenty, gained back twenty-five, and was now gonna give Terry and the detective hives for the irritation they were causing. She took the specimens, let the cop spend two or three minutes on hold while he looked first at the hooker, then Terry, then Terry's ID, then at Lynn and Bradley to guarantee they were on hold too.

"Feed them piss-poor hounds yet?" he asked from his receiver, just to spray some jittery tension as the female voice returned to say "negative" as if her noun were a reproduction of one of those pounds she'd melted with a "black beauty," unrequited, unforgettable, beyond hope of recovery.

As the cop walked back, Lynn picked up the heavy lock, turned the key in its seat, said, "Sit."

The dogs obeyed the command and watched the cop.

"Don't like no one, but sure as shit they hate yer ass on sight, Crofchec," Lynn smiled and drew back the gate.

"Hope to hell you gave'em one'a'yer special snacks then," the detective ran it by the adjustor's face, twice as ugly, twice as mean.

Lynn looked at Terry. "We'll go over to the shack and sign some papers. And don't mind Crofchec here. He got rabies ten years ago and it's bin'a slow recovery."

The cop smirked, but the smirk contained just enough chloroformed humor to go with the sting of morning air.

Terry followed the insurance adjustors as Crofchec walked back to the line of cruisers, all less than a year old and each one already half-drowned in the almost ocean-like battle mists of the city that fed on steel, rubber, glass, and naugahyde. The "shack" was a refugee trailer from an army or juvenile detention work camp. It had desks, typewriters, a heater; and was saturated with coffee stains and the rotten smell of the too sweet shaving lotion these men wore. Lynn directed Terry to a chair, put paper to typewriter, got name, address, phone, social security number, told him he'd be paid nine dollars per hour with an extra buck thrown in "cause sumtime during any day yer here, you'll need a beer, or sumthin stronger, sumthin to chase it away." He let the pronoun crawl under the door as if "it" were that secret cousin who got himself strangled in a whorehouse, the catastrophe serene, polished, nearly soundless.

"Ten bucks ain't bad. But you'll probably come

to think twelve's better, skip over the thirteen cause everyone who spends sim seconds here gits the superstitions. Fourteen; fifteen's the top at yer end. Sign this line here. And this line here, Terry. That way we'll start our day. Dogs have names too. And don't fergit'em. The one there we call 'Rooster.' The one next to'im's called 'Leroy.' They live and'll probably die here. They're OK. Until the sun goes down."

Terry looked at the two German shepherds. Ninety, ninety-five pounders with huge paws, thick tongues. Knew he didn't have to wonder or ask about the hours when these animals assumed their true devotions. "Make damn sure they stay away from one'a yer immediate assignments, that's all," Bradley said with a no non-sense warning, "and take these." Terry grabbed the expensive "Kodak Instamatic," and the clipboard holding a stack of simple blueprints, followed the adjustors out the door.

Crofchec and the four other cops were outside, along with the hooker who had looked remarkably small, even child-like with her face framed by a back-door cop-car window, and now, standing in a tight expensive skirt, legs framed in riding boots, stood nearly six foot tall, a rich man's purchase for a rich man who'd need a pocket full of repairs after tricking with this machinery.

"Name's Noreen," Crofchec said, not wanting to get trapped too long in the diphthongs. "Wanna have her look at a nice Buick yer holding sumwhar in this lot."

"Color"? Bradley asked.

"A light blue Buick Century. Clean. No more'an two, three thousand miles."

There was a pause in the breathing, then. And then Crofchec finished the description, "Somebody important got killed in the front seat. Think Noreen here knows who fed'im to the Angels."

They began to walk toward the cars. Some of'em, Terry noticed, didn't even look like cars or steel anymore, but unidentifiable immigrants from the temperature episodes that'd raced over the Nevada Test Site simulated parking lots where the fires of that thermal radiation, Terry remembered, ate glass, interiors, and paint, but left the shells intact.

"Rooster" and "Leroy" trotted ahead and the main detective tried to stay out of their way.

"Anyone got another smoke?" Noreen asked. Bradley dug for his humidifier, pumped a *Lucky* out of it.

Noreen offered a simple, murky call me if you wanna do business sometime later "Thanks" and added, "Hope the puppies sniff you up after sundown, Crofchec," staining the cool end of her cigarette with some unforgettable hoodlum girl red lipstick.

The other cops were eyeing the goods too, had dropped the image of any Buick and were figuring how much out of a monthly check could be bent for this excursion, kept out of the shadows of a household budget.

Suddenly the dogs started up running, saw a couple of pigeons land on this forest, and interrupted the civil servants' bitter-sweet raptures about groceries, electric bills, the price of kids' tooth decay, and whether a $1000.00 sex feast'd get'em to the first day of a next century without any regrets.

"It's over there, Crofchec," Lynn announced, "only one outta the whole stack production line fresh."

They walked down a slight incline, careful about the ice, the dogs snarling off in a short distance letting the adjustors know they were close by if needed.

"Goddamned things'll kill sumone one day," the detective spat, warning the other cops, who like Terry and Noreen'd never been here before.

"Relax Crofchec. They're yer closest relatives just doin their job," Bradley challenged back. "Besides, doughnuts and coffee's waiting in the shack."

The Buick was just like it'd been described. Expensive. Lot'a elaborate filigree and plastic.

"Git yer clipboard ready, Terry," Bradley announced. "This an'everythang after this'll take sum time."

Terry looked down and saw the "blueprint" packet more clearly now:

| DASHBOARD | WINDSHIELD | Steering Wheel |
|---|---|---|
| Front Seat | Front Floor Board | |
| Back Seat | Back Floor Board | |

Door Windows        Door Wells        Back Windshield
Back Windshield Well        Trunk

No ornaments. Nothing to impinge on the desolately drawn, humble images.

They walked around it, slowly, the professionals and the dogs on full alert, Terry and Noreen at the edges standin like first grade strangers on the first day of school.

"Over here, Terry," Lynn signaled with his hand. There was a pool of not quite dried blood in the well where the inside left edge of the windshield met the dashboard naugahyde.

"Draw that right here on the print and print the words 'small blood puddle' next to it."

Terry did that while Noreen gagged a little threw up a little, but stood hard, didn't say a word. Knew every sound would be held for, or against her.

"Sumone wanna open the driver's door?" Crofchec asked quietly.

Terry knew if he wanted the job he'd have to open that door in front of the other motionless figures in the shadows of the downtown skyscrapers that gave them an automatic extremity, no one really hungry in that light to rent out their own personal autopsy, or just the bodies in general poised as equal chunks of shadows around them. So he pushed the release, pulled open the whole show of steel, glass, false leather and design.

"Hinges are still perfect," said Lynn who added,

"Take that camera, Terry, and we'll start with some pictures."

The passenger had been shot. Scattered under the brake pedal were bone fragments with dried brain jelly clung to them. The driver's window had grease stains from where the head leaned. There was dried foamy spit on the rear-view mirror. Under the heater, one spent case of a .22 pistol shell.

"Killer likes'em high velocity, huh?" one of the patrol cops half questioned.

The adjustors stared up at the policeman .

"Stuff that goddamned mouth a'yers, now," Crofchec ordered.

Noreen looked over the man, caught and roasted for a moment in his stupidity. She didn't look for long though. Didn't care what she betrayed or revealed. Let it fade as she turned her back and watched the dogs chase each other through their maze of contorted steel and glass.

"Terry, git a picture of them skull fragments," Bradley instructed, "and that spit on the rearview mirror an' be careful. Don't fuck with anything else. Add it to yer blueprint too, so's' ta double record everthang. People from the police lab'll be here soon. But it's gotta be on our books."

Terry understood they assumed it was one of those "incidents" where especially this kind of driver dies; heart stopped from an injection of over-delivered glacier smooth heroine and a greedy snort'a cocaine mixed with paid for mirage intensity sex washed down by a fifth of brandy and a burst aorta. Wife'n'kids  waiting hours at the yacht club for the no-show patrician father, no more than thirty-four, thirty-five with waves of family connected success waiting to coronate a future. Noreen was some high-strung service for sure, but Terry thought death hadn't necessarily come with "works" along with a nostril sized spoon. MaryJane, acid, hashish more to the point to unstring the green along with a tall shiny dark red dress blow job, use those to sneak up to the border of death, scout the edges but not a fraction further. No cop trouble except for this every other day ugly kind with its eavesdrops and threats, some jail where you could paint yer nails and drop an emergency dexamil to git the watry eggs down. No prison at the other end though. Nothin worth that price. Put some cash away. Start up a bar with a home-tested boyfriend in *Beersheba Springs* or *Bell Buckle* or *Chewalla* or some other Tennessee place named after Other Ladies she might'a been from like *Edith* or *Edwina*, *Elora*, *Eliza*, *Eulia* or *Eva*. Bring down a parfleche full'a savings from fancy and not so fancy tricks and attract customers there. Sex time's one thing. A simple prison second gotta smell stuck to it that will flatten a world.

So Terry knew they'd made a mistake with the Buick. Brought it to the wrong destination.

"Noreen, honey," Crofchec's voice said, "Cum over here, wil'ya?"

The words, each of them, were assembly line vicious and made the dogs flinch for a second, stopped their circling around another not far away car. Noreen crossed her arms over her chest feeling the real cold slicing at her. Went a tone greyer from hearing the detective's vocabulary. Walked toward the Buick. Beautiful legs carrying a not yet overly spent beautiful body.

"Want yew ta'luk'it the front seat there, fer'a second. See whut yew cin call up. An'don cut out iny morsels."

The policeman let his words break over Noreen as she grazed over her wounded lip with her fingers wincing at the still tender shreds. "Don't know anything. Do'wanna know anything," Noreen said. And backed away from the door.

The detective's eyes shifted. Went dark.

"Don't touch her. Least in front of us, Crofchec," Lynn warned.

"Noreen. Maybe she knows enough of the law. Maybe no," Terry thought as he stuck the goods on a shelf for that moment. If there was no safety at least there was respite from what could happen on a twenty minute backseat journey to an interrogation chamber where the Fathers of the City would draw their form of bloodlessness to cleanse one of their wandering sons and any Noreen whether she knew the story or not would be carefully drained then sent back into her world, where the damage sweet and pure was discernable only to the creatures who lived there. Terry hoped her statement about personal knowledge couldn't be fragmented or carried off as unstable excess energy. Truth having no more than say, the structure of rock, and subject to the shapes and sizes of various pressure waves as a police panel and tow truck pulled up to the front gate, red lights straining.

The experts from the Police Lab took pictures, wrapped the Buick in a canvas shroud, hooked it to a lift. Drove the steel away.

Time had drained out for Crofchec and the other cops too as they wrapped up Noreen, and pushed her body down into a cruiser.

"Couple'a days. And have those doughnuts ready," Crofchec winked at the adjustors who nodded their heads while Crofchec walked around the property of the Police Department, opened a door and sat next to somebody's far away daughter who didn't know yet if she was gonna wish she'd never been born.

It was 12:40pm. More than five hours had slipped by.

"Hungry?" Bradley asked Terry.

"Not sure," was Terry's answer.

"First day. I'll buy," Lynn offered. "Usually it goes slower. Dipped in shit. Came out clean. Let's go for a beer."

The beer included Big City sandwiches and an added double shot'a whiskey for the adjustors. For Terry, those pieces of foamy spit on the rear-view mirror reminded him of letters from his closest childhood friend, a girl named Danni who'd trained to be a nurse, joined the army, shipped out to a field hospital in the Mekong Delta. Her letters weren't about the everyday war she was seeing trying to wash it away with elaborate skin searing showers. She'd always wanted to write something and some of her ancestors had been horse soldiers, escorted the Franciscans, Juan Crespi and Junipero Serra into the forbidden eighteenth century unknowns of California and its untapped soul vineyards. She decided to take it back a few centuries though, to Cortez and incidences of Aztec gold which had escaped the smelters of the "King's Share," the gold masterpieces like Isabella's jewels becoming almost air, pawned for funds to finance armies and even as Columbus himself begged for his first voyage the borrowed monies her jewels had obtained disintegrated nearly as a fallen orange.

Danni had been drawn to the letters of Cortez to his Emperor describing what had not been smelted; crocodiles "wound round" with many golden wires and as well there were bells with delicate savage sounds, and ducks that seemed to be either caught in flight or to float once more on the waters of Lake Texcoco which surrounded the Aztec metropolis. Spain gathered in Toledo in 1520 to see "gold butterflies which seemed of such lightness and agilities they might themselves begin hovering over living flowers for their pollens or snails' heads with tentacles, the gold itself seeming to exude a slime, so uncanny were these renderings that they seemed more than the value of the gold itself." Cortez registered a shipment from Tenochtitlan, September 1526. The list included golden turtles, tadpoles, fire-fly heads as well as Christian crucifixes Moctezuma ordered his goldsmiths to craft for the Spaniard. But the majority of those objects the Aztec himself offered at the beginning of that legendary end in 1519; golden skulls, collars of turtles and turtle shells with snail or cicada-shaped links, eagles with bells in their tails, crayfish, jaguars, all produced with the greatest precision of natural detail had become lost or rare by 1524. Other uncounted masterpieces were lost by the Conquerors on "Noche Triste," the Sad Night of July 1520 when the Aztecs forced the looters to throw those ransacked tons into swamps along with the questions the Conquerors might have had about why those small golden fish, serpents, animals, and birds so frighteningly resembled the Living Creation that they were an offence to the Christian Soul.

Among the gold objects brought before the Spaniards in those earliest days were a fish with scales of silver and gold, the two metals joined not by soldering, but in the casting itself, which stunned the Conqueror, along with golden parrots with moveable tongues, wings, and heads, and a fruit eating monkey with equally movable feet and head; featherwork so convincingly wrought that it looked like enamel, every piece technically beyond the abilities of contemporary

European goldsmiths.

Danni wondered whether the Marquisate del Valle, as Cortez was known, may have seen in these things the completed animation of new more smothering witch-worlds his and other worlds so irreversibly became. Had these lost charms and spells become the desolate, senseless financial talismans of the wars of her world scurrying over humans and the worship of their own cleverness convulsing in "uncanny" gold "slime" and penetrating more exactly, through their withdrawn evasions, the corpse reservoirs of modern war?

Terry thought her corner of hidden presages was like one of those traceless parrots or tentacled snails as he heard the irresistibly rising voice of an adjustor.

"Rest of the day, put yew thru sum beginner paces, Terry," Bradley said, "an' lemmi git yur side'a da' bill. Next time's yur turn."

# II

When Lynn applied his key, Leroy and Rooster, eyes only gone half-hard, ran up to the gate and sniffed Terry's crotch.

"Till'em they cain't have yer balls, lest till sundown, there Terry," Lynn smiled. "After tamarraw they'll be yer companions. Git used to'em. We'll show'ya wut tih feed'em. Ain't fancy. But we kip'um up strong."That part-day and the next were devoted to the office trailer. Legal codes gone over, paper-work, cameras, responsibilities, keys, dog food ("Combo'a hard'n'soft an'be sure to pol'eece the dawgshit"). "Keys fur the box in the bottom desk drawer Terry's right'cher on yer key ring. Par'tah Indin Tertory" (a snub-nosed .45 with two boxes of bullets).

"Wan'cha tih know it's thar," Bradley said. "Won't lech'yeh furgit. Sum'ah wut yew draw'an sign'll sind sumone onna dir'ec stagecoach flight tih'sim hard steel. Nobuddy's tried yit, bit'chew nevah know," Bradley let the observation trail off. "Case'yur wunerin, accent's Southern Ohio. Be sure tih'hav doughnuts and coffee fur visiturs too. You'll git plenny'a warnin. We'll be around ever fiew days so yew won'git that lonely."

"Me? I'm frim right here." Lynn made sure the question couldn't get asked. Delivered it shriveled up, stirless as the petals of the streaked tulip Terry saw on the passenger-side floor of the Buick.

Wednesday: 7:30am. Terry arrived like the adjustors said to. Alone.

Rooster and Leroy were running in a vicious, expectant circle. He applied his key to lock, unwrapped the chain, pushed the unsecured gate. For a moment he saw their breakfast; his balls along with his not yet tested ever enough prick, the three bottom of the barrel stooges that'd been assigned to him, the one's he hadn't given permission to fly away flopping in the canines of these direct mail German laboratory toys, the ones those blond science boys hauled outta their closets, mixed up some wolverine, some gila monster, a musty pinch of SS sperm, come up with this pair of spelunkers who make removable all those with genitals who enter here.

How would Terry get their names out of the bottom of his vocal chords (before those got torn out too) as they, yeah, galloped toward him looking more like small deeply insulted bears ready to peel that salmon who slithered away last fall in their run for eggs and another try at birth and being and death, and wouldn't, by the look of things, accept any substitutes.

"Leroy." Terry yelled that name next, but the dog didn't respond. Didn't seem to care. So he tried the name "Rooster," strained the vowels through his winter parched lips and the two beasts pulled to a stop. Sat down. Stared at the pile of human meat standing before them.

Danni sent a letter, one mostly of notation and fragments gotten to defiantly, Terry thought, as he stared at these dogs, on some afternoon between her exhaustions when the only bodies to take care of were the dead for their flights home. She cleaned faces, if there were faces in those hours to possibly lessen the shock of the bereaved, to convey this unsigned message that someone saw them and helped them into their dying. Something, anything to distract the firmness of the violence.

"To the alchemists who crafted the bird-like eagle

pendants," one note began, "the dry texture of gold resembled the surface of dried blood. The metal itself was full of erotic connotations: the liquid a menstrual divination filled with peril. The mixed smell of copper and gold resembled certain female frogs when they are filled with eggs, the hallucinogens extracted from their poison glands become very rich: metal, sexuality, menstrual and metallurgical combinations were executed as co-attendant unbroken realities. The lips, noses, eyes; flesh of golden faces hanging as if ready to be boned. Their expressions are austere, heartlessly meticulous and the austerity in itself is glamorous, offering no luck, no ease, only the curvature of an untouchable promise lurking with the aftertaste of spasmodic debasements. Gold was implanted under the skins of forgotten Amazonians up from their River bearing the morbidity of sleep that accompanied the fragilities and vices of the wearers whose ancestors in their first earth hungers may have feasted on ants and become anteaters. The pendants which resemble eagles have huge beaks and one carries a beautifully detailed fish. Its wings are crescent moons. Abstract crocodile jaws extend as framing devices behind the head and from the edges of each ankle. In these and other objects the erotic questions about gold, metallurgy, the types of fantastic strangulation which accompanied Venus' alignment on the twilight horizon with Jupiter and Saturn begin to be defined and to find form. The piece itself could represent a month which mysteriously swelled one of the older calendars with days none of the inhabitants of that Earth could possibly bear along with the ancestral abandonments which allowed such an added penetration of time."

She included more unfinished references about "ancient bell-making centers which may have existed in Honduras, Oaxaca, Central Mexico, and Western Mexico. There are myths and stories that refer to parrots and macaws; it was they who taught People to speak; it was they who carried human beings into this world; it was the parrots who handed over their tongues."

And a closing fact about the Inca, Atahualpa, the ransom collected by his People for him, that "nine forges ran four months straight in 1533 yielding 13,420 pounds of gold; of silver, 26,000 pounds without any crafted object surviving as well this Conversion."

She was trying to discover through these facts and details of her heritage extending from the two Conquests of Mexico and California (one of her ancestors having ridden with the Crespi Expedition in 1769) why she'd "signed up for a war that posed so much anguish over the life or the death any nation might claim for itself as if it were a poltergeist finally able to digest nothing but its own accelerations." She called these soundings her "monophthongs" and if she could get to one articulate vowel then perhaps there might be an answer to her own sudden, generative imaginings. And the force of suffering crushing her could not be washed off no matter how refined her cleansing rituals. That much she could write. "Boys with their brain jellies dripping out still unaccountably conscious, asking me and the other nurses if they were gonna be alright even as they were being overwhelmed by unconsciousness and coma."

"All of them," she observed, "who know so little or nothing of their deaths. Didn't seem to know they had died."

What about Noreen? And what puzzles might ring in his ears if he asked why one went to one job open to women; why one went to that other job open to women and what each would come to know about boys and men carefully harvested in any of the worlds that did manage to come alive, be the offerings to destiny and decay, and who was the single woman Danni referred to in her letters, before the invaders came "who was resurrected and who told what she saw in the OtherLife" about the Invaders impersonating the "Tzitzimime"; the monsters who will descend with the death of the Sun.

Was that what she was, the nurses who accompanied her, the boys sliding into their deaths, too young to even know what had invaded them?

Terry walked toward the Olds remembering the time when they were in high school, spring of their eleventh grade year. Danni read about Cleeter. Not even a town, five, six hundred miles away in Arizona. A religious cult had moved there from New York State.

Didn't call themselves Mormons, Shakers, Aurorans East or West. But one of their congregation told them to migrate to that country with the women and children. There wasn't much time left either. Ten years at most. The clock'd run dry in May of 1962.

They were still in waiting when Terry and Danni arrived about three weeks before the End was to occur, had breakfast, bought a jar of marmalade (didn't know why), and talked to elder sisters and brothers who'd settled in, became sort of local business people calm as armchairs on a garden shrouded verandah sure about the "Rapture" as they were about the price of "Cornflakes" they sold in the settlement's only version of a supermarket.

No one appeared to be really crazy. Girls were pretty, but Girl Christians, sweet as their flesh could be sprouted under the night flowers of local Sahuaro cactus might have a taste of goodness more fantastic and evil than heartless sin, suck a Jew like Terry into light that might be the author of mongrel darkness itself, arrived pitiful, broken and broke, provoking even the unfriendliest angels to up and flee Paradise.

When Terry got around to asking one of the male elders if "the End'n'all" was gonna hurt, that Brother and Son of the Gospel looked straight into his eyes and answered, "Son, only a heathen'd ask that sort'a question," put his hand on the boy's shoulder and offered yer ass is'a goner no matter what smile reserved for the doomed who'd never be able to experience the vineyards of the chosen young female taking a buck twenty-five for the box of doughnuts and two 7ups he was just then purchasing in case he and Danni got a flat in the hills beyond Cleeter and Cleeter Time.

On the way out they stopped to take pictures of a small herd of Brahma steers a local rancher kept for the Bothers and Sisters. Terry and Danni thought it was either the meat locker for "The Journey" or for the hungry crew of a clandestine flying saucer that needed supplies like those earlier earth sailors who raided their own planetary islands and a lone bull decided to chase Terry who didn't believe it at first, that a Hindu Beast formed a personal grudge and nearly beamed up his Unbeliever's Ass, the chase down a cactus studded hill nearly as funky a jamboree as the Day After when the Chosen of Cleeter had to explain the meaning of the Delay and its Persecution to a craven, grotesquely unhumbled civilization.

Shepherd the AfterLight. Let it grow out of that desert equal to the wilds of Galilee itself.

# III

The Olds' front end looked like a hair-sprayed wig that'd been crushed by a bad tempered bird. Probably two days old. Nothing in this place had an age beyond five days. Pushed by insurance and the spasms of the law, each wreck had to be charted, recorded properly, its secrets stripped. Terry looked at the fact sheet. Head on. Family with two children. No survivors. Pieces of human hair, skin, frozen blood and teeth lodged in the cracks of the windshield calling the eyes to ache with longing for the victims to be whole and alive again, a longing which seemed to appear unbidden, hastily rummaged from some faint unresolved mountain that held the profiles of these immediate dead and the provisional clockwork Terry applied to them. Something they, the luckless, could not belong to even though the blueprints and graphs would transform the remoteness and finality of their residue into a trustless mosaic of inch wide starlight heaved out of its sockets.

Just before he opened the door of the Olds, he remembered that Danni had come over to his house on a Christmas Day when they were twelve. His parents called after Terry heard the noise of an early morning crash. Another family drove into a sunken culvert. Negroes apparently lost in an impenetrable Southern California December fog hit the cement ditch and its street bridge at 40/50 miles per hour. Terry was first to see it. The injured children. A father wearing the steering wheel half way through his chest. Dying mother trying to talk, to whisper through a collapsed face. Danni spent the morning with him, especially on Christmas to make sure he'd be ok, after a neighbor who'd seen it too said it looked like Guadalcanal grenade corpses. The wreck, and the colored people in the white, still orange grove enshrouded town, cleaned up before dawn as if the whole thing hadn't happened. No report in the local papers, no one hardly curious, the penetration of the Christmas Hush sewed back tight and shut. And even though she was only twelve, Danni called the local hospital to find out, angered over the attempted cleansing. Wash away the interruption, the town workers not missing even the slightest shard of glass on that Christmas Dawn of 1955.

Danni's parents owned a grove, nothing elaborate the way it was starting to go then, but enough acreage and yield to get by. Other fruit growers selling off, buying new cars, pulling their trees out by the roots with D8s, setting the valley up in orange wood fire and smoke as if it were a miracle come to free them and what they ever had been, killed and poisoned every last trace. The oldest families turning themselves inside out for the scramble.

She lived in a small wood-framed "Grove House." The mother and father loved cactus for, and rather than a lawn, they had prickly pear mixed with succulents and rocks, roses and manzanita that had somehow crawled down from the mountains, rooted here and attracted hummingbirds and quail, even a scraggled flamingo or two escaped from a mysterious house in the foothills, said to be a kind of prison for an aging silent movie queen who'd gone to rot there, dressing in costumes, letting her 20s Rolls Royce get covered in bird shit and crusted pollen, eating only avocados and water in her lingering last year.

Her father was an "Okie," mother a Mexican/ Cherokee. Somehow they'd got up enough to buy a grove after World War II where, it was rumored, the shy father won some medals, though he never showed them, even for a moment hinted such objects existed. Hot summer twilights Warren and Bernice shared fresh squeezed lemonade and homemade tamales with whoever the visitor was. Often there were coyotes not more than thirty yards off through the tree rows. The twilight and its margins made it possible to hear them running down ground squirrels. Danni's father loved their kind of noise along with the scents of tamales, lemonade, the settling dusts from a day of tractoring cut with the probing musk of orange leaf. Their tractor was not new, but it served them, hauling spray rigs, trailers, plows, ladders through the grove rows, the family dogs scrounging at the edges of the equipment. The fenders of that Massey/Ferguson were stripped by the constant scathings of orange tree, looked like big, thin pieces of silver dollar slowly being eaten away. Which was true. But only by common orange branch and thorn.

Danni spoke Spanish, "Okie," and if she wanted to bait Terry, she included some Cherokee, throw'im a ripe orange along with it that they'd peel and share. Her father and mother had some corrals with horses, burros, and they'd let Danni and Terry once in a while saddle up the animals, explore the foothills that flowed to the edges of the groves, where, even into those twentieth century decades, they could spot one or two last condors drifted into their ranges from the desolate Sespis. They'd look for ancient bones, arrowheads, rattlesnakes, hawks nests, even an abandoned mine. But they'd be careful about that one since they'd heard stories of other children who'd, against the warnings given to them, walked into such darknesses where ceilings collapsed; a drowning in a water-filled cavern ending with sheriff's divers and an eerie couldn't be found body, "each child gnawed invisible by the mountain" as her mother put it, the words traveling no further.

They crawled too, in the manzanita and ceanothus under-scrub, into what they thought to be an old grizzly trail, hoping to see a paw print. But that never did happen, though they knew the huge bears ranged over these exact hills. A neighbor family had a grizzly trap hung over their fire place, tall as a man with terrible teeth and jaws to eat the rage of a bear and the bear with it as proof and truth of the once upon a time bear world hovering real and near. They'd have their lunch of burritos and fruit under a sycamore, joke, take a nap, try to catch some brook trout by hand as the horses grazed, dogs dozed, squirrels watched, and woodpeckers hammered at some of the four hundred year-old oaks of those canyons, trees curled with sun and rain, wind and heat until they were mangled with being alive, carrying the rumors of their living centuries as unsubdued, repellently fierce inscriptions of shade, hard and direct as the moistureless heat and air of the summer droughts. They watched the turkey buzzards out on a mid-day cruise, heat tumbling up from the earth pulsing at their bellies and wings, their recesses of hunger. Once they even found what looked like a group of weird still partially joined rocks that they brought home, and turned out to be dermal ossicles, the pebble-like armor-bone embedded in the skin of a huge ground sloth, washed down by the thousands of years rains and seasons. A friend of Terry's family, a fossil prospector from the museum in L.A., going over the fossil with a magnifying glass pronounced it "a real specimen worthy of a La Brea Tar Pits display" and told the children these bones formed a kind of solid mesh which protected the animal from *smilodon fatalis*, the great sabre toothed tiger. The dermal ossicles brought them back to the same spot with the hope of finding a legendary *fatalis* canine but instead they felt the shaking of earthquake, their part of hillside rising up into clouds of scary dust and they knew next day pictures in the newspapers would tell them about Bakersfield or Arvin where buildings had fell in, mothers and fathers shaking their heads over the wandering goddamned shame of it and glad, as the children knew, the quakes hadn't come yet for their town, but everyone knowing there would be a "sometime". It was like gophers, Danni's father said, trying to be gentle and graceful so as not to scare the children, try to drown'em, poison'em, but they always come back, the whole thing that way relieved of its grudge, though you'd hear behind the words other things he's seen and was now re-embroidering the heartlessness of it so it couldn't ever touch anyone again after touching him.

# IV

A tall impeccable stranger came to visit for only a few days every year or so. Danni's father saved his life in an ambush in Northern Italy. They were the only survivors of their platoon. Obviously close but not talkative in front of others, the two ex-soldiers went for long walks through the almost ready to be harvested groves, up into bordering canyons, the visit quiet, Danni's mother cooking, letting these men have their time. The visitor had become some kind of celebrated artist in New York City. A painter who spoke other languages, and who wrote too.

He made these periodic journeys to see his friend, always alone, both of them needing each other even though it was ten long years at that point since their war ran itself out. When they were on their long walks Danni said her mother often, waiting for their return, sat, stared out her kitchen window with tears running over her face, knowing the horrible distance both men shared, their need. So she cut flowers from her garden, set out, when her husband and his friend got back, in simple vases. She served them chicken mole with thick hand-made corn tortillas and chilis, some strong coffee. He stayed out on their screen porch, reading and writing the three or four nights of his visits. At the end of it a car arrived from LA. Never a fancy one, with a chauffer. He'd go back to the great City and they received invitations to the shows at galleries and museums both knew Danni's father would never see. It wasn't that he didn't want to, didn't care. He put all these wonders in a box of orangewood he formed by hand. Sanded and varnished it for the moment one of those objects arrived to be savored over an afternoon lemonade, admiring his friend's worldliness and accomplishments. "Travel" had taken him so directly to death and war out of the solitudes of Oklahoma. His friend knew. Grieved over the fragility which hovered over Danni's father, his sixteen hour workdays. His body strung taut with orange labor and what he'd had to do in those mountains of another world. The friend sent Danni's parents letters and pictures. For Danni there were post-cards from New York City, London, Paris, Barcelona, Florence, Athens. The handwriting was muscled, sure. The accompanying notes told of mountains, people, food, cities, ruins; other worlds and that someday he'd take her on one of his journeys. Danni hung them in her room letting them keep watch over her sleeping body.

By the time she was ten, Danni could drive the tractor, hitch up trailers, clean corrals, watch over horses and gardens. She and her mother, adoring the father, afraid of his work and its toll while an occasional drawing or small painting appeared through "special delivery" to be hung on the walls, the father subdued, recognizing their beauty, their emotion, the excitement, but wordless for days after. Danni's mother didn't quite know what to do. She felt the objects posed too harsh a contrast for the modesty of their home, but she loved them, and loved her husband's friend for the gesture, and the thought of it was, for her, at those moments when she let herself cautiously know it and think it, too harshly overt; she understood it was not an intervention in their struggle. The gifts given with the intimate reluctance and ceremonies of a battlefield incident that had grown gingerly into a living and needed friendship.

Whenever Danni's family invited Terry to stay a summer night, he'd go into a small alluvial canyon with Danni and they'd watch the Milky Way, the constellations, try to name *Cassiopeia*, *Antares*, *Scorpio*, *Lupus the Wolf Star*, *Sirius*; find *Polaris* from that point in the *The Big Dipper* and look for Mars and Venus, discuss "The War of the Worlds" which they'd seen from the balcony of their local theatre. The movie scared them, with its interplanetary marauders who were more like Nazis to them, their parents' terrible war still so close, the death rattle of its violence fresh, impassively rooted in the adult gestures around them with or without talk. The references to wounds, battles, malarial fatigue contracted in places like Tarawa where men were eaten by sharks. One of Terry's uncles was assigned a station in the jungles of Central America before heading off as an "Island Hopper" in the atolls of the Pacific. The fear was a Japanese landing off some remote coast, those elite Asian troops gaining a foothold in Panama, capturing the "Canal." The harvest of such a catastrophe didn't have any estimation. So that uncle and the other soldiers under his command were sent into the American jungles to patrol, accurately map, recon the terrain. At least half of them were killed by poisoned darts, the Indians with their frog toxins patiently, soundlessly murdering these and previous invaders with exactions of death almost completely unreal to the victims. The way those men died. The simplicity, potency of the otherworldly triumph transformed Terry's uncle into a haunted killer whose homecomings and after war visits plunged those who loved him most into a confused unease which, though it flickered, they never let rise into a flame to hurt any more a man beyond repair.

The children memorized the geographic heaviness of the war as a kind of uninvited helpless thrill that explained finally so little about the silences of these mothers and fathers, aunts and uncles. "The War." "The Depression." Fact and legend which enfolded them in an arrested, dry peculiarity, stunning them even in the supposed cleansing prosperities their "victory" provided. And they'd add to their star map the names of *Bill Haley and his Comets*, *The Platters*, *Little Richard* and the local *Olympics* who Danni's mother liked nearly as much as the homemade string beefed burritos she'd chew in that rock'n'roll/country darkness swelling dried oak and sage.

Danni that summer was going to visit her father's friend. "Connecticut" she told him. The cut and bite of the noun nearly injuring him. He was happy for her. Afraid too, about who'd come back after the two month stay. Her father's friend sent pictures, and they looked at the straight forward photographs; a house on a hill with a barn, the lake the buildings overlooked, the thick unfamiliar woods and trees behind it. The note accompanying the pictures said:

> *Some photos, Warren.*
> *Danni will stay here with me,*
> *Louise, and her two kids.*
>     *Fondly, B.*

Terry's boyhood friends belittled him for being, if not a sissy, then something next to it for his closeness to Danni, which extended past childhood. She was a girl they really didn't want to ridicule. Not that they wouldn't have, but she was turning into a beauty and her skills as a "grove girl" undermined their communal innocent stupidities and meannesses which always lingered on an edge no matter the unwanted scruples over her transformation and a possible kiss, a touch of titty in a seething, but so far empty-handed future.

During her two months "East" Terry received only a single letter. A fairly long one describing the daughters, Karen and Penny. "Both of them are tall and thin and can't wait to go to college. Their beauty has a streak of distance to it, and they're conceited and often won't let go of being polite which makes me feel like they're tolerating my time here for "B's" sake. I don't think they really want to be mean. Maybe it's just caution and my being from such a different world. Sometimes we do talk, and though that's ok, our worlds will never touch. "B" lets me ride horses, canoe and fish in the lake, wander the woods while he paints and works in a barn he's converting into a "studio" with presses and other tools. He lets me draw and pull prints, and every day has a stack of books for me to look at. He is a great cook too and has big summer meals at least three times a week filled with guests and talk, mostly about art and about just about everything. When I think about it I ache for home a little and miss you and western saddles because these English saddles they use around here take some real patience. Don't like them much, so I ride bareback. Karen and Penny get all dressed up and I know they don't approve but they don't say anything either. There are deer everywhere. The heat's so wet I feel like one of Dad's sorry gophers. Summer thunder showers not like home at all, but "B" takes me to the movies, to his favorite diners, shows me books and talks with me. Most times Louise spends in her garden and it's really different. Like a painting too with flowers and vegetables mixed together and certain weeds she uses as herbs. She has truckers bring rocks and soil and writes magazine articles. We talk about cactus and she even lets me help her spread chicken manure with her daughters who ask more questions then about where I live and what it's like. We're going to have dinner soon, so I'll stop. XXX Danni."

She came home with a cardboard "tube." There were prints wrapped in it with a note from her father's friend about Danni and how much it meant to him to have her for a visit. A month later they received a Western Union message from Louise. They found her father's friend lying over one of his printing presses. There had been no indications he was ill, no reason to suspect. The death shocked everyone and would Warren be willing to fly to New York to attend the memorium and funeral? The message was accompanied by a phone number. When he called, Louise said his voice was just as their friend had described it and began quietly to cry.

The eulogy said things about painting and art; what it meant to live through a war and to come just this far into giving one's life over "to the desperate, quietly real implications held in a single man's attempt not to be alone." Danni's father was praised for saving his friend's life. Other delicate and gentle things too were said about the "orange groves and walks in the California hills." Not too much though. "Hard to hear," as Danni's father with his gnarled fingers shook the hands of dignitaries, artists, and hundreds of guests who came. Louise at the post-funeral dinner could not control her trembling hands as she thanked him for coming and would not let go of his arm as she sat through this last necessary public ceremony.

The trip took a week. When Danni's father came home he spent a day making a batch of tamales with his wife and daughter. Then he went back to his orange grove and gardens more remote and condensed, "without shade," Danni's mother said of him with a kind of straggled frankness offering not the slightest gratification. Watched his daughter grow into a tall, auburn-haired 17 year-old who read the books which arrived in special boxes after his friend's death. Books about artists and poets she'd linger over at night after doing homework. And people came to their house, to their collection of prints, small paintings, drawings. Some offered to buy. Some wanted to use the "art" for shows and "landmark exhibitions" as they called them which traveled in America and other countries. The mother quickly learned about "Art" and the business of "Art" keeping a clear, precise watch over these beloved gifts, covering them with proper insurance and legal contract. They looked at Danni too who wore faded levis, a female version of hard-worked cowboy boots, chambre shirts cut off at the shoulders as she tended the daily care of her parents orange trees, directed a trusted workman in Spanish, fed chickens and horses, weeded gardens, watered her mother's zinnias. Her shoulders were freckled and strong; long fingers with nails unselfconsciously cut short. Her auburn hair was tied in a subtlely swaying bun and at mid-part a gracious, even palpitant aberration she'd come into this world with, a streak of gray hair shimmering, drawing boys and men as if it were a ripple of melted pearl, as did the small mole at the left crease where her lips met. Her walk had a vivacious surety and pitch of cool, direct intelligence which marked each of her close unevasive labors as the men and women from the far away New York and European addresses sorted with their trained, reserved eyes.

These people wanted Danni's father to assume a personality for the unstated "sake of his friend." The phrase locked and guarded, but for that, just the same, impatiently bunching into designs he could not accept.

The mother and daughter wanted the spectacle, wanted it to immerse them. And they passionately did not want to be drowned. Danni's father watched. Saw no retraction of grace, or scorned their flirtations with the shrewd, ingratiating intrigues. Perhaps it was because of the killing he'd done, the gore sealing up his mind in erosions he allowed to stalk him only to the sinews of his fingers. The sinister extension of the death roar coming to an arrest in himself, and falling as the tenth part of water or the tarantula hawks who actually, ceaselessly arrange the days, sucking each one, to be spit out, these eaters who hunt the days as living creatures who have not begun yet to yearn for the more vulnerable sustenances lying below in a purer cold masquerading as the warmth each day partially touches and cannot so far be smelled.

Danni's father occupied his refusal about as much as the time it took to say "no" and let any further sullenness die there over an amount of money or fame cutting its way deep into them. The curators, the art historians, dealers, collectors, they'd rephrase it, he knew, and keep rephrasing it, dangle each version as if it were a jewel, or a resurrection layered with the ceremonies of "lunches" "dinners" which he refused neither politely or impolitely not at all wanting to make a squalor of his basic Oklahoma courtesies and manners. But the refusal was hard as the granite hills which loomed over them and though the mother and daughter might entertain, even enjoy these transactions and their lure, Warren placed himself aside. And perhaps this too he learned from the heartlessness of the war he'd survived. He didn't want to stop any life that came to touch his wife or daughter. And what further could he bring to any of this other than to carry the ache of a home-ground that'd come to both him and his dead friend at the moment of a singular violence which had grotesquely shredded every immediately previous living body around them?

# V

Terry opened the door of the Olds and noticed a man's left shoe. The sole was split nearly in half. LeRoy and Rooster watched him, ears pricked up, thrusted and summoned. Terry called out the name "Rooster," deliberately told the animal to "sit," and LeRoy followed the example. It partially dissipated the wash of fear he didn't want clinging to him around these dogs. Knew couldn't be afforded. The arrival of the lures which stunned Danni's family was accompanied by the arrival of another war. Her father read the papers. Understood this one, though it had hardly appeared. Yet, the will of it, the pre-debris of its lurching, not yet attached mockeries reminded him of other veterans, two he and "B" had talked about over their long walks in various arroyos that curled down to the edges of his fruit trees where they encountered what they thought was their mutual "Luck" again in the form of a cougar lioness playing with her single cub in the protective outcrop of a large boulder where she let it romp over her body and try to capture her wand-like tail; charming it, teasing it, the mirage of it rippling over them. "B" told Warren how these other men became artists too after their service. One from L.A. One from Montana. Westermann, the first; H.C. Westermann whose ship was hit by Kamakazees in the final sullen battles of the Pacific. The spectral "Zero" pilots inflamed with suicide, their alien vows of retribution, of a sky stupefied in unbearable waste rains presenting the would-be conquerors' armadas with the deathbaths of their victory and its nurseries of expressionless sorrow. "The artist fixing," "B" had written in an article about both artists, "new momentums to wood, metal, glass, plastic, steel – sculptures, coffins, mystery houses, wandering nightmares demanding as yet unincarnated myths of self-destruction for their identity, questions never before asked that fit nowhere. Unanswerable 'Death Ships'; each one a warning carrying us to the point of No Days. Humans entering every verb for death forming the brain out of dwindling sensations of emergencies broken open by the truths and lies a Westermann 'Death Ship' floats upon. The artist's despondent, fierce humor rips at the order of the world dispersing its assumptions and transmissions of slaughter. Each thing reaches toward a stinging, unsurrendered scrutiny of breakage and its undertow."

The other, Peter Voulkos. A Greek from Montana who'd been a tail-gunner stuck at the witch-end of a B26 with a machine gun flying over places like Saipan and Iwo Jima and later "Turning the traditions and crafts of ceramics," "B" wrote in the same art journal essay, "into an outpour of scathing invention and courage" that seemed to Danni's father, as he read his friend's words, examined the accompanying photographs, like seeds set adrift by pouring machine gun fire; and reading over and over again "B's" closing phrase about the Greek/American artist, "His own touch of answering humanity stalking the codes of violence and their fixed gravid unlife as if he were what those promises and codes needed most to fear."

Warren finished the article, Danni told her childhood friend, and then placed it too in the orange wood box so carefully wrought it closed with the soundlessness of thread to needle.

Danni's mother knew the walks her husband and his friend took in those arroyos covered endless discussions; they were immediate, each man sounding the other, even momentarily perilous, the effort often radiating, then exhausting them. She thought it was a way of passing into and belonging somehow to their survival. But she knew it was more. They stirred a truth for each other and came away from those long nights increased, had some dignity before the violence which had come for them, would always come for them. She knew that too.

She had no idea Danni was to be the first and that she and her husband could be bypassed by the currents of noiseless rapacities as if they were moths at wingfall searching a split screen. The daughter's fascination with writing, with art began to increase, grow firm. And she hungered for experience, particularly her rides through the groves drinking, smoking the sweet marijuana friends left in her high school locker, speeding at ninety to a hundred miles per hour on the back of a chopper or an altered Ford pickup with fuel injection conjured by an auto-shop boyfriend over those meager two lane streets bordered by four foot flood culverts on both sides was one place to begin, then to move forward. How could she manage to get to war? A daughter, an only child. Undergo somehow the fury which had transported her father and his friend as she grew, tall, boys and men shifting their eyes at the pronouncement; the hesitant, even evasive flickering of a young woman, sharply attractive, unwilling to be stifled.

She left one morning, a month before high school graduation. Took a boyfriend's car to L.A. Drove through old "Chinatown." At Pershing Square she watched the hustlers and drag queens deal up some meth, some obvious soldiers home on leave looking to score a tab of acid or heroin. She began to recognize the fury, whatever that might be, that was the malicious certitude shifting, embroidering its endless predations which had hollowed out the young men she was watching not more than one or two years older than herself. Then why take an oath of allegiance when another more relentless oath beckoned that could rot tongue or eye with the equal morbidity of the sweetest bullet? The young men she saw were ravished, but unlike her father they seemed almost sterilized, throbbing with expulsions and boredoms no other war had so fastidiously extracted from its common soldiers.

At 3:30pm she opened the door of an army

recruiting depot, talked to the sergeant there, signed on to be an army nurse. 18. The contract sealed. Her father couldn't eat for nearly a week after she informed them. The mother. Near overfed one of the horses, almost killed it. During the three months before boot camp and training, Danni spent the time reading, helping her mother with contracts, letters, requests. Her father let her work the grove with him, let her have the time, refused the anger and distance that would have been so easy. Told her the house, the orange grove'd be there when she got back. Didn't know to say it any other way. When the note came saying Danni was taken prisoner, her hospital compound over-run in a notorious battle her father and mother understood no one knew if she was alive.

# VI

Terry heard Krofchec's voice off in a distance as he braced himself for the last blueprint that'd tie up the Olds in an insurance molded knot. He marked the place on the backseat where some blood had dried, took a picture. Rooster and LeRoy. They were running toward the detective.

There was another body there too. Noreen's. Krofchec was clumsily slapping at her face and Noreen was fighting back. He'd done a detour. Got some liquor.

Taken the call girl for a ride and the deal had slammed shut.

"Fucker. Ugly fucker," he heard Noreen say. "Try ta'kill me."

Rooster got to'em. His initial lunge hit Krofchec about mid-calf, took some detective meat and wool, some blood, twisted his head with the prize while LeRoy got the receipt; swiped at the man's elbow. Left a raw, exposed site of shredded cartilage. It was like a butcher had slipped on a smudge of wandering fat, the knife flung and carving whatever it touched.

He thought of Danni even as he watched Noreen reach for the detective's pistol, the savage failure of the war and the rush to embrace the labyrinths of desertion coded to its certainties as they were coded to the blueprints he'd made that day. The cold stench of a Noreen pulling at the .45 and its holster, trying to tie her fingers over the trigger, Rooster clamped to her shoulder, taking half its flesh, coming back immediately for more. He thought he'd seen Danni in one of the images on CBS after Walter Cronkite tried to say something beautifully, morosely useless. He knew he'd have to stop the dogs. Krofchec was sinking into shock, the liquor curling out in waves, leaving him stranded, vomiting. His wordlessness as ugly as his words. And Noreen. Her shoulder and ankle were half gone, reaching for that pistol. Terry suddenly realized the core of the images that'd stolen Danni. Stolen a huge clump of his and the previous generation; his own uncles humiliated by battle slaughter and living the hells that only men can imagine for each other as an ocean of afterlife nightsweats. He had to be quick now. The dogs were moving into a frenzy and would kill. Noreen hesitated, eased her fingers off the butt, began to crumple in pain as the dogs bit at her and Krofchec. What were the sanctuaries of those images, the vocations of innocence mixed with trustlessness penetrating each successive future they had been allowed as Terry reached for the pistol, got it loose from its holster as he killed the dogs and heard a line from one of Danni's final letters about where she'd been:

"That they have learned to breathe cruelty and love the smell."

# Doomed
# To Be
# Rich

He'd hardly said a word for three years. "Breath hadn't stopped but what rode it had," he commented to nothing in particular but the wild flower seeds in his hands thinking of the ways words can sort'a dry up same as the soil had in his section of the Valley. Not gone to dust yet, but a light brown no matter, brittle, as if it'd been snuffled by four generations of hogs. When his granddaughter came Mr. Woodward prepared. Didn't want to seem too strange to this beloved girl so he picked strawberries, baked cup cakes, and warmed peanut butter sandwiches. And he spoke to her, when it seemed he couldn't avoid it, in a whisper, which made the girl giggle.

"You jist talked Granpa," she'd say, as if the world was truly the brand new miracle it ought to be.

"I did?" he'd answer, letting the girl see the sting of his surprise which delighted her, made her hungry for a cupcake.

It was really the only time he'd allow himself "this excursion" as he called it. Otherwise he kept to a late-life kindness that made the child's mother, his daughter, sometimes ache with grief.

"Ole Man Woodward's gotta a garden coyotes'd drool over," one of the local big growers noted with almost a sheen of envy, though it was only a little more than an acre. "Walk into his shed. Be damned you don't see newspapers filled with dried up wild flowers, boots claimed by black widows, hoe'r two sharp enough to shave a goose pimple, seeds wrapped in foil names on'em lined up in trays like they wuz San Bernardino whores." And with that the grower grabbed a church-key floating the fender of his field pick-up, stabbed the top of a virgin beer, and let loose a little geyser there to cool off the four o'clock boil of a summer afternoon.

Mr. Woodward attributed his garden, the tastes of vegetables and herbs, a string of lemon, orange, peach and plum trees to the chicken manure a local egg rancher dumped every year, a Jew from Russia who seemed to be able "to smell them good eggs with his eyes" and carry what the big growers identified as "some memorable shit. Ain't caught no one prayin over it yet but yew never know what them fuckers might think up next. A mound of it, by God. Filled with feathers too. Practically to the point where you could hear that goddamned thing flappin over the Sierras."

The image of that flyin shit and the superior crop that poured out of that miniature plot which received its treasure held the tones of bewildered respect from the local small thousand to the larger twenty thousand acre and more families who made their millions by keeping a choke-hold on the water first, transform an acre into a streak of money, transform twenty or a hundred thousand into a casino, each head of lettuce, each bushel of "potatas," them sweet jungles of orange and lemon trees and cotton fields chips to be cashed in. But even so, when old Mr. Woodward trucked a load of his goods into town the wives of the biggest growers heard, drove the hot miles to fill their baskets as if the best their husbands could do was grow weeds and salt.

Didn't cause jealousy. Couldn't pin that one on no wanderin donkey's ass as the locals might let such a stray harmless image pass through; but a tinge of consternation to stay shrunk in the corner of a warehouse would be more accurate. And that small crop sweet or tart drew a comment at the close of each growing season from the newspapers which his daughter and granddaughter made into a scrapbook. "His truck shined, oiled, ready to go up a mountain pass in compound low for an almanac year." Pictures of an elderly man and his goods, work-thin, not unhandsome, face hardened from sun and wind, intelligent eyes staring off into the distance of the camera. There were baskets filled with peaches, onions, lettuce, tomatoes, flowers, corn, plums tasted better than a bowl of homemade ice cream grown in soil so carefully preened and sheened that itself smelled like a branch of the flower family to the noses of those farmers trained in botany, agronomy, entomology, biology and money; every word of the run ending in the sometimes vowel of "Y" with its all the time deluge of cash.

Mr. Woodward started out at fifteen haulin trucks for the nearest growers. Oranges, plums, grapefruit, artichokes, walnuts, pecans to Stockton, Sacramento, LA or San Francisco. Once in a while far as Humboldt and Eureka. As a boy he was tool ready and bull strong meaning he was smart, didn't have to be told, fix any busted thing himself rig it up with hay barbwire and spit to make his deliveries load and unload tons of boxes and do that for days without a break.

"Hell. Worker like that. Feed'im a hand full'a popcorn. No questions asked. Makes the banker smile," said a rancher as he rolled a cigarette, licked it shut, lit it wet. "Let the wives once in while have their day. No harm in it finally. But why when he does do his talkin caint he plug his goddamned mouth shut then?" the rancher asked touching a lip blister. "Say nothin too much since he signed up in '39; what wuz he thirty three thirty four drivin tanks from Tarawa to Saipan?"

There was that respect which kept a partial lid on the whispers. Most of the people Mr. Woodward worked for, his age, took the federal deferments which identified them as Essential Contributors to the National Good. Meaning they grew food and what the food grew for them arriving careful and intact. Through the whole Depression Mr. Woodward wasn't sick a day, was known to have quietly helped or hired as many Okie swampers as he could "Ta keep a family or two in dignity and clothes" as he said knowing at some point that help might result in a beating, slashed tires, or worse in those ugly years when so many walked the two thousand miles they did. May be, if it hadn't been for the Pacific, they walked to old Venus up there festering like some hornet unable to find her sting.

One of those wives told Mr. Woodward, "When the winds came, at first no one really understood. Crops still green then and the plains dipped with them seasways all the way to somewhere in Texas. Then them other things got let loose so mean it put the Satan Himself back in the Book. Made you wish it was the Terrible Visitor who showed up. Least he had some manners. Water sunk away. Air withered. Soil turned to stingy snot. Even fires choked to death like a three day infant."

She thought it might'a been her father's fault. Told about his arrival in the 1860s.

"Came in a bone picker and one afternoon found himself wandered down in to a hid stream bottom filled with Cottonwood and Box Elder. It was peaceful he was reported to have said, peaceful enough to cut a chaw looked around let the juice fill his teeth. Sametime seemed a bird let loose hit his hat square. Looked up thinking it was a raven, a magpie. Listened too cause the angers was still ripe then in them hours and you could be murdered by anyone anything a stray buffalo bull waitin down there; last one of a herd of two hundred thousand? So he changed the location from up to down, took off his hat. Not a stain'a nothin there. Leaned over. Brushed away some grass at his feet. Won't be damned if there wasn't what looked like finger bones with some finger nails and some parched up skin. Thought anyplace got tornadoes, an ocean of skeletons far as any man's nightmare could take root may as well have a small rain of fingers on a cloudless day. Father took a sniff cause in them hours sniffin and seein and hearin was still important. Didn't make no difference if you was a man badger antelope nuthatch better use what's given. Use it not and just as well turn to every other dust creatures turn into. Well, his nose and eyes didn't have much to say. And them fingers? If they weren't dancing or turning the strings of a fiddle they couldn't be heard by his ears or anything elses'. He moved. But slow. Draw no attention to even a cricket cause he was scared. Didn't know if he'd have time to pull a knife or if he'd wandered into a prairie hole that punched out corpses. Heard about one where there was skeletons, wolves and men and birds just laid and gone to sleep like each had been visited by some child and put to peace. He listened close for footsteps. Watched for them small hands and feet. Don't know if he could'a murdered and dowanna know but I heard he did look up at the high branches of a cottonwood. Saw a bundle there with old moccassins sticking out one end and knew it was a tree hung corpse snugup ten twenty years? First branches too high so he rigged his saddle rope, managed the branchless first twelve foot then climbed that old tree like he was a child himself to the death bundle. An old warrior still had some dried flesh on his face. There was hawk and magpie feathers and some small stones in a rawhide pouch, pipe too, carved face of a crane out of red stone of some sort. Took the pouch, the feathers. Left'im the pipe and as the man headed down somehow that bundle started a slip and before he could reach, whole outfit smashed and scattered like a tiny boat reaching the hell of this world, not a chance to reach the hell of the next. He thought right then, though he was still young, goddamn him and his ways. Cain't even let the dead alone of Others though they hung'em in trees. And I'm still here to tell what I heard though; once anyone goes cold no matter what they did with their earthly flesh, those Indians thought everyone went to the same place. No heaven or hell. The walk could take a billion years. The good the bad fallen away. No one to remember or care. The power of darkness coming too to its final rest. Gave'im a burial asked he not hold too much grudge since him and our kind invaded that corpse's life. Then went and invaded his death. My granddad watching those dust storms build into their terrible daytime blackness thought it was his doings," the old woman said, "Died on the way to California holding that little pouch of pebbles in his hands."

Mr. Woodward took to the habits of listening and may be he listened too long. Got his own words stuck in some lost depot. People came in hungry. Got hungrier and stayed. I always thought if you're gonna starve better to try it many places as you can; stay in one, start turning to bone in front of yourself, your mother, your grandparents with veins practically big as hoses pumping in their skulls and wasted arms just hollows the land, everything that walks, everything that accompanies what it means to walk and talk and let your eyes wander over what's alive. Here daughter have a rotted onion for breakfast dinner supper. See if yer teeth'll fall'in'r'break time yer twelve look like a flash'ah lightning got trampled.

And there was plenty of those. Girls and boys with that kicked-in look even a buzzard couldn't eat away. Ran deeper than skull or bone or eye sockets. Shacks scrumped up outta tar paper piss thin as could be. One fork for four people. Sulphur stunk water ready to gore your nostrils. Couple'a over-stained plates. A picture of Jesus other things mothers and grandfathers from Georgia Germany Ireland Carolina burned either by exhaustion or raging dust sumwhars in Kansas Mizzura think it was a so long ago lie sum one chopped it up with'a pick ax.


Mr. Woodward had a boy helped him once and later he asked me to help him too. I'm the grandson of that boy who was fifteen sixteen in 34', five years after the Crash. Said one Sunday to the old trucker him and his family ate watry potato soup for three years. Last horse gave up watching a dust cloud on the Dakota horizon. Roze 'bout high as'a thunderhead started to blot out the sun. "Blot" wasn't the best word for it but you try to reach for things anyways. Even a word here and there no matter how cold it comes up in your hands. Started to go dark by 1:30-2:00 in the afternoon. Sky seemed to have the breath of cholera and God wouldn't tolerate that dust in His teeth or nose.

Winds blew through the clapboard, pocked the windows. When it got bad they laid on the floor and listened to the furniture scrape over the floorboards not like they was ghosts but just a bunch'a other poor assed demons locked in some misery. Then when they crawled to this Valley'yer it was the water was the enemy. Cold and hard and driven by an immensity no one in this time can properly witness or name. Water mixing with the steepness of mountains and sluice of rock and canyon makes for a country either treacherous or handsome or a mix of both to grind the unwary man to a thing worse and far less than a pulp. Water fill a canyon one day with weight motion and roar. Pick the flesh off Nebuchadnezzar the Nebraskan shine his bones and then turn his bones to Sitting Bull's own dust itself and drown that too. And within two three days that swollen reeking thing with its waves and spray and bulk of fury withered to a trickle.

Mr. Woodward tensed up over this story thinking it was a mouth full'a words and a brain full'a who knows what'll hold a world together half Osage half some goddamned Irishman who appeared over a hill of plains flowers one day and not one girl of those villages in the following months could figure out how to refuse. Boy picked up a cut from a rusty haywire, nearly died of blood poisoning not far after on another day round '36 '37 no one to represent him but a sister, my aunt; hands and arms blown up from handlin too much fruit and insecticide. Fingers so strung with poison didn't look like she had more'an month herself and Mr. Woodward tried to help her in her last hours.

He did on occasion, not necessarily disappear but "loaded up" his car more exactly with one seat for the driver, the rest of the interior stripped for the proceedings. Long weeks of solitary travel into the desert, Sierras, canyons, or plains. "To look" as the old man said. Nothing more than the two words, and the trail they might leave, each vowel or consonant having the drift of cliffs visited, a crevice where certain wild grasses might sprout, the transformations of rooms or ceilings into small arroyos where he could hear desert big horn sheep sniffing the wind for the odors of his single human body in their vicinity.

He might take three or four shoes, some friendly tools, well gathered to the palms of his hands; a shovel, an ax, a hatchet, a trowel. Not always in that order nor having the pronouncements of easy formality accompanying him, as those objects often did, to flash flood creek bed or rattler haunted boulders. If something wore out he could stuff it with newspaper, or with newspapers carry a certain cactus which otherwise could exact damage "bad as the bite of a horse" as he said letting a grain of humor cover the worries of his grown daughter whose own daughter, the one who still can't refuse a cupcake, eventually became my wife.

The worry was always over water, imagining her father too easily dead from thirst and unfound and dead and as to his approaches to food; eat whenever hungry, rise at the winks of dawn, sleep with the first shades of darkness and what gets passed from one garden to another.

He loved the moment of a desertion from the world of moisture to the worlds of granite and sun and leeching winds of a Sierra dome and the tones of lichens sprouted on the hardest curls of a sheer three to four thousand foot cliff face. The plants and tendrils of hardest light, a bee wandered up and adopting a similar scorn for the clusters of uneasy prosperities lying a thousand to four thousand feet below on hillsides not more relaxed in their terms, but accumulable, and where, in the highest stirrings, the first melt of snow hovers between being eaten by granite or being the eater of granite, the greed of each poised in the hidden trickles and smallest cracks of rock.

What likes rocky exposed ledges in 11,000 to 13,000 feet of withering sun in this Grandfather's story?

The wars up there with their showiest blue and pink flowers, or the Sky Pilot aloft at 14,000 feet hovering in its crowded deepest blues, how it restored the sky for him, thinking as he often couldn't help thinking of the sky above the Japanese city he'd walked into and could find no way out.

"Does water come from the Pleiades or Cassiopeia?" he often playfully asked his granddaughter, letting the question, as I later came to hear it, rise toward the insulations he needed in order to regard the tufts of stunning flowers born of some possible radiate hell, or the as yet ungathered water forming a stillness in highest unfallen drips having no fearful flood or spread or roar of giant sea lions buried in roots of the San Andreas but half shades of boulders and split cliffs. A Sierra mountain flower might follow sun or water as a cougar might stalk ever weary sheep of the highest rock country and in that journey become a wildly decorative or stunted ledge master, wind and light nibbled as if it were some elder still-allowed-to-breathe corpse here sprouting fragrant yellow or pink splashed flowers asking for no mercy as its roots seek a shambled fissure and the sun above were itself a broken stick weed.

"Saprophytic." He'd pronounce this word, and so many others he began to memorize after his return, wanting those pronunciations on his pallet and tongue as counter taste to what he knew could not be left behind or abandoned. Flowers he saw that obtained their food by absorbing dissolved organic matter. And sun itself might be the Saprophyte feeding the strange host no other Guest has yet been able to sniff out as single flower plume or congregate colonies on the face of a wind cut granite spire.

And what might accompany water at these highest noiseless seepages where he could on the Third Day hear voices from various clumps of black rained rubble begging for a drink. Just one. One was enough?

There was Malacothrix Californica, the Desert Dandelion thriving in blistering suns of spring over Mohave alluvial fans those baked to near iron geologic tongues formed to a soft yellow haze and he'd spend hours watching the shimmer until it glowed windswept and soft with sunset. And he remembered the embers he saw who were once people still hot from what he later came to understand were beta particle residues covering his clothes his testicles puddles of gama rays and the legendary storm of paper fragments fluttering everywhere. The civilization not turned over to a final dust. Did such a rain of paper mean he and everyone else became "tresspassers" on a planet?

How could he comprehend and then describe to himself the word for water which had erupted in his brain and in that household; "Mizu" "Mizu" they asked out of the indescribable withering he saw the world become and the Word for him so simple, permanent. An ember. A keloid. And what was the temperature that day? Six thousand a million degrees as if it were an instant unnoticeable commonplace receding into a nightly weather report as other wars formed and immediately followed. And "Water" the one real spoken word in his own Valley his own body describing what actual greeds thirsts and growths.

What were these things? And if he was ever going to talk again then what talk and what was Death now as he spoke of an old seaweed woman and the shape of first cruelties as they were described for him out of which a thing called California might have begun to emerge and what was he hearing and seeing as he picked up the eagle feathers given to him in the Land of the Yolla Bolly?

Lagoons of wild flowers as he watched them, letting them gently impinge on his image of a flower from that City. The one-flowered Gentian no more than four inches high its petals edged with blue, interior white with greenish dots as he considered its life. And the Sierra Juniper, "Juniperus occidentalis" he'd see at over 10,000 feet, a fifty to sixty footer, five foot thick trunk folded in by the arc of a house-sized boulder, limbs seared by heat and cold turned white in death as some stranded seacrumb, white as peoples' white lips he'd seen, that part of their faces turned to stone which had made him "sort of talkless" as his daughter tried to apologize, not knowing what else to do in those "Victory Years" full of new chevies and mercs and muscle cars and she'd let go of her apologies to high school friends and their parents often not knowing where to put any of it.

He breathed more easily when he saw another high alpine figwort, "Mimulus primuloides" as he memorized the formal scientific identities, hoping such memorization might yield, at least for his daughter and granddaughter, when he did talk, some sense of safety, a world fastened to a flower's name no matter how silly or curious its excess. And this flower with its yellow petals, silver-haired leaves forming carpet-like reefs over moist small meadows, decaying stumps.

Once following the instructions of an old miner still given to long wanderings with a burro, he found that friend's "Mimulus" meadow in a crisp first light dew and swarms of High Sierra yellow-legged frogs leaping and glinting there, as if each of their horde were the first beam of an impassive uncertainty he wanted personally to tease him thinking of the legends of those frogs "so thick" it was said, "you can walk across lakes on them" as if you were, not Jesus, but a mountain Keechee warrior, one of the first to be hunted in the local genocides when there were no questions over who to hang or murder.

Simple rumors equaled simple exhibitions of hatchetry over who did or did not steal and eat cattle to keep from starving. A chief, whom they called "Baptiste" presented himself as one out of a Tale of Courtesies on a Sierra crag asking the many who hunted he and his women and children what were their losses. And when asked himself said not a one of his own, any count of the dead included "only a few strangers." He apologized for not making a better fight of it then vanished into the chaparral as if in that knitted undermass of twigs and leaves and cankerous ground cover words were born for such dignities.

# II

Mr. Woodward's parents and their second settlement friends still held the immediacies of the spring days of 1851 as news, if not fresh, then disturbances not yet gone to any faintness, and having, for more than fifty years certain uncomfortable strengths and outcomes rooted to that moment when the Mariposa Battalion set out to drive even the ashes of the Valley and Mountain Indians out of this world.

Destroy the "Acorn Belt" on all the highest and lowest foothill country below snow line and its variations of ancient trees. The massed life there a hindrance to the other abundances and waiting riches for those shrewd enough to see beyond the years of huge killing and the time when even a sniff of bitterness would smell more like cash in its slipperyness than the threads of cold sorrow or the chapters of truth covering the rewards of gore.

So on a Monday April 14th 1851 the Mariposa Boys set out after the more resistant Chowchilla.

Robert Eccleston, of the approximately 200 men in that private militia, was the only one to have kept a personal record. He wrote the party of young hunters "Made a display at once formidable and romantic." And Romanticism at that moment may have had more to do with a kind of Miwok "Sacajawea" "acting as guide" the diarist recorded. Mounted astride a large rowan horse, "She wore a hat under which her black straight hair hung down gracefully upon her shoulders, which were partially covered with a scarf thrown negligently over the left shoulder, her bodice was white muslin and her skirt of blue figured calico, and her small feet and ankles showed to advantage." The expressive surge of prose, if you'll care to notice, holds more detail than the recording of the discovery of Yosemite of which Eccleston at that moment was not a part. It appears that those members of the Battalion who were party to this curve in the mission were either benumbed by snow, the hunt for human quarry, or plain had no eye nor care for the marvels into which they stumbled. One of the scraggle later said if he'd "known the mountain haunt was going to be so famous" he might have looked at it. Thus it was on March 27th eighteen and fifty-one that that segment of the "Butterfly" Battalion stood completely blinded before all but slaves or gold.

But the "Guidess" of Eccleston's eye, though she had no recorded name, "every little while" glanced back to make sure of that hungry male company's gaze. She led them through steep snow covered valleys ("exceeding rough country") for ten days finding no Indians. They did however reconnoiter a "Rancheria" where they burned "1000 bushels of acorns and many old" bark huts. "Exceeding rough" meant perpendicular terrain, almost impossible to traverse rivers and streams, slopes of smooth granite where any slip by man or horse meant broken bones, a plunge over a cliff, or fatal exhaustion from the visiting extremities of sun or snow or "small feet and ankles" showing to advantage for which no man had a single immunity.

Every small "Rancheri" was burned. Acorns first, the nutrient larders gone to sparks and smoke signals the fleeing small bands of Yosemite and Chowchilla could hardly have failed to see or whiff and quietly keened over the images of starvation in forms other than hunger about to engulf them. At one site the diarist writes of astonishing "brush fences" constructed as protective surrounds for what must have been permanent "camps" and at this point in the recording that author mentions yet another such "fence" like those previously set to flame. The description, though spare, holds a tone of admiration, even stingy awe for its more than just a "primitive" haphazard "fence". The less than a paragraph account describes at once a subtle engineering marvel, a warning device, and a snare for small game; a maze capable of deflecting grizzly and wolf; a mindful masterpiece that only these great basketmakers could imagine and devise. "They" (the fences) "are some two miles long & made with chaparral cut off & stuck in the ground so close in a row a bird cannot pass through. About every 10 or 15 feet a small opening is left & in it is fastened a snare made of small pieces of green wood & twine which is sprung when any thing touches either of two little cross pieces. It is so well arranged that it is impossible to touch it with your fingers & pull it out again with out being caught..." This too was burnt and the loss though faraway and obscure rises to the tremblings of those Fairy Tales which may be more attractive to the soul than the most beautiful werewolves who are said to ride the clouds of Mono Lake saltflies conversing with the bones of the drowned. A thing so delicate, imaginative, and tensily heaved in to this world bespeaks of a mind which though gone beyond whisper or ghostliness calls us to, in spite of ourselves, the harvest of desertions hid in such still and cornered diary passages as if it were a plucked American Door not yet surfaced in either the oceans of the day or the oceans of the night where the dead have grown too hot for the planets which nursed their supposed being.

"The scenery here is magnificently wild. Whole mountains of solid rock are not infrequent & many beautiful pictures of tremendous waterfalls on stone by the oldest master enliven the stream. The snowy peaks, the summit of the Sierra Nevada, show out nobly. The majestic pines & C." The record of these lines, though written in haste and exhaustion, is observant and sparse, balanced by a sense of crushing dangers and fatality as the party spotted Indians walking on "smooth rock" as if they, in contrast, were in the last steps of a lonely infancy and outrage needing to be scoured away in the mists of grapevine twined-ladders ascending what to those men of the Battalion were and still are cliff faces so forsaken even the spider would think twice about being unloosed in those winds but to them who were hunted it was the face of home, and the cliffs, though they had no easy intimacy, had no fixed oblivion either.

In mid-May of 1851 the diarist reported snow four to five feet deep and noticed "Indians" watching them from the higher hills. There were, in those more desolate heights, "several Rancheri" which the hunting party "burnt" as if the Day of Reckoning had been left to the Fools of Mire who would in the faraway time to come of their own howlings mishear the warning to save their souls and instead hear only the murmurings of disoriented fish in the new seas.

There is the description too of a small "furlough": a foot race between members of the Battalion and another Indian "guide." The race: a sprint of approximately one hundred yards. The Miwok runner: "We'll built, tall, very muscular with small wrists and ankles..." Is this another luring "Sakajewean" with ankles also showing to advantage and if such a man were the commonplace, and the diary does not indicate otherwise, does that information tell us, whose only familiar is our irremediable distance, about nutrition, training, constant disciplined exertion, and lifetime study of one's own immediate surround. What is further to be discerned by the writer's comment that this Indian "ran extremely pretty". Did such a quarry, "extra pretty" as the author said he was, lead to a "present" given on May 29th 1851 to Captain Balen of the Mariposas; "an Indian Boy about five years of age ..." The captive was an orphan, as were countless thousands of others whose parents were killed for the traffic in children by many of the white immigrants who brought slaves with them into the new territory. Is the reference to this orphan an underdrift of stories Mr. Woodward heard on his rounds of delivery through the old Yolla Bolly country and the remnant Yuki/ Wailaki workers who assisted and gave him shelter in the cruelest years from 1931 to 1937?

Some of those people he met told about their own hard times and meaner winters as they unloaded and loaded fifty to eighty pound boxes for hours in that ancient California country. Hard winter to him meant something different to them and while they didn't exactly laugh over it they didn't exactly avoid laughter either as they told him about snow time, the one where you'd gladly eat wolf puke if you could, and the fierce Yuki women who picked up the flayed faces of their enemies killed in battle in their teeth and danced and everyone had tattoos on their faces, noses pierced, loved to eat wood rats, squirrels, rabbits and for sure fish souls were immortal, the only such beings in the whole fleshly world. "Why the only thing that comes close Mr. Woodward," they told him, "was beautiful words, good as salmon spiced with clover" and they did that at the end of a sixteen hour day, cooked fresh salmon over an open pit along with quail and lark and told of the oldest Indian trail stretching from the Columbia River to Sacramento and that this world can be recognized by rivers, streams, rivulets—water the names of water what is watered who drinks who slurps who bathes who listens who drowns who swims who gets cool who freezes who floats alive who floats dead.

And when they sang for him for some reason he didn't feel tired, as sore, the burning sensations in his muscles seemed to wander in to a sleep separate from himself and he didn't worry anymore about whether he'd wake up at dawn with a cracked tooth sore jawed and barren, unable to figure if it was him who'd kicked his dreams or if it was his dreams who'd kicked him, some body a dream decided to visit and settle in, thought the first night was good stayed for a second, for a third, start up the household labors.

It seemed to him his friends could go straight to a dream like that, pay it not to go to someone else but give up being a visitor and wander back into roots of berry bushes where for centuries it'd been happy and content.

He woke one morning and there were two eagle feathers on his chest braided together with deer hide and abalone. One of the women told him to take it home, put it under his bed. "Keep things a little calmer even for a white man," she said preparing some herbal tea. The emergent August morning was already hot with the tang of dried earth, withered poison oak, a small stiff wind that made the Milky Way look like the Queen of Sheba's diamond fillings.

He knew by mid-day the flies looked for shelter, birds went into open mouthed pant. The only creatures dumb enough to stay put under dust and sun, himself and the men around him. Each one of'em being goddamned about what they went and done. Got good with labor, got stuck, and since nobody come with any miracles then may as well watch for black widows one Yuki said with a kind of squint to emphasize how to keep a mind on what's under its nose otherwise begin to go vacant and you never know when a man'll wander unexpectedly in to his own waiting corpse.

"Learn that in the Bible, Dave?" another Yuki asked.

"Stopped reading that thing when it made me bowlegged," Mr. Woodward said was the answer.

They'd take a break, share some wild plums, the best Mr. Woodward said he ever had. They laughed over the thought of sending him to the local car salesman. Give'im the number of the local whore house for a free visit in honor of the purchase. No outward laughter but talk like that to keep pace with the wandering sun and changing shades of afternoon sky.

"Tastes good. Good as bad luck pulled up for a rest" the streamlets of plum juice draining over fingers and wrists. A small swarm of hornets joined too, came from what cave in the air no one knew. Hovered over plum juiced hands of Mr. Woodward and the small covey of Yolla Bolly Indians. No one delivering a threatening swat. But letting the insects land for a second on knuckle or thumb, go to buzzless quiet unable quite to figure how to move. The skin of a human hand too sweet, too sun thinned for other consideration.

"Wild apple tree blossoms mixed with smell of corpses it used to be. Drift from here to where the whales floated in dead. Grizzlies came. Them and the lions ate the world to the bone. By the nose you could say. Everything by the nose. Tastes in the air. Taut eye thick with tricks about murder and worse. Du nobuddy no gud. But it's there like the Flood when there's more mice than fish. Sweep the country clean of everything with hair on it."

Mr. Woodward took the slow drive back then. Sometimes it was firewood, redwood shingles. "Two-by-fours so raw, they was meaner than'a drop'a syphilis" one Yuki who rode with him said of the labors. He'd carry the tall tones of those humors through the forest and coastal mountain country down into Sacramento and the odors of the Delta. Fire and insecticide and oil smelling like the rotten toes of Molech. Flood scourge so huge and repellent it could hold the glare of even the Donner cannibalism that most peculiar ornament of unloosed heavens and hells. Every boiling pang of it sly and unhinged as those 1847 winter feasts. Whole backbone as if it were the firefly come out of God's own eye who recites by the path of its light each of the dissolving frenzies allotted and loosened and smoldering in those hovered fire tides of nether wildernesses.

He remembered his Welsh grandfather who lost his health to the vapors of arsenic and mercury while cleaning the scrubbers of the New Idria mines in 1862. Volunteered for the not more than five days labor and on the third emerged a ruin. Aged 22 having inhaled his lungfulls. Thinking an upturn in wages bought time to heal. "Not'a one" the grandfather known for his moods said, "was moren'a shell. Three to five days all it took with a new line of recruits waiting down the hill. Every year the newly injured wandered off half-brained or lunged. Each of'em smelling like they'd eat a garlic field. Some'a them far as Chile and Cornwall come down with far worse cinnebar fever than me. Couldn't remember the names of their mothers after day-'n-ahalf."

# III

He didn't know exactly where he stood as a truck farming laborer. Was it between his Welsh grandfather and those Yuki who seemed to thrive on sun-stroke and nerve and a shroud of humor that might wear the civilization away, hollow it out without its ever knowing, as he looked at blisters sprouted between his ring and middle fingers? Hundred ten hundred twelve for a week turn anything rightsidein and he wondered what those Yuki would do when the last seven days of the world come within reach.

He recalled a water break. They were covered with sweat/heat rash took off his shirt noticed a man still work-able into old age who'd been watching him. "Maidu say there's an orchid," the old Watcher spoke, "not more'an two three hundred left from the Last World. Grows near streamlets of the old meadows beyond the shadows of the Big Trees. Say you can pick one of its little flowers and it'll whisper about the prettiest girls and boys. Makes no difference to those old flowers what they tell. Maidu say them little blossoms got more trouble in'em than the last call of a bar."

"Don't mind Old William there," others interrupted. "Bring an extra gallon of water and he'll flirt all day hoping the misty morning will come for him."

It was said more as kindly fact. The kind where

everyone comes out for a long watch so the dead can hear the children laughing and go back to their side of the River where, if there are answers, at least you can't ride to the day when Mr. Woodward heard a Yuki he worked with unloading hay on a Yoola Bolly afternoon in 1938 say, "The Lord never get fat on mercy" letting the thing sway and dangle on his hay hooks without more comment as to the Mysteries that delivered them of the Round Valley into the twentieth century.

The trucker from Madera wondered what those Round Valley Indians meant.

Their words had a sound at bottom "studded with bear teeth" he noted, "whether dull or sharp" as he set to driving the dangerous miles with Shasta, the huge volcano in his rear view mirror, and the Sequoia Country ahead where there were still people named "Capt Wawa" "Mellie Chepo" "Julia Flamingbill" "Goodeye" and "Banjo." Some from Crane Valley "Flume" "Ahwanhnee" "Coarse Gold." Some had land. Some went without. Yokuts Miwoks Miwaks and "Chicago Dick" who showed up some mornings if he felt like it undrunk and unstunk and signed up for the Marines same day as Mr. Woodward. "Otherwise," one of the hundred thousand acre growers said "Weed'a took up a petition. What with carryin on with Indians and niggers churnin up a death'a Sundays gott'im sent to Camarillo for them baths they dump people in. Do that for a year. Empty all the funny ideas stuffin a man's sinuses. Come out a proper citizen. Never be the kind of thorn in yer ass Woodward is. Corp got'im first and look how he come back. Man know how to drive and repair trucks, haul loads of vegetables and fruit. So why bring up these damned poisoned things? Least we got Chicago Dick. Kept him from drownin in a furrow. Sent him down for some improvement even if he was a decorated Marine."

Maybe it did have to do with being a "trespasser in your own house." The roots of those words spread at their own pace as roots are bound to do. No, and they didn't cause a parade either, Mr. Woodward knew. But still. So when he drove up into Covelo and the surrounding country he remembered the seaweed cakes they baked for him like nothing he ever tasted. "For your night drives. No other time." Felt like he could smell deers' shadows through at least two miles of redwood darkness and easy to swallow as a ripe tree-pulled peach. And an elder woman, one of the last to remember the old soup and cake and jam recipes told Mr. Woodward what her grandmother saw. "1820 or so. Trappers from the Hudson Bay Company come down the Old Trail. White men with Indian wives and their kids like a wanderin circus. Them and their horses dressed in quills and feathers dances and songs for the night feasts. Good enough talk to talk you out of the three fingers of your lover's best hand and have no regrets. Beads, moccasins, knives, pelts. Some of them Indians Nez Perce Blackfoot Crow come down for the Long Walk sometimes for years. You heard 'em coming for miles and runners told of it days in advance. Quickest white men anyone ever seen. Pick up enough of your words in less than two hours and the prettiest signers talk with fingers and bodies made you feel doomed to be rich."

He was afraid sometimes, of hearing. And he was afraid not to hear. "Indian shoots, they were called," the woman said. "My mother memorized an old newspaper story from Mendicino. Must have been in the late 1860s. She was stole too and sold into labor. But the family wanted her to read. Felt bad enough about it after keeping her for twenty years. She taught me and one day gathering and drying seaweed repeated those newspaper words:

The Indian murder. They are only Digger Indians.
Women who had their brains dashed out the other
day a few miles from town and old and ugly at that
who had therefore outlived their usefulness.

"Mother told me about men who fed women and children strychnine. Slavery lasted right up to the new century. People who bought my mother said she was the best order ever filled."

# IV

When he walked out the door somedays he felt he could throw rocks at the wind, chase it to someone's hell, or to the still windless days, chase them to a place further where hell's beams jeer at the most ancient dead like a malathion sunset casting the shadows of fifty spray rigs as if such sunsets could thaw out a human throat or finger or lung. And though some asked, particularly the wives of various growers, about the seeds he kept, and the habits of flowers that came from those seeds, the types of soil and rock, sun or shade, a wildness or fretfulness a flower did have, distinct in its nervousness as a bobcat or fox; though some asked, the inquiry stopped as flowers sway in late afternoon Valley breezes, no one suspecting such small attentions with their attendant journeys up into the remote and dangerous spire worlds of the Sierras at eleven to fourteen thousand feet were his direct and carefully mapped challenge to the fire blast.

The voice of that seaweed woman told of mad horse races between white and Indian vaqueros straight down the steepest coastal mountains, hills, and ridges. Race could take a couple hours and them horses bred directly from the grizzly chasers, by the time they reached the finish line had their shoulders tore completely loose from their bodies, fell where they stood, losers or winners, bones left to bleach until they washed away. Riders killed too in a downmountain race. Everyone in them days a kind of runaway specializing in fire, poison, murder, and scheming. Language loose as pollen mixed up with Wailaki Maidu Pomo Pohoneechees Nook-Choos Spanish English and frog burped Russian didn't get spoke enough to water a sprout tree. And sure most of the murders of Indians took place in the name of precaution; not one man was ever charged or caught in all those years.

Say there were over eleven thousand of them Yuki in 1847. By the census of 1910 no one who could count could count over a hundred. Hogs got set loose to eat the near starved and dead. Miners needed fresh meat so all the land turned into a molasses bowl laced with strychnine. Then she'd tell Mr. Woodward that blue blossoms and ceanothus can be made into soups and sweet baths for the body; freshen face, hands and feet. And blue elderberry, boil it into jams and jellies, sauces for abalone and muscles, or make it into baskets and straight arrows. "You wanna kil'ah fish without killin yerself? Why ground some buckeye seeds, enough to end a hard day."

He'd think of those words as the oldest island hopping tank gunner in the Marines hitting the beaches from Tarawa to Saipan where he watched the nearly thousand women and children jump into their mass suicide while he and some Navajos begged them in whatever language they could think to shout not to. The murder and butchery and after smell of butchery and the horrible unbelief about it often more terrible than the violence itself and the rage and the lurking stink of gut stained sea smothering and permanent as it was compared to those women and children jumping to their deaths that made whatever it is about being human more frail more a molesting hopelessness as he and the ones still alive watched from the perches of their weapons seared by that maybe more than the other killing.

# V

The daring courage of nature or flowers or what makes flowers possible. Is it ghosts, dreams of the dead, or the dreams where the dead catch the living in their moments of being alive and know by that the living will ebb and turn the shades  allowable for beings and their bodies and the deaths of beings as if a world and its hells were a flower attacked by age and the colors of ageing red first, then transforming to lavender in a given wild Lupine or fields of purple-blue.

Bluest of certain wild things that might helplessly astonish a woman or man who chooses one memory or another of wide valleys filled with the combination of light yellow cream cups or the brightest magentas and blues of Calandrinas which once covered hills where anyone could follow the contours of a land and its canyons.

Hillsides swept by flower tides. Their touches of blue creams, still whites and orange, root runs in leaf mold, sharp rock. How would Mr. Woodward trace those feelers up a four thousand foot monolith? The trouble of it. The raspberry red of a floppy flower fully exposed to sun and wind, cut snows of late spring gone a little too profuse. Three-lobed coarse toothed flowers, short stemmed partial to half suns, sprays of part-light one day at a time. The erect day which makes for sharp toothed leaves, life zones and companionship.

Moist ledges of granite is one flower's "meat" and if sun dries it ferments it what uneasy mindedness will undress itself there among such pure and brackish repulsions?

Some flowers are especially a lure when bee-shaken. Such motions at those moments are not of the wind, nor even wind-like in the deft fragilities mixing insect and flower in proportions older than sun-rotted glacier or crushed granite slabs with their dredged up six thousand foot sheer faces.

In mid-afternoon summer stillness one can watch such dips and sways letting the eye glisten with the small lushness which seems to touch experience more lightly than the lips of the Polemonium confertum, the Jacob's Ladder of the highest crags and scant ledges at twelve to thirteen thousand feet with its curious name having to do with the Daughters of War and Preludes of Cruelty surfacing in the higher granite brittlenesses in clumps of solitary blue. And the Calf's Head. Except this one waits to forage not on grasses or to chew some deliciously snotty long-morninged cud but drown insects in the little ocean of its carnivorous head. Not like the Bovid's. But some smoothly primordial seal's skull uncovered in the San Joachin Hills, four or five of various miniature sizes sharing a central stalk. Each of them curled and flexed with their flappy two-forked appendages hanging from their snouts. Who would sup the water there? The lure of that well not "ghoulish" as some have accused. But holding perhaps each in its egg-shaped mouth some smaller remnant of the Deluge and the rainbows that appeared there and sea hauls full of buildings and whispers and cackles of Mohave hyenas he thought he could hear under wind under breath in the desert night.

Is the foliage fragrant or does it hurt, itch, cause sneezes. Does it sting, swell eyes or lips. Does it call afresh to your deepest losses or charms. Suggest the faintest smell of apple, lure of wild honey, stain of blackcaps on fingers for days. Or the longaway assurances of sex and flower veins with the lightest purples, the half-shades of a fern, the littlest doors to the placentas of various herbs mixed with sun and wind-shocked syllables of Searles Lake where he'd gone to see another Lily in April bloom; the "Desert Mariposa" in its Eastern Mohave array of yellow and orange. Late afternoon mixing with wind cupped flowers and their shadows moving him farther away from the "Beyond Help Dream" the Yuki said he'd come down with.

And what was the name of the other plane? The B-29 on its hide-n'-go-seek excursion flight waiting for its escorts. An hour was it? It wasn't the "Enola Gay" but "Bock's Car": Arrival Time: late for that City's huge arsenal of virus experiments, bombs, poison gas. FAT MAN'S original feast. "Sweeney" the pilot's name, Major Charles W. The flight itself tense and full of a swallowed terror, lightning and fuselage pounding rains so highly charged there was worry the plutonium FAT MAN might detonate. Bombardier, Captain Kermit K. Beahan (these names we would sometimes find scratched into the handle of an old shovel or pick axe glazed with his sweat). And what was that arsenal's flower image stamped onto the millions of weapons and bayonets it produced? "Was it a sixteen petalled chrysanthemum?" Mr. Woodward asked the Jewish egg farmer over a delivery of shit one day after the War and taking his guest to look for an Arisaka he'd taken at Tarawa in a cobwebbed closet. The Imperial symbol:

accompanied by the:

Kokura arsenal mark which for him resembled one of his favorite Mariposa Lillys, the Calochortus leichtlinii, common at a Sierra mid-altitude 7,000 feet having nothing to do, as he may have, at that moment of examination, reminded himself, with Mariposa Militias but with plutonium mushrooms and what cultivated that "family" and its possible distributions as he carved the outline of the Lily in to the handle of a masonry hammer, his favorite for tomatoes and other vegetables:

He introduced Xerophyllum tenax to his garden with its various common names: "Squaw Grass" "Turkey Beard" "Bear Lilly." Got it to bloom where it never did before; right in his garden below Yosemite. A confluence not known to nurture such wildness. The Hupas of the north made beautiful clothes and baskets from its fibres the treasure hunters yearned over and when those last stitches were synched, the root bulb, properly roasted, became a feast good for the heart, the bones too, strong big toes for good running and betting on races.

Who tries out the world through the choice of a flower. Pays the toll for a thirst can't be slacked no matter what dust arrives to digest memory. Rears a garden by hand then loses a finger or two to infection or sweat in the eye blindness by way of the hatchet and chopped kindling. Does a man's life begin or end with storms of irradiated paper as if those were water holes to be memorized at the beginning not when time becomes endurable but a parcel inextricable from the foolish generations who convince themselves in the names of their Atomic Fires that their Atomic Fires will not one day come to sear them. The whole reckoning of it somehow starved out purely pure?

Mr. Woodward: who was he?: "The Man Who Did Try It On For Telling" or "The Grave Name The Growers Love to Piss On?"

So many men to be going waterless, blind, going to wood or monotony. Crawling wind drift that eats the blue of mid-day skies in a desert canyon filled with mind-scratches of ghosts?

Hardly anyone ever saw this flower mass bloom in these parts. A wife sometimes from the local ranches

came to see though. From England. And she stayed
for tea and a little admiration. Had gotten some fame
it was said for her chores and studies; wrote some for
magazines far away as Europe. But there she was in
her light blue sundress big floppy hat asking over such
things as soil and manure and what sort of crushed
rock was applicable to what roots. A beautiful lady
with callused sunburnt hands come to claim, as the
other ranch women who marked the visits, sniffing up
their ravages of local guardianship and gossip, "either
the meanest or dumbest rooster" so inclined were they
to dwell as their husbands in the ores of cruelty and
blight. The flower she came to see has a stem two to six
foot high and the flower head's got a plume to it with
thick masses of thousands of small white to cream
colored flowers. The thing so delicate and tough you
wish it was Jack's Beanstalk flexed for a climb to the
racier Heaven of Your Choice or Funniest Hell that
looks like Heaven tastes like Heaven and only Heaven

knows what roots Hell sends out into
the farthest altitudes of the Sierras. This
plant also likes the terrible fires that
plume up in California and it'll follow
after a section of broiled earth settle
and bloom all over a hillside that looks
like some vomit a demon blew out her
ears so's to sniff the edges of torment.
The flower, though Mr. Woodward
didn't say so, didn't aver to it, it was

shaped like that cloud he couldn't stop claiming was his even though it made him a nuisance and he wished those fire lillies he'd brought to blossom had followed that fire. His daughter knew he didn't say much to an English Lady but she came twice a year for tea anyway. Could it be attributed to bad lungs, sore feet, the long-term damage of ear wigs? What was a town to think of any man's return from war and the triumph of a nation he seemed to want to spit on by describing what he'd seen for anyone who'd listen. What address had he been to and only a fool licks off the honor he earned and deserved. "No hell could make a man go that far astray while shoveling shit with that Jew. Who knows what got settled but by God when them other Kikes from Livermore showed up one day to record the Old Man's story. Them son-of-a-bitches sent practically the whole town in to a secret church meeting. FBI even sifted through a pile of chicken shit one night thinkin they'd find somethin. Thought the egg farmer was like them Rosenbergs fillin the Old Man up to his hat brim. Lucky too, the Federal snoops pulled up nothin cause some people 'round here can still twirl up a good enough noose. Least he could'a done was pretended. That was the way to some money. Not a whole fish bowl's worth but who sneezes at a little floated up bite-sized change?"

# VI

Wooly Blue Curls. He watched the plant and its purplish-blue flowers, its wool painted lavender or white; crimson in its mix of color. Trichostema lanatum. The names he memorized hoping this would allow breath again. The Greek "trichos": wonder glories of hair, sexy curls, straight silks, pubic mats, spongy kinks filled with sweat or rain; smell of sage and soils which touch hairs of nostrils over a long desert sunset?

Go for a sniff.

He thought if it had anything, anything to do with how the world might rediscover its natural right to health again it might have to do with the pollination of this plant as he watched, not wanting to be intrusive. Bee or butterfly come to this flower and get caught by a foot in the flower's cloven gland or its "slit" as he learned of it, and the insect drawn upward, drags a pollen mass over the other flowers of the plant, going from slit to slit cloven footed as the highest meadows he visited.

Achlys triphylla; "Deer's Foot": "Akhlys": Oldest Girl. She of Death Mist. Clouded Eyes. First Being even prior to Chaos. Most treacherous "dirty dry" nose drip full of epidemics and called locally among the earliest white settlers of the Northern California woods "Sweet After Death" for the delicate fragrance of its bunched fan-shaped leaves; such was the prize of it, leaning toward the OtherWorld as those years of the California genocide might have known it, its winds luring the fresh ghosts forward with their feet transformed.

Milkweeds with a preference for mountainsides turned to the deserts or valleys so hot they smell like unwatered about-to-die trees set to startle the tips of an eye, a wash of really stern heat to stunt the skin there. Let the rest of the body know nothing can be assumed. Not even a next step. Flowers with hoods and hair, lobes and wool so dense it might need a sheep dog to be herded properly, or properly fixed in the bear's eye for festivals and dances of the weir being which once rocked the valleys and canyons my wife's father said he knew, as much as earthquakes. And who, if it was secretly whispered at all, would know one from the other at shearing time?

A milkweed sprouted on an old flow of lava. A costumed princess ready to tango with the hardest rivers of stone or bone resenting commonest raindrop or speck of nutrient soil? And what courage does it take to track one's own knowing and where that leads and where that courage drops away, grows sour with neglect. Women or men the melt of it another age of glaciers in itself unmapped which has escaped discovery or fossilization. And who dying of that thirst attracts the glare of the highest vultures Heaven's reach cannot or will not touch?

# VII

Often in November and December Mr. Woodward walked the foothills. He knew these as the Months of Waitings. The great dormancy settled over the land, the ripenesses, whatever they were ripe for; snow and wind, hard colors of sky and granite, sting of ice and lone eagles up in the acute steadiness of their flight matching the invisible winds-a journey up the ladder sixteen/seventeen thousand feet and a flower to match the nearly invisible clawed and hungry spectre, The Glacier Lilly, a First Appearer after the snows also called Lady of the Avalanches, as he'd heard it, its dramatic yellow petals shaped like canines of extinct dire wolves biting through the ice-locked world.

And as in so much of the Valley mixed with his afterwar musings and searches, the one sprung from the on-wards of Sutter's Mill, everything, every inch of everything having to do with water and land and rivers of people to come has to do with mining. Doesn't matter what you name the exhumations or the certainties which follow them; farming, lumber, human migration, university laboratories specializing in the sleekest plutonium warheads nuancing death below breath, below what it means to fix breath to creatures who are bound to it or rendered by it, the worldly harbor of it.

When he came back too, one of the things he noticed was the absence of various lilies he always looked forward to seeing, carrying loads as he did up into Mendicino and Humboldt. He thought primarily the stands of Coast Lilly with their thin delicately swaying stalks and flower heads bent downward, as if in their stately lean they called the landscapes around them to a moment, not long or interruptive; no fuss—just the combinations of wonder and fear and breathing—and to be ravished by this pause and the sudden flush of curiosities it awakened. And one afternoon he stopped. For a relieving stroll into a roadside meadow, the cab of his truck having turned into a furnace. He noticed there were small craters in the bordering turf, hundreds and maybe thousands as he walked in his afterwar astonishments, lost in his steps forward and in the realization the wild bulbs had been dug up by bulb hunters, the landscape so quietly and shabbily gone morbid and final. There was, apart from himself, no one else under that sun. The name "Fort Humboldt" came to his mind, as he later told it to his daughter, long after their years of misunderstanding.

He had in the decade leading up to the War, been more than a stranger, carrying truckloads of produce and fruit. Those who helped him unload stacks of carefully tied and balanced boxes were often mixed bloods; Yuki, Lassik, Wappo, and a few, but rarer full bloods, carryovers from the post-1849 slaveries and years of child stealing, men and women whose fathers and mothers were forced into "indentureship" for decades and carried the memories of those exact hours when their people, within not more than a day, did become tresspassers on their own lands. He knew them as fellow men who also understood how to get through the hours of hard labor by way of laughter, a well delivered joke, sharing water and food, sharing the grinding silences and watchful gestures guiding each man to sundown without crushed ribs, wreckage of knees tracking the injured into mean hunger and sickness. A 5:30/6pm, still two hours of sun left twilight, but time for that day on count. They told the story without notice or overt emotion as I understand it, a kind of peculiarly glassy monotone, though, which let Mr. Woodward know they liked his company, knew his hands were at the same work as theirs. The year pinpointed: "1862". And what happened? It'd been going on for a while. The "Fort" put up to protect Indians from the "night" though you might not want to know the answer; local white settlers, soldiers, squatters. An eighty-foot diameter corral was built. Had ten-foot high walls formed of 2 inch thick planks; each one of them things 12 foot long, anchored at least 2 foot into the ground to keep the "night" from raping and stealing women and children.

Nearly a thousand herded into that circle. Took not more'an week for everyone to start dying. Fever and food no one ever seen'r smelled they told'im tasted like rotted bluejay only a mad one would consider swallowing.

They kept their dignity before the changeless finality of the story. There was, as Mr. Woodward tried to tell his daughter and when he could partially relax by the addition, myself, a sense of necessary comedy over their description of the materials used for "protection." The huge horizontal planks, ground depth of verticals made any "night" after 1862 in California for them the habitation of bloodless, frenzied ghouls coming from no recognizable dream or squalor, as if Indians and whites and everyone else were part now of ancient "Fright Illnesses" drifted into the currencies of the unnoticeable, no one not stuck in the "Beyond Help Dream". Them sharing red beans boiled in fat and fried deer meat soon as it got dark.

He often wondered how a flower, overlooked in its wandering capacities, might be the hardiest and bravest explorer raising nothing more than the carriage of its petals, anthers, swaying stems, supping and tasting the world, creating swarms of themselves over wide valleys and hills, marking soil and air and rain into an intense quickness inseparable from the silence which had overtaken him. He felt completely alone and for the first seven years after his return there was the strict censorship over any comment of all that he saw. And he knew those who saw the damage and those who suffered from the keloids and lukemia and blast pressure injuries became instantly inconsolable, like the Mujina he heard about. But now whole cities rather than single ghosts were transformed into "Faceless Ones" covered in bluish-white glare.

What are flower surges enveloping whole countrysides in shades of crimson and yellow, the seasons of zenith and disappearance, and what of umbels in the peculiar certainties able to carry the burdens of forty and more flowers in single clusters? When he entered, the city was still smoldering. He didn't know what a "dose rate" was then, the "half-life" of an isotope, the residual radiation of the beta particles covering his clothes; what happened to ovaries, testicles, bone marrow, lungs, fetuses; what "thermoluminescence" might be, the "hypocenter" he walked into, puddles of gamma rays, rads, the "Black Rain" which stuck to the skin, each drop a curse. How could he comprehend and then describe the, to himself first, "triplet" of injury to a human body, then for his San Joachin community. Begin there and stay there in the only world he knew?

> Thermal Injury
> Radiation Injury
> Blast Injury

All three never experienced by anyone prior to 8:15am Hiroshima Time August 6th 1945. Atomic Bomb Injury followed by Atomic Bomb Illness. What were these things and if he was ever going to talk again then what talk and what was Death now?

# VIII

The first words he spoke when his town was buying its Cold War televisions, air conditioners, kitchens: a couple of local ministers came to see him then told their congregations the Old Gardener was lying and worse, weakening the spirit of the nation and its ability to defend itself. And he saw the dying. Walked into it. Had no personal shield against it. He thought of the "Old Maids" drifting in to and out of various forms of shade, and variations of full sunlight even coyote or lizard might not suffer. "Bloomerias" bearing their nectars from one hill to another not acting like "Old Maids" at all, but girls set adrift, and sure about the folds of land they'll come to, how they'll shake and maybe grow older than any winds come to spread their flowers.

By December he knew 80,000 were dead from direct exposure. In the first eight weeks he didn't know exactly what he saw. Human bodies turned to disintegrating charcoal, cars and trucks melted, soil kilned to poisoned glass. His own town either hating him or thinking him a disgrace better having come out of Camarillo than Nagasaki. At least the one was explainable since every town could claim one of its own to be among the missing.

What was "Whole Body Irradiation"? What and who were those suffering from "Thermal Injury"? He realized after seeing and attempting to help the injured he had flexed his hands with such intensity without being aware of it; he thought he'd broken his fingers and wrists. Whenever he could, he offered those people food and water though their skin hung from them in flaps.

Their injuries were different. He'd seen battlefield wounds. Grotesque mutilations were to be dealt with. He whispered to the wounded, administered morphine, held the dying. The violence was what the gods of war, whoever those bastards were, ordained, and he was there. But the world turned to afterwinds, smoldering anemia, subcutaneous hemorrhage. He knew Death itself was new to it.

"If you gotta puke," he whispered to Death, "I'll hold your head."

He thought the word "desecration" might offer something. But he knew how best to deliver food. It was not so little a thing; bringing food. Loading and unloading the boxes by hand which he taught me to do; that his handwork and patience, a shared peach or plum brought stories and that a man who worked by hand saw that even Death was unsure how to feed on this poisoned stump.

"Even you. You don't recognize this feast," he said to Death on the twentieth night not knowing who else to talk to; that Death too had gone far past what the abysses of desolation will allow or did allow. If there ever was such allowance. And the flaring rim world where desolation achieves its calms where one could vaguely hope to be sobered and healed as the incertitudes might lure such brokenness.

Of unsound mind unsound body and their downplunges Mr. Woodward figured it for himself not wanting the genius of either to spread first to his Valley and the Valleys beyond where his was filled with enough mirages lifted and thinned out and become noxiously tolerable every word under it beaten if not to death then to the outreaches of a seductively smotherable panting.

Only later did the new words arrive. "Epilations"; hair falling from bodies by the roots. "Ecchymosis"; blood patches appearing first and then lethal hemorrhages from face, head, upper arms. Gangreous mouth ulcers, blood collapse. When his search for flowers brought him to the western slope of the Sierras he'd check for warnings about nuclear tests and prevailing winds from Nevada and what "minute" for the "Doomsday Clock" as he walked through the stands of bristle cone pine in the White Mountains, each tree five thousand to seven thousand years old girded by wind and curve of sky.

His daughter remembered one of her birthday parties after the war. 1952/53. Her eleventh year. A young cousin came. There was a large pot of boiling water; for spaghetti it was, and the cousin accidentally dumped it over her shoulders and chest, a terrible childhood accident, happened suddenly, as we later came to know it always does. Her small cousin survived, began to heal, but the scars that appeared on her shoulders and chest protruded and looked like shiny patches of stretched and swollen rubber. A new word entered their household from these cities and her childhood kitchen: "Keloid" and by that pronunciation she was hardly allowed to go swimming in the community pool. She knew he warned her cousin's mother about "sun exposure" and recalled for the months of July and August she joined the rest of her friends and their parents in a unanimous judgement—her father was spoiling their sense of victory and prosperity—got the attention of one of the Valley's largest water hoarders:

"What should'a got squeezed outta him didn't. 'Stead he come back. Whenever he does talk sounds like we better be ten years poorer and our shoes shined for the grave. Shames the whole town. Be no shadow in the sky other than him doin that mumblin'a'his. Think spreadin shit with that Jew must'a put water behind his eyes. S'pose one night you send a plane over his house with some of that pure brain death we spray. Claim it was a mistake. But his daughter sleeps there too. Gotta find the right note and pour money on it."

His daughter, wondering what else might have precipitated his versions of silence heard a nearly whispered conversation one Sunday while visiting her father's garden. A group of ranchers' wives telling what she thought might be a new wives' tale about one of her father's favorite flowers, those he visited in King's Canyon: Mimulus moschatus, the Musk flower.

"Its fragrance," one woman said, "is gone. No explanation."

"A flower losing its scent?" one asked.

"How could that be?" reckoned another.

"Some say since the Great War. But which one, now there's two?" a fourth insisted more loudly than the rest.

And she went one day into the foothills to find out for herself. Found an outcrop of the by its other name "Monkey flower" in a small spring-fed meadow: pinched and sniffed one flower, then another, until she tried nearly the whole of that ground and felt nearly rotted by a sense of unwanted superstition about such an obscure thing she'd done. What it meant or what sort of sign it was, especially for her father who'd become, when she was the one most cornered by being his daughter, a girlhood absence, remembering how close her bereavement was as she went on her dates to the only theatre in town which featured in those years movies like "The She Creature" "Zombies of Mora Tau" "It! The Terror from Beyond Space" and "Invisible Invaders" with its lone physicist so much like her own father who became in the movie the world's leading voice against nuclear war and she'd wept in the theater, her tears snuck up on her to both her own shock and her closest high school acquaintances who thought the sudden emotion was a line in the sand no matter how faint; her own isolation beginning at that moment.

His granddaughter, who never lost the taste of those Sunday afternoon cupcakes, recalled the particular flower he found most mysterious, and for himself, as important as water and breath. It was a kind of Snow Maiden, but the one who comes in the depths of Mohave summer nights out of the boiling soils of those days. "Evening Snow" as he hinted to her, called up by the burrowing owls who sound like frightened lost children flying in the hot night anxiously summoning a parent. Their pa pa sounds freezing the throat for a second of anguish—or their laughter—their "queeing" turning the ridges of the ears cold as if some ghost were giggly over the mortals who take the emptiness too much for granted saying "Mizu, Mizu" in their fateful seconds of breathing the dead can no longer touch or smell and want for themselves as some token, some anything to feel what water and breath would be again. Or a chuckwalla waving its tail. A beacon for these flowers which rise up in the night and swarm around the sleeper with their accumulate perfume and on a late June morning melt back, away from one hundred twelve degree afternoons, the petal a snow white and the edges a lightly brushed purple letting the white undergarment bleed through. And how could one gauge such nights and their flowering visitations or how humans can be visited?

Or was he a fool coming into the evil hours of the night unboned as he'd seen others unboned?

"And what took root in him?" a near to death rancher asked. "Come back talkin like a windmill full'a worms."

Maybe it was the onset of ecrus. The brown of summer and heat lashes and what takes to climbing chimneys, pissing in shoes. Or a wild flower that loves to sprout and take hold in shales. Unbind sterility for just a long enough second. Drench it in the taste of spit and meat and sweat of a possible lover.

DAVID MATLIN is a novelist, poet and essayist who lives in San Diego, California and teaches at San Diego State University.

# S PUYTEN  D UYVIL
*Meeting Eyes Bindery*
*Triton*
*Lithic Scatter*

Made in the USA
San Bernardino, CA
16 August 2013